MURDER ON A MAINE TRAIL

A Nora Lassiter Mystery
Book 3

Bernadine Fagan

MURDER ON A MAINE TRAIL

Also by Bernadine Fagan

Murder by the Old Maine Stream
Book 1

Murder in the Maine Woods
Book 2

DEDICATION

This is for my family.
Their support means the world to me.

CHAPTER ONE

Sometimes life skips the lemons and hands you the lemonade upfront, something that rarely happens to me, but a joy when it does, like right now. I am officially in a lemonade phase. Everything is going well. Three minor issues need to be looked into, and I will be paid to do that. Since my bank account is in the desperation phase due to a few online purchases I was unable to resist, the part about being paid resonates.

I'll have to stay in Silver Stream, Maine, a while longer to solve these cases, but that's okay. My one-bedroom New York City apartment is no longer empty, thanks to my friend Lori who is in charge of leasing it to Whatshisname, my cheating ex-fiancé, and good riddance to bad rubbish, as Great-Aunt Agnes would say.

I hope it wasn't a mistake to lease the apartment to him, but I needed someone to pick up the tab and yes, I'm overcharging him by quite a bit, and there are moments when I feel guilty about that, but those moments pass at the speed of light and leave a nice warm glow in their wake.

Great-Aunt Ida doesn't seem to mind that I've taken up residence in her house. When I arrived for a four-day visit after Great-Grandma Evie passed away, the leaves were on the trees, the weather was mild and winter seemed beyond my concern.

Today everything is covered with snow, and the temperature has settled into the single digits, an increase from last night when it dropped to seven below zero, a temperature I hadn't experienced since I'd lived in this part of the world as a child twenty years ago.

Although the roads have been plowed, I rattled through this wooded section of Maine at a glacial pace in

my wonderful little Ce-ce. Ce-ce is short for Chevy
Charlene, the name I've given my old silver S10 Chevy
truck.

"The Eye of the Tiger" blasted from my cell phone
indicating a call from Mary Fran. One day when I was
recuperating from the assorted cuts and bruises I'd incurred
after a run-in with a Sherman tank, I'd programmed my cell
phone with different ringtones for my frequent callers.

I pulled off to the side, although not completely, due to
the snow piled by the plow.

"Where are you and that bucket of bolts you call a
truck?" Mary Fran asked as soon as I answered.

"I take offense at people calling it a bucket of bolts.
That phrase has been tossed in my direction more than once.
Ce-ce has character, plain and simple."

"Right. So where are you? You told me you were
leaving more than two hours ago."

"I'm a short distance from town."

A horn sounded in back of me, and I waved my hand
out the window, signaling the driver to pass. He beeped
again and pulled around me like a maniac.

"What's that beeping about? What are you doing?"

"Nothing! I stopped to talk on the phone. I'm not
going to drive and talk on the phone."

"Did you stop in the middle of the road?"

"Of course not. I pulled over a bit."

"Someone's cursing you, aren't they?"

"These roads don't compare with New York City
streets where plowing entails scraping down to the asphalt,
creating potholes and spraying salt and sand as if the goal
were to deplete the world's stockpile. Here, on the other
hand, they just leave a bunch of snow on the road. People
have to be extra careful."

"You're turning into an old lady driver. I'm
embarrassed to know you."

"I'm just careful. Other people, not so much."

"Oh, Nora. You are not a Maine driver, for sure. Well,

I'll be here until around noon. Stop by. Maybe I can help with the case. I need to get away from here before the rush starts next week. Ay-uh, I need some action."

"And I need to get warm. Ce-ce's heater doesn't work, and my long underwear is no match for the drafts that attack through the floorboards."

"Hot Heads Heaven has heat."

"So I've heard," I said before I hung up.

Both hands gripping the wheel, I finally eased onto Main Street. I could see Nick Renzo's Silver Stream sheriff's vehicle parked in its usual spot. The sheriff was in the building. Slowing further, almost to a five-mile-per-hour crawl, I picked up my cell phone and hit his number on speed dial. I'd see Mister Handsome and Appealing later, but I'd call now. I finally came to a stop in the middle of the street.

Despite warning myself again and again about the need to hold back where Nick was concerned, I couldn't resist the desire to connect with him. Sometimes I am a weak woman, a thirty-year-old weak woman.

But I had to be careful. Although we were definitely more than friends, Nick and I were not a couple, not exactly anyway, so I couldn't allow myself to fall in love. I was a New Yorker who planned to return to the big city, he a Mainer who loved his town and his work; he was an honest-to-goodness sheriff, I, an out-of-work computer analyst, presently working in Silver Stream as a private detective-investigator.

Actually, I'm not a real detective. That rumor took hold when my great-aunt Ida, desperate to make someone pay attention to her concern about a possible murder, took wing when she bragged that her niece, the "hotshot New York detective" would investigate. I never corrected the misconception because someone wanted to hire me, and I knew I had the computer skills needed to solve the problem.

The "detective" designation is still in place, but I'll handle that as soon as I've cleared up these three small problems.

Nick finally answered.

"Nora, I'm going to give you a ticket for talking on your cell while driving. Or maybe I'll just arrest you."

I did not bother to tell him I'd finally stopped driving. I smiled and kept the words, "I might like that," from tripping off my tongue. I simply said, "Hi, Sheriff! Surprised I made it into town?"

"At last. Where are you?"

"If you had traffic cameras on Main Street, you'd know."

"How was your first trip alone in the snow?"

"Piece of cake."

"How long did it take you?"

"A little over two hours. Maybe closer to three."

"You could've walked faster than that. Why didn't you take the northern route instead of looping all the way down here? Marney LeBeau lives closer that way."

"Road's too narrow. It makes me nervous. Besides, I have another case. Margaret the librarian has a little problem. I'll go to see her after Marney. And I also want to drop in on Mary Fran. Have lunch with her."

"Well, be careful. Although I suspect you are too careful on the road."

"I'm a cautious woman. Maine drivers are reckless."

I knew he was shaking his head.

"No mishaps so far, I hope."

"None. Except," I paused and took an audible breath. "Well, not exactly." I paused again. "If you don't count . . . " I paused again, dramatically, and heard him take a deep, patient breath. "If you don't count the star I scraped off some big SUV with a rack of official-looking lights on top. Parked on the street, right in my way as I drove past. It was just a minor scrape. I don't think anyone saw it."

He laughed and suddenly appeared at the door of the station house. He hurried over to where I'd stopped, and I rolled down the window. He leaned in and kissed me.

His lips were cold and warm and wonderful.

"Hi, sweet stuff. You know you're parked in the middle of the street."

"No, I'm not."

He chuckled. "Okay."

"So, Sheriff Renzo, it's good to see you." I only sounded breathy because of the cold air rushing in around him.

"I've missed you. It's been too long."

"At least we'll get together tonight. You cooking?"

He hesitated. "There's a change of plans for later. Dinner is out. I have to go to my mother's. For dinner."

I waited for him to ask me to join him, but the invitation never came. Just as well. Mother Renzo did not like me, understatement of the decade. Arianna Renzo had made her preference for his ex-fiancée crystal clear, and how apropos that the favored one was named Crystal. I wouldn't think about it.

A pickup truck pulled up in back of me, and Nick waved him around.

Then his cell phone rang and he answered. "Renzo."

His cop persona kicked into high gear immediately. "When?" he asked, his features hardening as he listened. "I'm on it." He clicked off.

He leaned toward me. "A body was found by a couple of kids on snowmobiles, north of here on the switchback not too far from Ida's."

"At least this body has nothing to do with me, thank heaven for that. I know of no one accused of a crime, and I didn't find the body."

"Yes, I'm relieved about that."

He gave me a quick kiss. "I'll call you later. Gotta run."

Since I'd been in Silver Stream there had been two murders, unprecedented in this normally peaceful town. Both victims were connected to cases I'd worked on, so it was good to be out of the loop on this. Otherwise, people would talk, possibly wonder whether I'd come here to start a new version of Murder Incorporated. And who could blame them?

All was okay.

Lemonade still flowing, I drove off slowly.

I planned to start two of my cases this morning because neither would require much work. First, I'd see Marney LeBeau whose husband Floyd was missing, sort of, nothing the law was concerned about, but money was involved. Hers, she thought.

After that, it was back to town to visit Margaret the librarian who complained of stolen reference books. Both sounded like elementary cases. I loved this.

My third client, Aunt Ellie, would have to wait. She really didn't have much of a problem. Most of the family thought she'd invented that peeping-tom story to get attention. Personally, I agreed with them. She'd been lonely since her husband went to prison, and had been keeping to herself most of the time. Maybe this was her way of breaking out.

I passed Mary Fran's beauty salon, aka Hot Heads Heaven, and turned onto the road that led up and around to Marney's place. A truck that had been behind me rocketed around me before I completed the turn, sending a spray of snow across the driver's side window. Through a misting curtain of white I saw the driver shake a fist out his window at me.

The nerve. I would have shaken my fist back, but that maneuver would have involved lowering the window, which would have involved taking a hand off the wheel while turning, which everyone knows is risky, unless one is a trained stunt driver, which I am not.

I finally arrived at Marney LeBeau's house and rolled to a stop in the snow. Taken aback by the sight of the place, I sat with both hands on the wheel, staring.

Something was off here.

CHAPTER TWO

Even if I had followed Marney's directions precisely—I only made a few wrong turns, a record for me—I'd know this was her house because she sat in a rocker on the rickety-looking front porch, bundled in a puffy red down coat with the hood pulled tightly around her head, allowing only a small portion of her face to show. No one would ever mistake her for Little Red Riding Hood, of course. The wolf maybe, the little girl never.

Despite misgivings, I finally opened the door of the truck. The driveway had not been cleared, so I had parked at the end. I paused, hearing an echo of my father's voice as he recited one of his favorite poems, which had always annoyed my mother but delighted me. Phrases popped into my head, distracting me from the woman on the front porch.

Whenever I go to Suffern along the Erie track
I go by a poor old farmhouse with its
shingles broken and black.
It needs new paint and shingles
The tragic house, the house with nobody in it.

I felt as if I were seeing the embodiment of that house now, transposed, unkempt, empty, but mostly sad. Of course, this house wasn't empty, yet the feelings it evoked were similar.

Crowding in around the words of the poem was a very unkind thought. How on earth could this woman afford to pay me? I shook the notion from my head. Marney was a woman who needed help, and I'd do my best for whatever little money she was able to pay.

My hand rested on Ce-ce's door handle as I closed the door and took a more thorough look around. My kindest thought was that the place needed repairs. It was a ramshackle mess. One peeling shutter hung askew, and scattered around the front property beneath the snow were oddly shaped bumps that I knew were not artsy sculptures.

The fingertips on Marney's left glove had been snipped off, probably so she could get a better grip on her cigar. Maybe she was sitting out here because she didn't want smoke in the house? My dad smoked a cigar occasionally. My mother insisted he go outside with it. No one, not even me, wanted that smell in the house.

Marney waved a fully-gloved right hand, took a quick puff and tapped the glowing cigar tip into the snow.

"Nora Lassiter. Hello, girl."

I smiled and waved.

Marney was a big woman, husky and tall, probably close to five-nine. About her weight, I couldn't even guess. Her coat added bulk. Traces of gray hair mingled with the dark strands that escaped from the tightly-pulled hood framing her oval face. According to Great-Aunt Ida, Marney was in her mid-fifties.

At my first meeting with Marney three days ago, she told me her husband had raided their joint bank account, an action considered legal, but certainly not moral. She wanted me to find him and report his whereabouts. I could understand her need to find him, although I wasn't sure what she intended to do with the information. None of my business.

On the surface she was an innocent, needy woman with a simple request, but I had a strong feeling there was something she hadn't shared yet, something she wanted from me.

"Was beginning to wonder if you'd changed your mind," she called through the haze of blue-gray smoke that eddied around her. Squinting, she waved a hand to dissipate it, and stood.

Her words activated a strong urge to turn back. For long seconds I did battle with my sense of obligation. I believed in keeping promises, so I thought *lemonade, lemonade, lemonade* and tossed aside the host of excuses scrambling for purchase in my head.

I was here. I'd do this.

My traction boots handled the foot of snow easily as I tramped to the porch.

"Of course not," I lied, walking slowly, arms out for balance as I tackled the snow-covered steps. I grabbed the railing, felt it wobble and decided it might be riskier than the steps. As I hit the top step, Marney yanked a narrow envelope from her pocket, and handed it to me.

"I did like you said. Made a list of all them places I could think of Floyd might go. First one's your best bet." Her breath came out in white puffs that got lost in the gray-blue smoke. "He has a room in the residents' housing unit, actually he paid for it ahead of time with a check from our joint account, so technically, it belongs to both of us. Here's the key and my note giving you permission to search it."

With a gesture I thought held a hint of defiance, or perhaps pride, she angled her oval face to the side and stared down at me, waiting for me to speak.

"The key," she said finally, "is a master key. As head carpenter, he had one. He gave it to me a while back, when he first started working there."

"I take it you haven't heard from him recently?" I said as I fingered the outline of a metal object in the envelope. The key. With a sinking feeling, I unclasped the envelope— yes, it was a key—and pulled out the list. I hoped she didn't want me to unlock a room he might be living in.

"Not recently. That's everything you need. I think. General stuff. Name, cell number, photos. The key's to her place, too, just in case you want to check there. I duplicated it a while back," Marney said, pride in her voice. "I guess I'm a bit of a key collector. I have hundreds of keys."

Her place? I hoped I'd misheard.

"A woman?*"* I asked, conscious of my voice shifting into a higher frequency. I cleared my throat. "I thought you wanted me to look for your husband."

Something crashed in the house, and my gaze shot to the window. The curtain fluttered. No, not a curtain, a sheet, one with faded pinecones imprinted on it.

"Yeah," Marney said, as if nothing were going on inside her house. "But Beverly TheSlut will know where he is. He's been to her place more than he's been here this past year."

"TheSlut?" I said. "What an odd last name. Hyphenated, is it?"

Ignoring my facetious question, she continued.

"She works at that mountain ski place. In season she lives there in her fancy room. Don't know if they're an item any more. Who knows? He told me he relates to her. That's why he took the job up there, I think. So he could be close to her. He comes home every few weeks to see what's going on. This is still his house. We're not divorced."

Marney puffed on her cigar and stared at me. I sensed a screen around her thoughts as thick as the blue smoke swirling around her head.

"Got me that money in a settlement when I fell on an escalator in one of them big stores down in Freeport. Should never have put it in our joint account. Dumb thing."

"We all do foolish things at times."

"Beverly had a husband. Eddie Binderwig. That's him there in the photo I gave you with her and Floyd. Don't know where he's at these days, either. He's an electrician up there."

I glanced the photo.

Marney snorted. "I went to high school with them guys. Instead of calling me Marney, Beverly Sue called me Marmaduke. Real loud. You know that Great Dane in the comics? Anyway, then she went a step further and took to calling me the Great *Dame*. Big joke!"

High school for Marney must've been over 30 years ago. "That's certainly not funny," I said, knowing the insult was carved in her memory like bas-relief on a cornerstone, knowing the hurt had never gone away and probably never would.

"Some kids started woof-woofing when they saw me. And the fool I've been married to for twenty-two years became chummy, more than chummy, with her. He's a traitor and a thief. Anyway, she'll know where he is. She'd never tell me, but you could get it out of her, sneaky like. She's a gabby one. Or maybe follow her and she'll lead you to him. He's got a room at the lodge, but I haven't been able to contact him. They keep telling me he's not there. Poo on that!"

"Where is this mountain?"

"Little over an hour or two from here. Years back it was part of that camp place Rhonda runs. Can't remember when her family sold it off."

"All Season Wilderness Lodge and Campground," I said, my heart sinking as the possibility of woods travel loomed in my future. "I've been there. I remember seeing mountains in the distance. Those the ones you're talking about?"

"Yep. Called Jason's Mountain, after the owner's son, I think." Marney took a second thick envelope from her pocket. "Beverly's a ski instructor. Or maybe she teaches folks on one of them board things. But I doubt that. She's way too old to even be a ski instructor. That's for young folks."

I didn't comment on that.

"Won't be a problem for you, will it?" she asked.

"No, of course not," I fibbed as I remembered how difficult it was finding my way along roads or paths that weren't as clearly marked as New York City streets. A GPS wouldn't include most of the trails, so the possibility of getting lost, which has happened a time or two, definitely existed.

Almost two hours travel time? I think not. Double that in this weather. It would take me four hours. I needed someone with me.

Mary Fran, of course. If anyone had told me as a kid that the day would come when I'd seek her out, I would have thought they were crazy. Amazing how life changes.

I'd spent my childhood wishing I possessed a magic cloak that would make me invisible whenever Mary Fran was within attacking distance. She was a horror, a demon child who caused me to shake in my Keds, a tormentor adept at inflicting painful little surprises.

Marney handed me the second envelope. "Lucky for me, Mr. Slimebucket didn't know about my secret stash. This will cover your expenses for a few days, plus extra. There'll be a big bonus if you get me the information I need."

Information? Other than his location? What was I missing?

I opened the envelope and stared at the pack of hundred-dollar bills. "Marney, how much—"

"No need to count. Amount's written on the back along with the date. I want you to do this right away."

I glanced at the amount. To my credit I didn't jump up and down, and the word 'Yippee' never escaped my lips, but I did think of the bills I could finally pay. However, good manners as well as my code of ethics compelled me to protest.

"This is way too much, Marney. Our agreement—"

"I remember exactly what our agreement was, girl," she interrupted. "If you can do this for me, it'll be worth every penny. Actually, there's something else." She paused and managed to look a little sheepish. "Serious snooping might be involved. I was hoping you'd go the extra mile, if you know what I mean."

Here it comes. I should have known. I. Should. Have. Known. I wondered whether it was something illegal.

"And that would be?" I asked.

Something else crashed inside the house. I glanced at the window again. No sheet fluttering this time. Marney ignored the noise.

"I heard you was real good with computers."

Oh, no. Something illegal? I almost said no before she asked, but I gave the short answer.

"I am," I acknowledged modestly. Computers were my specialty. Not that I had the ability to break through the Pentagon's firewall, but I was better than good and way above average. And given time, I thought, I might be able to breach the Pentagon's computers. I shook that felonious thought from my head.

"When you find him, I want you to investigate a bit more. Find out what he did with my money. He may have spent some on her. But more likely, he's up to something illegal. Anyway, this will probably involve breaking into his laptop. Opening his files. Whatever. I don't know much about computers. But I know him. And he always guarded that laptop like it was pure gold, so it hides a lot."

When she hesitated, I prompted, "Go on." Although I was ready to back out now.

"I know him real good, and I know he's up to something fishy. He can't be put in jail for gettin' ahold of my money, but he *can* be put in jail for something illegal." She shrugged. "Like I said. Serious snooping. I want to hold all the cards. I want to be able to send him to jail."

Jail. Finally, I understood.

A third crash inside the house turned my attention, and I looked from the door to Marney, my brows raised in an unarticulated question.

She said, "I woulda asked you inside, but the two newest ferrets, Bonnie and Clyde, are biters. They also don't like smoke. They're young. Wouldn't want them to nip at you." She smiled when we heard another crash. "That might be Ferret Faucet getting into the act. She doesn't like the new ones yet. Sh-ur are causing a ruckus this morning."

Ferrets? Oh, geeze. I didn't even know what a ferret

looked like. Besides, I was probably allergic to ferrets, like I am to most animals. The sneezing, oh the sneezing . . . but the biting would be worse. I shivered, glad I wasn't inside.

"Are you still going to take the case now that you know what I really want?"

Interesting that she handed the money first, letting it act as a hook before telling me what she really wanted.

In spite of this realization, my thoughts were colored more by the thousand scenes flipping through my head like images in a massive document folder, traveling at the speed of light, but not too fast for me to remember them vividly. Images of me and Whatshisname that I wished I could delete.

Her husband, the man she should be able to trust above all others, had cheated on her with another woman, had stolen her savings and taken off. She felt helpless, the way I'd felt when Whatshisname had done something similar to me. But I had managed to get back at him in a small way. I didn't think Marney had that option unless I helped her. More than anything else, this convinced me to accept.

"Yes, I'll take the case," I said, hoping I wouldn't have to break into his computer.

"Thanks. Sorry I didn't tell you all of it from the start, but I was afraid you'd say no if you knew."

She was right about that.

I nodded and turned to go, but her hand on my arm stopped me. "I've heard how good you are at figuring stuff out, and I knew if anyone could help me it would be you. You being a big city detective and all."

Eeesh. This was my chance to set the record straight on that bit of misinformation. A short, very short, internal battle ensued: the ethical and upright me versus the dishonest and deceitful me.

When the battle ended I finally spoke up.

"I'll be in touch, Marney," I said as I headed down the snow-laden steps with caution, not touching the rickety railing, placing my feet in my original footprints, backwards. "Next stop, the library."

"Library. Well, in that case, there's one more thing you should know," Marney said as I concentrated on navigating the steps without toppling to the bottom. Good thing I'd worn my super tread L.L. Bean boots.

As I stepped off the last step, safe, something else crashed in the house. After a pause to listen for more ferret antics, Marney said, "Don't know if you know, but Margaret and Beverly Sue are cousins. Second cousins, once-removed."

CHAPTER THREE

As I turned into the cul-de-sac behind the Country Store and eased to a stop next to the Silver Stream Library, "The Eye of the Tiger" blasted from my cell phone. Mary Fran again.

"I saw you standing in the doorway of Hot Heads Heaven on my way back," I said as soon as I answered. "No customers today?"

"You were here hours ago. What kept you so long at Marmaduke's place? You get lost?"

While I no longer felt the impulse to run when I saw Mary Fran, a trace of the child remained in her, as it does in all of us. So, her use of the pejorative didn't surprise me.

"Don't call her that," I said.

"You're sensitive?"

"I am."

"Okay. *Marney* then."

"Better."

"So, fess up. How many wrong turns?"

"Two," I said, counting the area I circled three times as one event, and not counting one double-back.

I aimed Ce-ce into a cleared area in the library parking lot. "You interested in changing those odds?"

I heard a happy gasp. "You have a job for me?"

"I do, if you can make it."

"Absolutely. I need to get away. I think I'm getting a sinus infection from the smell of hair coloring."

"Do you ski? Or snowboard?"

"I'm a Mainer!" she said with an indignant huff.

"Can you get away for two days, maybe just overnight? Not sure how long."

"Yes. I'm almost positive, but I'll get back to you once I settle my daughter with her aunt. Both of them would love that."

As soon as I got out of the truck, the wind whirled around, snatched my hat, carried it away and settled it on a huge pile of plowed snow. I retrieved it, stuffed it into my pocket and made my way down. Gracefully. I was halfway down when my boot caught and I tumbled forward, not so gracefully. The flag above me seemed to mock my arrival as I struggled to my feet. It snapped and waved, its halyard clanging against the pole in syncopated cadence. The rhythm of Maine in winter.

I scrambled up, dusted off, and went inside. The warmth and quiet of the library had the quality of a hug. I loved this place. I had loved it when I was a child and a permanent resident of Silver Stream, and I loved it now as a temporary resident.

Margaret stood behind the checkout desk, a massive oak structure lemon-oiled to a high sheen, and came around to greet me, her usual placid expression tinged with unease. All done up in her staid navy suit and a deep gold, ultra-proper blouse, she wore her hair in a tight bun that rested at the nape of her neck. The bun might work if she loosened it, maybe flicked a few strands around her face.

"Nora," she said, a decibel above a whisper. "Good to see you. I wasn't sure you'd make it today." She glanced around surreptitiously and tipped her head toward the back room. "Follow me."

I glanced around, too, not sure what I was looking for. The coast was clear, but I had no idea why that was necessary. Feeling a bit like an agent in a spy novel, I followed, smiling.

"Not come? I told you I'd come, Margaret."

"Ummm. Yes," she said, her sensible low-wedge heels

thumping on the well-worn wooden floor.

A movement in the research section caught my eye, and I glanced over as the dentist, Margaret's boyfriend Harold, bobbled his basketball head at Margaret, a white toothy grin or grimace or smile pulling his lips apart. It was so out of character that I wanted to ask him what was wrong. Perhaps a digestive problem. If Great-Aunt Agnes were here, she'd know.

Margaret gifted him with a perfunctory smile and kept walking. I had seen them at the Harvest Dance together a while back. Obviously, he was still interested. Whether that was true for Margaret was hard to tell.

As soon as we were ensconced in the back room with the door closed, she pulled an envelope from her pocket and handed it to me.

Déjà vu with that move. Today was certainly my day for receiving envelopes. I felt like a bagman picking up the day's take. Margaret tipped her lips in a facsimile of a smile. It was an odd movement that showcased her pearly whites, but failed to brighten her face. I caught myself before I mimicked the action.

"Nora, I don't think I'll need your services after all. The problem has been solved. But I want you to have this for making the trip unnecessarily. I should have called you. I apologize."

"So the reference books have been returned? That's fortunate. I know you were very worried. Who was the culprit?"

"I can't tell you. It's a family matter that I'll take care of personally." In a move to dismiss me, she reached for the doorknob.

I didn't move.

Although I nodded my understanding, my gaze remained on Margaret as the word 'family' fluttered through my thoughts like a red flag, setting off a mini dilemma. *Family?* Could this involve the second cousin, once-removed, the notorious Beverly Sue Binderwig, aka Beverly

TheSlut, aka Floyd's LeBeau's former girlfriend? I'd wager the contents of one envelope on Beverly Sue's involvement. But reference books? I didn't see how that fit.

Marney LeBeau wanted me to get chummy with a member of Margaret's family and now a member of Margaret's family was the library thief? Correction: *possible* thief. So both cases might involve the same person. Gee wiz.

Since I couldn't say anything without revealing what Marney had hired me to do, I said nothing. But I did remember what most television detectives had to say about coincidences. No such thing.

Margaret released the doorknob, folded her arms and stared back. "What is the problem, Nora?"

For brief seconds I was looking at a mirror image of me in high school being cornered by two tough girls who wanted my lunch money. I had refused. I'd held the same pose Margaret was holding, staring down the opposition while my stomach churned, my knees threatened to buckle and my mouth went dry enough to keep my tongue pasted in place.

The difference was that I had not threatened Margaret.

This "case" threatened her. All of a sudden I wanted to reach out and tell her everything would be okay, but since I didn't know that for a fact, I said nothing. She'd have to come to me. Tell me what she was hiding. I figured the reference books or library materials were a smoke screen she'd concocted to get me here. Well, I was here.

For several seconds I wondered whether she'd committed a crime. On the heels of that thought a host of horrid criminal activities ran through my head with murder, burglary and major theft topping the list. If that were so, I was well out of it.

I stood there with the cash-laden envelope in my hand. What to do? What-to-do?

I couldn't keep this money, much as I wanted to. Even the devil on my left shoulder couldn't persuade me.

I extended the envelope. "I can't take money for something I haven't done, Margaret. Thank you for offering, but please keep this. Call if you need my help with anything. I mean that."

With the reluctance of a child being handed a list of chores to do, she took the envelope, never once looking me in the eye. I put my hand on the knob to keep her from taking the initiative and ushering me out, all the while trying to make eye contact. Impossible.

Ce-ce's wheels were spinning in the snow when she burst out the library door like a woman escaping a burning building, her arms waving frantically. I stopped and opened the window.

"I *do* need your help," she said. "I didn't want anyone to know, not even you, but I'm desperate. Please don't go."

I angled my head toward the passenger side door. "Hop in."

Margaret scooted around, her sensible shoes sinking in the snow, and hopped in.

"Sorry I . . ."

I reached for her shaking hand. "Don't. There's no need to apologize. Talk to me."

"This must be strictly *Entre Nous.*"

I had to think about the *entre nous* reference a minute. Nothing came. Enter? Enter us? Nah, couldn't be.

"It's my cousin Beverly Sue," she said, while I was still trying to figure out the French. "I need your promise that you won't tell *anyone* what I'm about to tell you. Especially Harold. He went to the men's room and doesn't know I snuck out here. You see, I've done something I shouldn't have done."

I skipped *entre nous* and let murder, burglary and major theft take another turn through my head as I waited for her to reveal what must be the crime of the century.

"Go on."

"We signed a non-gambling pledge, and I broke it. If he knew, he'd never want to see me again, so you can't share this with a soul. It would ruin me."

She signed a non-gambling pledge? Was she a gambling addict? Maybe I should give myself an out.

I leaned forward. "One caveat, Margaret, I can only promise if you haven't done something illegal. Could I be considered an accomplice or an accessory by keeping your secret?"

"Nothing illegal, Nora. You have my word on that."

"Good. Shoot."

That was probably a poor choice of words. I hoped guns were not involved.

Chin trembling, she said, "Beverly Sue and I have always been friends. We're cousins. Actually, second cousins once-removed."

There was that *once-removed* designation again. Who knew what that meant!

I reached behind my seat and grabbed a blanket that Great-Aunt Ida insisted I have with me at all times, just in case, and handed it to Margaret, who draped it around her shaking shoulders.

"Thank you."

"Go on."

She swallowed hard.

"I trusted her. Every month I gave her money"—she paused, then lowered her voice to a whisper, which was unnecessary since we were in my truck, the parking lot around us was empty, and my windows were closed against the Maine wind howling outside.

"Go on," I encouraged again.

"So we could go in on lottery tickets together." Her shaking intensified. "I'm not supposed to . . ."

She paused. I was about to step into the silence with a comment about what a good idea that was when she clutched the blanket with both hands, and seemed to push the word *"gamble"* out on a current of held breath. My first thought was she was having some sort of attack. Heart attack? I did not want anyone to die in my truck. Another body? How would that look! No and no! I reached over and touched her shoulder. "Margaret?"

Taking a deep breath, she sat ramrod straight and continued. "Same numbers every week."

No heart attack. *Thank you, God.*

"Our numbers came in weeks ago. Bev called. We were both so excited. I jumped up and down with such abandon that I dropped the phone."

While I was trying to picture Margaret jumping up and down, she was glancing at a shiny red Jeep Grand Cherokee, new, I thought, parked at the corner of the library lot. I'd never noticed this one before, nor had I ever noticed Margaret in such a state, her expression shifting from distress to outright panic as her hands clasped and unclasped the blanket around her shoulders. No great deductive skills needed here.

Calmly, I asked, "You spent some of the money before you actually had it? Bought the Jeep? And you haven't heard from your cousin since?" I asked as a gust of wind howled through the trees and sent a clump of snow whooshing off the library roof and onto the hood of the spiffy new Jeep.

"Yes, to all. Not a word. I've tried to contact her. Cell phone, home phone, work phone. I called the main desk at the mountain and was told she's been off all week. I don't know whether the woman I spoke to was telling the truth or not. I suspect she was protecting a fellow employee from what she considered an annoyance call, so I sunk so low as to call her ex-husband, Eddie Benderwig. He does electrical work at the mountain. Turns out I couldn't get hold of him either."

"You had a written agreement with Beverly, didn't you?"

She nodded. "Yes, of course, but I can't find it. I always kept it in the fireproof safe in my closet, but it's not there anymore."

"Did anyone know the combination besides you?" I

asked, suspecting I already knew.

"No combination, just a key that I hung on a nail in the closet."

Uh-huh. Such mind-boggling security. Any child of ten would be able to crack that safe. I stifled a groan.

"Beverly knew this," I said, hoping she'd contradict me.

Margaret bit her bottom lip, and tears spilled down her cheeks. "Yes."

"Anyone else?"

"Possibly. I don't know. I didn't tell anyone. I don't think Beverly did, but I'm not sure."

"Did Beverly have easy access to your house?"

Margaret nodded. "Of course. We're cousins."

"So to be perfectly clear, you want me to go up to the mountain, find her, and persuade her to give you your share of the windfall? Thousands of dollars? Maybe a million or two?"

I tried not to sound like that was the most incredible thing I'd ever heard, and I quashed the urge to hum *Dream, Dream, Dream.*

"What I was thinking," Margaret said, her voice hesitant, "was you could find evidence that she had taken the money and possibly confront her with that evidence and get her to return my share."

Like that was a possibility. Gee whiz, Beverly Sue, will you please, pretty please, fork over a million or two for your second cousin once-removed.

I didn't need to ask the next question, but I did. "Where do you think I'd find such evidence?"

"Her computer."

Surprise, surprise.

"Or maybe a bank's computer," she finished.

The bank's computer? My mouth dropped open. Did all these people think I was a criminal?

"I know she banks online," Margaret said, as the word *felony* swirled around my brain and took up residence. I'm no legal expert but what she was asking probably fell into the category of a felony. With a long mandatory prison term attached, no doubt.

The dentist stepped out the library door wearing a red plaid hat with earflaps, a black scarf, and a gray jacket that could probably withstand the winds on Mount Everest. He smiled, grinned or grimaced, when he saw us sitting in the truck, and headed over.

I said quickly, "Her bank account? I'm not a lawyer or a cop, Margaret, but I'm pretty certain what you're suggesting is a crime, the prison-time kind."

Both clients wanted me to commit a crime. Interesting.

"I know it sounds impossible," she whispered, "but I've heard things about you. I know that sometimes you can do the impossible." She glanced at Harold who was almost at the door. "Please keep all this confidential."

"You've heard I commit crimes?"

"No, no, of course not." She paused and looked at me. "Well, not exactly."

Really? This day was full of shockers.

Harold knocked on the window and Margaret, with a world-class smirk on her face, rolled it down. "I'll be right out, Harold." Her tone was gentle, contradicting her expression. She rolled the window back up, but Harold didn't take the hint. He waited where he was, doing a little dance in the snow that involved arm fluttering. Margaret looked at me, and said in a desperate whisper, "Can I call you later?"

"Definitely."

"Remember, this is between us, no one else must know."

Suddenly, the phrase *entre nous* kicked in. *Between us.* Of course. I should have known.

"My lips are sealed, Margaret."

She nodded, paused, and then jerked the door open with such force that Harold, whose head happened to be bent forward at that particular moment, got thumped roundly. I won't go so far as to say this was by design. I mean, it could have been an accident, but it certainly made me reevaluate my original take on Margaret the librarian.

Her back to the injured Harold, she yanked the envelope from her pocket and dropped it on the seat, not giving me a chance to refuse it. "A down payment, Nora."

I watched them walk away, Margaret in the lead, Harold several paces behind, massaging his forehead.

CHAPTER FOUR

Since Nick was involved with an investigation in the woods, I went straight home from the library. Great-Aunt Ida's old Victorian house dated back over a hundred years and was more like home than any place I'd lived since I had lived in Silver Stream.

The steps to the porch were shoveled and sanded. I'd done that myself before I left. Good thing, with the aunts coming and going despite the snow.

Great-Aunt Hannah's teal '65 GTO with the stick shift that she'd insisted I learn to drive a while back was parked in the general vicinity of the driveway. In their early eighties, my great-aunts—Hannah, Agnes and Ida—were back from their senior citizens' meeting, and probably rehashing the special announcement they'd been told to expect.

This morning when Hannah had arrived to pick up Ida, she informed everyone several times that she refused to guess about the matter. Ida declared that she was annoyed there were no rumors, and Aunt Agnes said she didn't care one way or the other about any special announcement. Her only concern was the lunch menu because Nick's mother, Arianna, was in charge of today's menu.

"It's scary what that woman does with food," Agnes had said, tugging her snowflake-embroidered black vest across her ample front. "That garbanzo bean mess she concocted last time she volunteered to cook? Vinegar! The woman put vinegar in the beans. Hard to get the taste, or the image, out of my head. Did I tell you I had a nightmare about those beans? Woke me right up from my nap yesterday."

As I opened the front door, I heard Agnes in the front room declare, "Well, he's always been my favorite, and that's that."

"I heard he met Frank Sinatra when he was a kid and Sinatra helped him get started," Ida said.

"Hogwash!" Hannah said. "I don't believe a word of that. Publicity, plain and simple. Trying to associate his name with Sinatra's."

I don't think they would have noticed me if it hadn't been for the burst of cold air that rushed down the hall and eddied into the front room announcing my arrival.

"Nora, have you heard the news?" Aunt Ida said as she stepped into the hall, closing the top button on her blue wool sweater and tugging the collar of her polyester print blouse over the top.

I quickly shut the door all the way. "No. What?"

I looked up from yanking off my snowy boots to see petite Great-Aunt Hannah join Ida. With a flair that I'd come to expect from her, she tipped her chin up and tossed a purple wool scarf more artfully over her left shoulder.

"They're making a movie in Silver Stream, and we're going to be in it!" Ida said.

"With Josh Rockford!" Hannah said, as if she were onstage announcing an Oscar-winner.

"Who's out there?" Great-Aunt Agnes called from the front room.

"Hi, Aunt Agnes," I shouted as I set my boots in the boot tray. "So," I continued, "You're all going to be in a movie? That's great."

"With Josh Rockford," Hannah said again.

"Who's he?"

Hannah and Ida gasped in unison, same note, same pitch.

Hannah recovered first. "He is only one of the top movie stars of the 20th century."

"We've seen every movie he ever made," Great-Aunt

Ida gushed. "What a hunk."

Hunk? Had my eighty-year-old aunt just called some old movie star a hunk? I smiled, kissed them both, and padded into the front room, a warm and cozy place with upholstered chairs covered in flowered slipcovers, doilies on lemon-oiled end tables, and insulated drawn drapes in an apple green that picked up the color of the leaves on the slipcovers.

"I suppose I've seen him, but I don't recall."

"He played a detective, one of Manhattan South's finest, in *Murder at the Garden*," Ida explained.

"Big Josh is coming," Agnes said, assuming I hadn't heard. "That's what they called him, Big Josh. And he'll be at our Winterfest this year, down by the lake. We go every year. 'Course we don't sit outside much more. Too cold. We take a sleigh ride. Then sit for a bit by one of the fires and have s'mores and hot chocolate."

"When he was around, all the ladies swooned," Hannah said.

Agnes's eyes widened in shock. "Mooned? Someone mooned our Nora? When did this happen?" Irate, she struggled to get out of the chair.

"Swooned," I said loudly, sitting on the arm of the raspberry flowered chair she sat in. "Women *swooned* when Josh was around."

Agnes sat back. "Well, 'course they did. And what a relief no one mooned you."

"I thought you picked up batteries for your hearing aid," Ida said to Agnes.

"Some woman once fell off her chair when he walked into the restaurant where she was dining. That was a big story at the time," Hannah said.

My jaded side kicked into high gear with that bit of trivia, flashing the words 'publicity stunt' in my head with neon-sign intensity. Only my love for these wonderful women kept me silent.

"I was shocked when I thought somebody mooned

you. And in this weather to boot," Agnes said. "It's cold enough to freeze his you-know-what off. 'Course that would serve him right, if he was so bold."

"Absolutely," I said to Agnes. Then, "The Garden? Because I'm from New York I figure you're referring to Madison Square Garden?"

"Yes. And Big Josh should have won the Oscar for that one," Ida said. "He was robbed. The man was brilliant."

"And handsome," Agnes added with a smile.

"They need extras for a few scenes they'll be shooting in the sheriff's office and the church basement. We intend to be there," Ida said.

"We're going to be in a movie," Agnes said, reaching for my hand. "Maybe you can be in it, too. A pretty woman like you with your striped blonde hair and beautiful blue eyes would be perfect."

"We intend to plan a little cast party, and I'm heading the committee," Hannah said. "Imagine. Planning a party for Josh Rockford. Never in my . . . " She paused, clasping her hands to her chest, smiling. "Well maybe in my wildest ones a ways back."

"If anyone had ever told me that one day I'd be starring in a movie with Big Josh I would have told them they were nuts," Ida said with the kind of sigh I'd never heard from her, and an expression I'd never seen on her face.

"Starring?" Hannah questioned.

Before I had a chance to comment, the theme from *The Lone Ranger* blasted from my bag, announcing Nick's call.

I smiled. "Hi, Sheriff Renzo," I whispered. "How's the investigation going?"

"We're looking at a burnt out mess of a Dodge Ram with a charred corpse in the front seat. No plates. Looks to be five years old or so. We'll have to wait for the M.E.'s report on the identity of the body."

I heard several people speaking in the background. Then Nick said, "Hold on a sec."

I tried to hear what was going on, but it was impossible. I moved down the hall out of range of the aunts' discussion.

I heard Nick say, "Some guy found it near the truck. That should help."

More muffled chatter flooded the background, and Nick told me to hold on again. I thought I heard the word *Binderwig*, not an easy word to mistake. But possible. Maybe the guy said cinder. A wig on a cinder? A twig on a fender?

My heart began to pound. I took a deep breath, and waited, the name Beverly Sue Binderwig front and center in my thoughts.

"Nora!" Aunt Hannah called from the doorway. "If that's Nick, ask him if he's met any of the cast or crew yet."

Straining to hear, I waved her away and squashed the phone against my ear, making the jumble of background noises slightly louder.

Ida appeared next to Hannah and called, "And ask him if we can meet them before the auditions. You should have some pull."

"Nora," Nick said, "I have to run. I'll get back to you. It'll be late. Can I stop by?"

"Yes, of course." Before I could add "anytime," he'd disconnected.

With a sinking feeling, I slipped the phone back into the pocket of my jeans.

CHAPTER FIVE

It was close to ten when Nick's headlights flashed in the window of the front room. Ida had gone up to bed, and I sat on the floral love seat, feet up, wrapped in a multicolored afghan crocheted by my great-grandmother, making a list of the things I needed for my trip to the mountain. I figured I might have to be there two days, possibly three, and I was not looking forward to it. The cold here was bad enough, but mountain cold was worse.

Tossing the afghan aside, I hurried to the door. Seconds later I was in his arms, savoring the feel of him, strong, tall, rugged, pressed tightly against me, filling my senses with the freshness of outdoors and maleness and him, hugging me like he never wanted to let me go.

"I've missed you," he said before lowering his head to kiss me full on the mouth.

My fingers slipped through the dark hair that curled over his collar and I melted into him like I belonged there, like I never wanted him to let me go.

When my thoughts clicked into place, I pulled away and stepped back, making a conscious effort to curb the errant thoughts that raced through my head, inflaming my body. If I intended to stay in Maine . . . if I were willing to give up my life in New York City permanently . . . if . . .

Then he would be the one for me? Was that possible?

"I missed you, too," I said, straining to keep the passion in my heart from spilling out with my words. "We've had so little time together in the last few days."

"We have a lot to catch up on," he said.

Arms linked, we headed into the front room. Instead of aiming for the loveseat, I headed for the floral chair. With a quick maneuver that made me smile, he outsmarted me and flopped in ahead of me and pulled me onto his lap.

I wondered how dinner with his mother had gone, was about to ask, but decided I didn't want to know. Arianna was one of my least favorite people, and I knew the feeling was mutual.

He said, "Tell me about your visit to Marney. Did it go well? Or are you ready to give up your *detective* career?"

"When I give it up I'll go back to New York. Is that what you want?"

He smiled and nuzzled my neck. "You know what I want. You know I want you to stay, just like you know how much this detective business bothers me. You're not trained, not qualified. You don't even carry a gun. You've been hurt several times and locked in a Sherman tank once. Enough."

"Not this time," I said, palms out in mini protest. "I've got a simple search assignment from two people, and the best part is they overlap. I haven't seen my aunt Ellie yet."

I explained what was involved, fingering the pleated roll on the arm of the chair as I talked about Margaret without actually revealing her "gambling" secret, and hedged about Marney as well. It's not a good idea to share everything with a man who has taken an oath to uphold the law.

When I finished, he looked at me for several seconds without speaking. He knew I was holding back. Nothing much gets by Nick.

He said, "Marney told me Floyd took off with money from their joint account. She wanted me to go after him, but there was nothing I could do, or anyone could do for that matter. You understand that, don't you?"

He kissed the palm of my hand, continued on to the pulse at my wrist, and then wandered up my neck again.

"Of course," I said, leaning into him more than I

should, greedy for the feel of his lips on my neck. "But Marney figures Beverly knows a thing or two. Which is why I'm going up to the mountain tomorrow to search her out."

That got his attention. "Beverly knows what Floyd did with the money? That's a stretch. Even if she did know, why would she tell you?"

"Maybe I can finesse it out of her. What's Beverly like? Marney mentioned a high school episode, typical teen stuff, but that was a lot of years ago."

He hesitated. "Beverly can be tough. There was an incident on the front steps of the Country Store just before I came on the force. It's a little hazy, but word was she sucker-punched some guy and then kneed him. Sent him ass over teakettle down the steps. Even with a broken arm, the guy refused to press charges. Only reason I know about the incident is the sheriff told my dad about it while I was standing right there."

His dad. He never spoke about him, never spoke about much that was personal. Nick held things close to the vest. I'd have to work on that.

I actually shook my head to clear the thought. We were not a couple with a future, period. I had nothing to work on.

"What?" he asked. "Thinking about how to get Bev to talk?"

Not about to tell him what I was thinking, I groped mentally for something to say. I took my time. I sat back, wondering what more I could share about Marney and Margaret while still maintaining confidentiality. Nothing came.

"I have a job to do for Marney and Margaret, and both jobs involve talking to Beverly Binderwig. Period."

When he said nothing more, I hopped up, grabbed his hand and headed for the kitchen. "Aunt Ida left out some of her blueberry muffins. And just so you know, I make a very tasty hot chocolate."

"Getting familiar with the kitchen, are you?"

"I have a wide range of talents, Sheriff Nick Renzo."

"I'm learning that."

"I may cook a meal for you one of these days." I couldn't actually picture such a thing, but it sounded impressive.

As I filled the kettle with water and placed it on the stove I remembered the aunts' request.

"The aunts want to meet the big star, Josh Rockaboard, or whatever his name is. Could you facilitate that?"

"Rockford," he corrected. "I can probably manage it. I'll let you know."

I set the cocoa mix and a spoon in front of him.

"Do you know anything more about Beverly that would help?"

He seemed distracted. From the way he concentrated on the blueberry muffins and fingered the spoon, I knew something was up.

"Not much. I really don't know her."

"Do you have any idea whose body you found?"

"I figured you'd get around to that. You heard, didn't you?"

"Maybe," I said as I removed the whistling kettle from the stove and turned off the burner. "I thought someone said Binderwig. Why aren't you telling me?"

"Because I'm not sure, and I don't want to upset you."

I gasped. "You think it was Beverly? You think she's dead?"

"No, I don't think so, but I can't be sure. There was a ring found near the truck and one of the guys thought it might've once belonged to Beverly Binderwig so I gave a call up to the mountain, and they said she was working. They offered to get her, but I told them to hold off. I'd get back to her."

"At least you know it wasn't Margaret's relative. That's a relief." I shook my head and smirked. "Some man remembered a ring? Sounds like quite a guy."

"He said his wife mentioned it to him years ago,

wanted one like it. It was a distinctive ring. It had the tracing of an EKG and a heart carved on the band. The initials B and E were inside with a heart symbol separating them."

"B & E. Hmmm. Breaking and Entering."

He actually smiled.

I closed my eyes. "I know. Her ex-husband's name was Eddie, right?"

"Right."

"You think it was him?"

"Don't know, but most likely it was a man's body. One of the shoes was intact, a large boot shoe, maybe size twelve. I have no idea what the ring means. Someone could've planted it."

I poured boiling water into two cups with cocoa mix. "So this was a homicide?"

He nodded. "Definitely. We think the person was shot before the fire was set. 'Course, we have to wait for autopsy results to be completely sure. But a gun was found on the ground."

"Like the killer didn't care if you found it. Can you trace it?"

"Maybe. Not sure. Forensics has it now."

"And you think the Binderwigs were involved."

"Don't know that. But once the body's identified, the Binderwigs will definitely be on my list of people to talk to."

"I'll see Beverly tomorrow. On the slopes."

"The slopes? I didn't know you skied."

"It's been a while. I skied once when I was nine years old. My father wanted me to go again. "With practice, she'll do just fine," he told my mother. "We'll buy her skis instead of using the rentals. That'll help." I didn't tell Nick the rest of the story, about how my mother had a fit and said, "We don't have money to throw away."

I smiled at the memory of her next words, which had stung at the time, but seemed funny now because she may have been right.

Nick gave me a strange look. "What's behind the smile?"

After brief consideration, I decided to tell him. "Mom said, and this is an exact quote: 'Nora needs a pair of boots with tire chains for traction, not something specifically made to slide around.'"

Nick smiled, but I had the feeling it was only because I had smiled. His eyes held a sadness I seldom saw in him.

"So you're going to throw caution to the winds and make another attempt?" he asked, adding milk to his hot chocolate.

"Since Beverly's a ski instructor, I thought I'd take a lesson. Get to know her before I probe."

"I hate to miss this event."

I smacked his arm and said, "Should I have Mary Fran take pictures?"

"Absolutely. Video would be better."

He finished up his hot chocolate. "I don't want to leave," he said, standing and taking the cup to the sink, "but I have to get some sleep. Tomorrow will be busy. And of course, I'll be worried about you on the slopes."

"You're not hungry?" I asked, noting the untouched blueberry muffin.

"No. I had a big meal. At my mother's."

Finally, finally, finally. The dinner. I waited for details, a few would be good, but he offered nothing so I grabbed the afghan from the love seat, wrapped it around my shoulders, and stepped out onto the front porch with him. He kissed me again in the icy cold of the Maine winter night.

"Better get back inside or your toes will freeze," he said as he hurried down the steps. I took one step back.

Then he opened his door, flooding his official SUV with a brief show of light, and giving me a glimpse of a plastic box with a fancy red bow and swirly script sitting nice as you please on the passenger seat. Leftovers? Special treats?

Arianna aka Earth Mother aka Nick's Mom was an environmentally conscious person who grew most of her own food, wore clothes as boring as road signs and kept her hair in a style popular back in the sixties. Based on what the aunts had told me, especially Agnes, Arianna added squash to her chocolate cake, beets to her muffins and kale and coconut milk to her New England clam chowder.

While Nick never complained, he rarely ate with her, and if he was to be believed, rarely took home the food she tried to foist on him. Yet there it was, plain as day, taking up a spot on the passenger seat, where anyone standing on a porch could see it. Unbidden, a wave of pain washed through my heart, knocking me off balance so that I had to step back to regain equilibrium.

A plastic box!

I could not picture Arianna *possessing* a plastic box, but the kicker was the dainty red bow.

Now who would do that? Let's see. What were the choices? Arianna? His deputies? Or could it be choice number three? His ex-fiancée, Crystal, who'd been flirting with him since she returned from Boston a few months ago. Hmmm. One didn't have to be a Mensa member to figure that one. Former fiancée Crystal had been there for dinner. I'd bet my last dime on it. No wonder he hadn't said a word.

He was free to see whomever he wanted to see; free to kiss whomever he wanted to kiss; free to eat whatever anyone tied up with an elaborate and way-too-cute red bow. Maybe he really liked red bows. Who knew! Who cared?

Not me.

Had he kissed her? The tsunami was back, tossing my heart this way and that as I thought of the kiss we had shared moments ago.

I took a deep breath, then without a characteristic final wave, I stepped back and went into the house, switched off all the lights and went up to my room, careful to tiptoe in the hallway so I wouldn't wake Ida.

It was good to remind myself from time to time that Nick and I were not a couple.

Without consulting my packing list, a first for me, I threw underwear, jeans, socks, and extra sweaters into my bag, brushed my teeth, changed into my thick gray sweats, pulled on heavy-duty wool socks and hopped into bed.

Images of that plastic box with the stupid bow marched in and out of my thoughts like an invading army, with Crystal, his ex with the shiny dark hair that swung around her shoulders like a silken mass, leading the line of march. Her hair was her best feature. He probably loved her hair. I had to admit mine was not that fine. Maybe I should let it grow.

Many hours of twisting, turning and pillow-punching passed before I finally drifted off to sleep.

CHAPTER SIX

Mary Fran was at the house bright and early, her black Kia Sorento loaded with enough skiing and snowboarding equipment to start a ski shop.

"Suppose I drive," she said, looking from Ce-ce to her SUV as I tossed my lone bag behind the driver's seat in my truck. "I'm a good driver."

"We're not going for a week's vacation," I said, eyeing all her paraphernalia. "We're going to work."

"And we need to look the part, right?"

"Of course." I thought I looked the part.

After my last windfall—perhaps windfall is an overstatement—instead of being as frugal as prudence dictated, I'd stood on the porch of Aunt Ida's house, watched the first snowfall and pictured myself schussing down a ski slope in a colorful and trendy ski outfit, something in blues or aquas.

Not that I knew how to schuss, but there was always the lodge.

Figuring I'd hit the slopes at least once while in Maine, I'd immediately gone online and found the perfect outfit, an aqua jacket, white trimmed, with an asymmetrical zipper for style, a high collar for warmth and white ski pants to pull the outfit together. Attractive, avant-garde, definitely smart.

I'd stopped short of buying skis and boots. No need to rush that part of it. Besides, a person could always rent ski equipment.

Aunt Ida had located an old pair of boots in one of her

many closets and put them in a black plastic garbage bag this morning. I'd thanked her and shoved them into my overnight bag. She said they were my size. I trusted her, and didn't bother to try them on or even examine them, which I hoped was not a mistake. So unlike me. But time was short and I was too indifferent to care.

"And with the possibility of snow tonight, we're better off if I drive," Mary Fran finished.

"Snow? The temperature is above freezing today. It's bright and sunny. Not supposed to snow for another two days. We'll be back by then."

"Maybe. But the temperature will drop."

Since I didn't feel like driving, I acquiesced. After we were on the road, she asked, "How are you going to approach Beverly? Want me to introduce you? Not that I know her that well. But still."

"No thanks. I want to get to know her on my own. See what kind of person she is. I'm not expecting much. Marney hates her guts and would like to see her stomped under one of Godzilla's clawed feet. That is, after she reveals Floyd's whereabouts, and what he did with the money.

"Margaret, on the other hand, wants information from Beverly but does not hate her. Not yet, anyway."

A half hour went by before we spoke again.

Mary Fran broke the silence. "What's wrong?"

Since I had no intention of discussing Nick with her, which would be akin to broadcasting to the entire town, I told her a partial truth. "I was wondering whose body was found in the burned-out truck."

"Body! What body? When did this happen?" She swerved a bit, causing me to gasp and grab the dashboard.

"Slow down! Watch what you're doing."

When she slowed a bit, I continued, "They found the body late yesterday. Probably a man. Murdered."

I went on to tell her some of what Nick had shared with me, especially the part about the ring.

"On what trail? Where?"

"He said on the switchback off this road, wherever that is."

Without warning, Mary Fran yanked the wheel and made a sharp U-turn that had me grabbing the dashboard for support again, this time with more force.

"I know where it is," she said. "We passed it. We should check it out."

"No. We have to get to the ski area. Business first."

"No one told me anything about a body," she said, her words spilling out rapid-fire. She turned so swiftly that her SUV narrowly missed a ridge of snow at the edge of the road. "Why didn't you tell me immediately? This is big news."

"Mary Fran!" I gripped the dashboard with both hands. "Watch out!"

"Don't worry, I have complete control," she said as she swerved back and I rocked to the other side. "I'm a good driver."

"Who says?"

Suddenly the Mary Fran from my childhood had replaced the hairdresser and needy woman of the last few months. The demon child was at the helm, her demon eyes focused on the road ahead as if I had never spoken.

So I said again, more forcefully. "There's no reason to go to that spot. What do you hope to see? We won't find any evidence. The police spent hours there yesterday. Turn around."

"A truck? How old? What year?"

"Nick didn't know. He thought it was about five years old. Why does it matter?"

"In case you've forgotten, I know a few things about cars. You do remember that I'm part owner of The Biggest Little Auto Mart in Maine, formerly run by my soon-to-be ex-husband Percy, the crook who is now serving time for shady dealings. The company has a close relationship with your uncle JT's auto body shop. Maybe I'd recognize the truck."

"Recognize it? A burned out hull? That's ridiculous. Far-fetched. Morbid curiosity is stirring in your head right now and that's that."

"You mentioned a ring. I remember Beverly's ring. It was made of titanium, and she bragged about it so many times I wanted to yank it off her finger and shove it down her throat."

"Shove it down her throat! What is the matter with you?"

She made another quick turn and we went bumping down a path in the woods. My sunglasses bounced down my nose and ended up straddling my knee. These were pricey glasses, and I didn't want them scratched. Fortunately, I was quick enough to rescue them before they hit the floor.

"Slow down," I shouted, lifting the glasses to my eyes.

In response, Mary Fran jammed her foot on the brake with enough force to throw off my aim, which caused me to poke myself in the left eye.

"Owww. I will never let you drive again, that is, if I ever decide to take you with me again, which will probably be never since you are incapable of following orders."

Suddenly, the demon look waned, and the adult Mary Fran reappeared. I rubbed my watering eye, which made it water even more, which made two Mary Frans appear, a scary sight, but one that would clear when my vision cleared.

She came to a full stop. "Sorry. I'm getting carried away just thinking about another murder. Do they think it could be Beverly?"

"Nick said they have no idea, but he didn't think so. He thought it was a man."

Looking meek, which I didn't buy for a second, Mary Fran took her hands off the wheel. "Can we stop on the way back?"

I blinked several times to clear my eye, then searched for a tissue in my bag. "Oh, for heaven's sake. Yes. Now, let's get to the mountain. I have to find Beverly."

"If she's still alive," Mary Fran said.
I rolled my eyes.

CHAPTER SEVEN

By the time we arrived at the ski area I was ready for a nap. Since that was not an option, I took a deep breath of mountain air and scanned the scenic view.

"The rental shack's over that way," Mary Fran said, pointing to a cluster of pine trees. "You should put the ski boots on first."

"You ski here a lot?"

"Oh, yes. It's close, and I love it," she said, unloading her equipment.

I grabbed the bag with my ski boots, set it on the ground and opened it. Mary Fran, being her usual busybody self, leaned over to see the boots Aunt Ida had packed. She yelped and stepped away. I gagged and staggered backwards. As luck would have it, my heel caught on a rock protruding from the snow, and I landed with a thud.

"What's that smell?" Mary Fran yelled loud enough to scatter little woodland creatures into the next county. Standing a few feet away with her nose wrinkled and her mouth open, she made a gagging motion with her finger, accompanied by what she probably considered appropriate noises.

"Don't tell me," she went on. "I recognize it. It reminds me of my grandmother, but it just doesn't fit my image of you. You used to be such a fashionista. Prissy Nora Lassiter, the fussy fashionista, fussy fashionista." She spoke in the sing-song voice of an taunting child. I wanted to smack her.

I pretended to ignore her as I struggled to my feet and pulled the mothball-marinated ski boots out of the bag. "Aunt Ida never mentioned the odor. She just told me they'd do the trick. I probably should have checked," I said as evenly as possible.

"Ya think?" She snickered as I stepped into my smelly boots. "You know, you could have rented boots here."

I took the verbal high road. "I don't need to spend money on boots." My tone was definitely snotty. "It's bad enough I have to put out money for skis I only intend to use for an hour or so."

She shrugged and set down her super-duper boots, a shiny black pair with purple trim, the words Nordica Fire Arrow emblazoned in flashy script across the top. I loved them instantly. I considered firing her on the spot. Petty me.

"I dislike the smell too, but it will dissipate in the fresh air."

She scoffed as she stepped into her beautiful boots. "Dream on."

I turned away. I had no time for this nonsense. I had to keep my mind on the goal. Once booted up, I said, "I'll head for the ski rental shack. You pick up lift tickets, and we'll settle up later."

I left her dusting off her spectacular boots and tramped off. The first thing I noticed was a sheet on the wall of the rental booth listing lesson times and instructors. Well, wasn't this a stroke of luck. Beverly Binderwig was scheduled for a beginner class in twenty-five minutes.

Good. She was alive. But when the body was identified, Beverly might be implicated. I had to be careful.

I might wind this up today. No overnight stay necessary. I'd talk to Beverly, get a feel for her character, then find out about the stolen lottery ticket, about her connection with Floyd and that would be that.

How well this was going! Everything falling into place.

Piece of cake.

I moved to the counter where a kid with spiked hair was busy on his cell phone.

"Skis or board?" he asked, wrinkling his nose and stepping back as he looked at me.

"Skis. Can I sign up for a lesson?"

"Pay here, and I'll give you the lesson pass."

Ten minutes later I was on my way, clomping through the snow, some of which had turned to slush in a few sunny, well-trod spots. It was amazing how the weather had changed. It was almost like spring.

With skis on my shoulder, poles in hand, lesson pass dangling from my jacket, I felt like I belonged. I was a fellow skier looking forward to a day on the slopes. I smiled at a young couple, acknowledged a family with three children, and smiled at two guys with 'instructor' emblazoned on their jackets.

Ahead, the mountain loomed like an invitation, and I pictured myself schussing downhill, navigating moguls and finally coming to a stop in a smart spray of snow.

I rounded the last bend, saw Mary Fran attaching a ticket to her magenta jacket, and headed over.

I considered the job ahead and thought about the best way to approach Beverly. Maybe I'd start by talking about men. Or maybe gambling. I'd seen a sign for polka night at the main building. Maybe she enjoyed that.

I hoped this ski trail would lead to the money trail.

"That's Beverly," Mary Fran said, pointing to a woman standing next to a ski school sign at the bottom of a long, slight incline. "She must be waiting for her group to assemble. You'll be using the T-bar lift. I'll be farther down, but I may be able to see you. I know you don't want me to introduce you, so I'll take off." She handed me a lift ticket.

"Thanks."

"I'll make a few runs on the intermediate slope first to warm up, and then it's the black diamond slope for me." She laughed. "Watch out for the slush at the bottom of the bunny hill. Don't fall in that puddle."

I smirked. "I may make the expert slope by the end of the day," I said over my shoulder as I headed for Beverly and my first skiing attempt in over twenty years.

Until I saw her, I didn't realize I had any preconceived ideas about her appearance. But I must have had because seeing her took me by surprise. She didn't come off like any man-magnet or tough broad I'd ever met.

Instead of a perfect movie-star smile, she had a slight overbite, instead of flowing, sexy hair she had, of all things, braids that escaped a playful floppy-eared frog hat. She was about my height, five-five, and seemed years younger than Marney, even though they had to be close in age. I tried to see a family resemblance to Margaret, but nothing came.

She was chatting with two children, a boy and a girl, both around ten or twelve years of age. They were all laughing when I joined the group of about fifteen people ranging in age from preteen to late fifties. One woman looked close to my age.

"Hi," I said to Beverly. "I'm Nora."

"Welcome," she said, checking my lesson pass. "I was just about to show everyone how to get up after a fall. That's sure to happen. The rule is roll to the side, sit up, poles to the side, knees up, stand.

She dropped to the ground and demonstrated.

We practiced, and I did pretty well, repeating the instructions to myself like a mantra each time. It didn't bother me a bit that I took a little longer to stand than everyone else in the group. I was just being careful doing the roll to the side. That part was tricky. My skis kept flopping. Of course, we were on level ground now, but still. Tricky.

Next we practiced the snowplow position. That went well.

I gazed at the mountain I was going to ski down— some would call it a slight incline—and tried to drum up enthusiasm for the task ahead.

I *would* enjoy this.

I *would* do well.

Going up on the T-bar lift would be fun.

I pointed my clumsy skis in that direction and followed my group. I was glad I was in the middle of the line. I certainly didn't want to go first.

At the head of the line, Beverly was giving more instructions, but the kids near me were making so much noise, I couldn't hear a word. Well, I'd ask her what she said when we got to the top of the hill. Actually, it would work to my advantage. It would be a good opportunity to talk to her alone.

Beverly went on the lift first.

I brushed a small speck of dirt off my aqua jacket and adjusted the collar. Aqua was one of my colors. Years back I'd had a professional season color analysis done that indicated I was a summer and looked best in pastels. Colors are a powerful design element. They must harmonize with your own individual coloring.

Mary Fran came swishing down a hill off to my left, and I waved to her as our line moved forward, but she didn't see me. After I befriended Beverly, I had no wish to swish down any hill.

The lift was in continuous motion, so a person had to be ready when the next T-bar came along. Tense, watchful, I awaited my turn. I observed the guide in his red Jason's Mountain labeled jacket as he made sure a skier was in position for the journey up the hill. A nice safety measure for beginning skiers, I thought. I liked safety measures.

The noisy kids ahead of me took off, and at last it was my turn. When I stepped toward the lift, my ski tips crossed. Scrambling, flailing my arms for balance, I smacked the lift guide in the shoulder with one of my poles.

"Sorry," I said as I managed to avert disaster and uncross my skis in the nick of time.

Finally, I was in position.

The moving bar connected with the back of my thighs.

Feeling secure, I smiled in relief, relaxed, and sat back for the ride up the hill. Immediately, which turned out to be way, way too late, I realized I'd made a mistake. The T-bar stretched like a bungee cord, and the next thing I knew I was falling backwards. To counter the effect I threw my body forward. Too far, way too far. There was no time to counter the thrust.

I landed facedown in the churned-up snow with itty-bitty pebbles embedded in my upper lip. Above me, the lift continued up the hill, my T-bar swinging in the breeze without me.

"Emergency! Skier down!" the lift guide called. "Next skier, hold off."

"Hey, Mom, did you see that? The lady tried to sit on the T-bar," some kid said loud enough for people to hear on the next mountain.

"Stand back," the lift guide said. "Stand back. Give her room to get up."

I struggled into a sitting position, saw the next T-bar heading for me, and ducked quickly, just in time to avoid getting slammed in the head. Unfortunately, the momentum created by my speedy move combined with the pull of gravity to send me backwards again.

"Stop the lift!" the guide yelled.

"Do we need an EMT?" someone called.

"I'm a nurse," someone shouted. "Does she need a nurse?"

"She's bleeding," the nosy woman with the kid announced to everyone within earshot. "Someone should at least get the First Aid people."

More people gathered around.

"Obviously she didn't listen to the ski instructor when she told us *not* to sit on the T-bar," the older woman said primly as I struggled to get up, attempting to implement the procedures we'd practiced earlier.

Roll to the side, sit up, poles to the side, knees up, stand.

With everyone watching me, onstage so to speak, it took me a little longer to complete the steps than it had during the lesson.

Knees to the side. Stand?

No, that wasn't it. I switched it around.

Poles to the side, knees up, stand.

I knew for sure the *stand* part came last.

Finally, with someone on either side of me, I was pulled to my feet and assisted off the T-bar path.

CHAPTER EIGHT

"Sure looks like someone punched you in the lip, honey. It's all puffy. If you want to change your story, I won't think the less of you," the heavyset woman in the white uniform with the Hazel nametag said as she dabbed my upper lip with a soapy gauze pad.

"No. I'm fine. This happened the way I said it did," I mumbled through semi-closed lips. I wondered whether the solution on the pad was toxic if swallowed, or if I could be allergic to it. I'm allergic to so many things. Dogs, cats, dust, certain soaps, perfumes.

Hands on her broad hips, feet firmly planted about a foot apart, she stood back and stared at me. "Umm-hmm. Well, I know a lot of people, a few guys who could take care of your problem, if you get my drift."

"No." One word was all I was willing to risk. I had already swallowed some soap. Probably toxic. I gagged.

"You look awful. A real blossom on this lip," she said, dipping a fresh gauze pad in clear water. "Such a mess."

"Bad Boys," the theme from the television show *Cops*, blasted from my cell phone, announcing a call from my brother Howie in Florida.

Relieved, I pulled back, flexed my fat lip and mumbled, "Excuse me, I need to take this call. It's vitally important." Big fat lie.

"I understand," she said, depositing the bloody gauze in a biohazard container.

"Hi, Howie. How's everything with my favorite cop on the Miami-Dade PD?" I said as distinctly as I could as I eased off the exam table and squared my boots on the tile floor with the smallest thump I could manage.

"You sound funny. What's the matter?"

"I hope it's someone who can help you," the nurse said in a stage whisper they probably heard in Alabama.

"What? Who was that?" Howie asked. "Help you. What's going on?"

"Nothing. I'm fine." I ran my tongue along my bruised upper lip and tasted the coppery blood residue and the antiseptic soap. The poison soap.

The nurse huffed loudly and shook her head as she ripped the used paper off the table, mumbling, "If a person doesn't count getting punched in the mouth a big deal. . ."

I headed for the door.

"Nora!" Howie said impatiently.

"I'm skiing today."

I gave a bare-bones account of the T-bar incident. A normal reaction would have been to ask, solicitously, if I were all right, would I suffer any lasting effects, and such.

But this was my brother.

He laughed. No questions.

"I'm glad you're so concerned about my well-being, Howie. I'll call you back later. I'm late for my lesson."

He laughed some more.

Finally, he stopped laughing long enough to ask, "What else? I know you're up to something. You took another case, didn't you? I thought you were returning to the City."

"I'll be going back shortly. I just have a few things to clear up first."

"Since you've been in Maine, I check the Silver Stream police blotter when I get it. An old friend in the department forwards it to me when something big comes across. And what do you suppose I noticed today?"

I rolled my eyes and gave a huge sigh. As if he'd seen my expression or heard my sigh, he continued. "Another homicide. So unusual for that area, don't you think?"

"You're as predictable as snow in a Maine winter, Howie. You want to know if I'm involved, right?"

"Are you playing private investigator again, Nora?"

"Of course not."

"I don't believe you. Just don't get too involved, no matter what. You've been lucky before, but your luck won't hold indefinitely. Remember that criminals don't play by the rules. You could get hurt. Or dead."

"There's no violence involved in what I'm doing. I'm not dealing with gangs like you are."

I hung up and made my way to the lift to rejoin my group so I could focus on my reason for being here in the first place, interviewing Beverly, aka ski instructor, lottery ticket thief, husband stealer, person of interest in the case of Floyd and the missing bank account funds.

* * *

Beverly skied over when she saw me get off the lift. Whether she thought I needed help or was just being nice was hard to tell.

"I missed your mishap," she said. "But I heard all about it."

"I hope that's not a request for an instant replay."

She smiled.

"I'm glad you didn't let a little tumble ruin your day. The others are on their second run down the hill. I'll help you catch up. We're still on the snowplow maneuver."

She explained the snowplow again—although I was pretty sure I could handle this—and I headed down the hill. I made it successfully to the bottom, and scooted over to the lift. After two runs I was feeling good about myself and my skills. This wasn't so hard once you got the hang of it.

I chatted with Beverly at every opportunity, keeping the conversation casual, unthreatening, mostly about skiing. Of course, by doing that, I had not learned a thing that would help me find out what I needed to know. If I were a professional investigator I would know a better way to learn what I needed to learn.

After the third run, I decided it was time to shift the focus of the conversation, get more personal.

As I watched Beverly help an older woman who was having a problem snowplowing, my attention shifted back to Silver Stream and the women whose difficulties I needed to address. Thoughts scrolled through my head as if they were written on the rolling ticker at the bottom of a news screen: Marney needed me to locate husband Floyd and the money he took; Margaret needed to recover the money she and cousin Beverly won in the lottery. Both money problems, both involving Beverly. Beverly might have had financial problems herself, or else she wouldn't have cut her cousin Margaret off. I wondered whether she had convinced Floyd to empty his joint account, and share some with her. Anything was possible.

To do my job, I had to get more personal. If I couldn't do that, I'd have to go the serious snooping route, possibly break into computers. I shivered at the thought.

Beverly skied up beside me in line. "One last run practicing the snowplow, then it's on to better things," she said."

"You seem to love your work. Is being a ski instructor a part time job for you, or do you work here year-round?"

"I only work here in the winter," she said.

"It must be nice having summers off, but hard on the pocketbook."

"I manage," she said, giving me a look that warned I was too close to a personal boundary. So I had a choice, either be tactful and hold off a while, or forge ahead with reckless abandon. I went with reckless abandon. It was that kind of day.

"I hope they pay you well or else you'd need another source of income. Since I'm single it would be a problem for me."

She didn't comment. We moved up in the line. If I were reading her body language correctly—tightened jaw muscles, narrowed eyes—she was angry and about ready to shut down, so I tried another tack.

"I tried skiing as I kid," I said. "Before my family moved to New York City, my dad took us to the mountains, maybe this one. I don't remember. But I do remember that I didn't do well."

"You're doing okay now," Beverly said as we waited in line for the T-bar.

"Thanks. I hope I'll be able to come a few more times before I have to go back to New York City."

"When are you leaving?" she asked.

"I haven't decided." Was that ever the truth. "My ex-fiancé . . . he said . . ." I let my voice trail off as the actress in me made a debut. I bit my bottom lip and looked away, reluctant to recount an obviously painful event in my life. At times like this I feel I should have pursued a career in the theater. Emoting further, I gazed at the mountain with what I thought of as my forlorn expression.

Beverly Sue stared at me. "Wants you back?" she finished.

Perfect. I nodded. "Yes. And he lives in my apartment building so I won't be able to avoid him." I paused after that partial truth distorted the facts, big-time. Whatshisname was renting my apartment and I could kick him out at any time.

Without actually staring at her, I was conscious of her reaction. A lift of her brows indicated interest so I continued. "He cheated on me a few weeks before the wedding. I can never trust him again."

"I don't blame you," Beverly said. "I wouldn't trust him either."

I wondered why she and her husband had called it quits.

I was glad there were still several people ahead of us. It gave us more time. I inched forward on my skis, and took a giant step.

"Money was involved," I said, keeping my eyes on the lift line, while keeping Beverly in my peripheral vision.

"The deadly duo. Sex and money. Men want both. I've

been around long enough to know how that works," she said, stabbing her poles into the snow as she moved. "Some men are users. You're lucky you caught on before you married the guy. I found out too late. I'm divorced."

"I'm sorry. That must have been hard. I know how difficult my breakup was. I hope you don't have to run into him often," I said, wondering if her former husband was dead in the truck.

"He works here. As an electrician," Beverly said as we moved toward the T-bar.

"So you see him every day. That must be hard, especially if you want to see someone else."

"Not at all. I ran into him just this morning. You have to be bold. You're young yet. Get to be my age, and you become bolder."

So he wasn't dead. "How do you manage that?" I asked, finding this pretense harder and harder to maintain.

Beverly laughed as she stepped toward the T-bar. "Date his best friend," she said over her shoulder.

"But what if his friend is married?" I asked.

No reply. I got that strained look again, and she took the T-bar without looking back at me.

At the top of the hill, Beverly said to the group, "We've taken enough snowplow runs. You're ready to traverse the hill!"

The daredevil kid in the group skied in front of me and said to Beverly, "Let me go first. I want to go first. Please, please pleeeease."

"Sure," Beverly answered. Then she addressed the group.

"To traverse the hill you will turn your skis while you're going down. Eventually you'll cut from side to side. It's fun, and it's not difficult. You need to go from having your weight evenly distributed on both skis to putting more weight on one ski. If you put most of your weight on the right ski you will turn left and visa versa. She demonstrated the weight shifting in place. We watched her assistant go down the hill, turning this way and that, a thing of precision and beauty. It seemed easy enough. I could do this. I practiced distributing my weight in place, repeating the directions silently like a child's nursery rhyme with each shift of my hips.

Shift, slow turn, traverse the hill. Shift the other way, slow turn back.

Piece of cake.

I put the rhyme to music, singing quietly, "Shift, turn, shift, turn. Traverse the hill." I had a lively tempo going that lent itself to rhythmic shoulder lifts as I stood and waited my turn.

One by one, the class started down the hill. Beverly watched and called encouragement to some, pointers to others. I listened intently, determined to seize this opportunity to make up for the T-bar fiasco.

Finally my turn came. I started off beautifully. Midway down I shifted my weight and began the turn. All was going well. A few of the class members hadn't turned their skis enough, a mistake I wouldn't make.

I was traversing the hill, my weight on the downside ski.

This was easy enough. Fun, even.

A few kids from another group zoomed past, almost knocking me over. Show-offs. I turned a bit more, just to be certain I was doing this correctly.

I heard Beverly yell something. Someone else yelled too, maybe her assistant. I strained to hear, but the showoff kids were making too much noise. Then I saw the kids at the bottom of the hill watching me with rapt attention. That couldn't be good.

"Shift," Beverly yelled. "Turn your skis back again."

I tried to shift. Nothing happened.

"Point your skis down!" One of the kids yelled.

"Stop turning up," someone else called.

I tried again. Nothing happened.

A chorus began to yell. "Turn! Turn! Turn!"

I wanted to yell back, but I thought the effort entailed in yelling might be enough to make me lose my balance. They continued to yell instructions. For heaven sakes, didn't they think I'd turn if I could!

An alarming thing was taking place. It was like I was in the middle of a Stephen King horror story, and I had no control. I was a runaway train; I was a semi hurtling downhill with failing brakes; I was a Coney Island roller-coaster plummeting on a ninety-degree drop.

I. Had. No. Control.

The skis had all the power, and they were taking me backwards down the hill at an alarming rate. Shifting my weight didn't help. The time for shifting had passed. My tips were pointed uphill. Period.

"Look, Mom! There goes the lady from the T-bar lift."

"Watch out! Clear a path," Beverly's assistant called from somewhere below.

"Hey, look! Some woman in a fancy ski outfit is skiing backwards."

"Is she a trick skier?" someone yelled.

"Maybe there's going to be a show," I heard some guy say.

Paralyzed with fear, poles dangling uselessly from my wrists, I stood rigidly on my skis, along for the ride so to speak. Since I couldn't see where I was headed, I tried to recall what was at the bottom of the hill.

Oh, yes. Now I remembered. A clear picture formed, none of it good.

Then through no effort on my part, I seemed to be angling to the left. To counteract that, I leaned forward slightly and a bit to the right. I attempted to put equal weight on both skis. That should do it.

No. Not so.

I picked up speed.

"Look at her go," the daredevil kid yelled. "I have to try that!"

At the top of the hill, Beverly's hand went to her

mouth, her face a mask of shock. No body language expert required to read that expression.

"Hurry! Get those people out of her way," someone called in an official voice. It sounded like the guide from the T-bar lift.

"Can't she steer?"

"Move! Outa the way. Hurry."

"This is amazing!" the older woman called.

I stood erect and slowed a bit. Not enough though.

"She's heading for the puddle."

Suddenly, I came to an abrupt stop as if someone had jammed on the brakes. The skis stopped. I did not. Arms pinwheeling to counter momentum that couldn't be countered, I fell backwards. Seconds later I was sitting in the mud puddle at the bottom of the hill, my aqua jacket splattered with shades of brown, my face spotted here and there, my legs and rear end very wet.

People surrounded me. A few oddballs clapped. The lift guide said hello, as if we were old friends, and offered me a hand. I jabbed my poles into the ground, missed him by a mere fraction and ripped my muddy ski pants.

My skiing career had come to an abrupt and undignified end.

CHAPTER NINE

I was changing into dry clothes, a pair of jeans and a blue wool sweater, when Beverly appeared at the door of the ladies' room.

"I never saw anything like that. Are you okay?" she asked.

I decided to be cool about the whole thing, suck it up as they say, so I didn't mention the abominable condition of my tony ski clothes, the damage to my self-esteem, or my aching body parts. "I'm fine. Well, sort of fine. I'll survive."

"You don't need to go to the first aid station?"

And deal with busybody Hazel again?

"Absolutely not. A glass of wine in the lounge is all the medicine I need."

"Want company? I don't have another class for several hours."

Perfect. I couldn't have planned it better. "Yes, that would be good."

We picked a table next to the window, and I saw Mary Fran heading for the big lift, chatting with some guy, and marveled at how fast she worked.

When the waiter came we each ordered white wine.

I figured it was only a matter of time before Beverly realized I was here to investigate her, so I wasted no time with please-pass-the-salt conversation. I needed to find out what she knew about Floyd as well as the location of Margaret's portion of the lottery winnings.

"I figure you're not here to learn to ski, so are you up here looking to meet someone?"

Unbidden, probably because it was the last thing I

wanted to consider, images of Nick Renzo flashed through my head. I felt him pulling me onto his lap, kissing me, holding my hand, whispering in my ear, dancing as we had danced at the Silver Stream Harvest dance, close and loving, holding me as if he never wanted to let me go.

No, I definitely wasn't looking to meet someone.

"Not exactly. I'm company for my friend. While she's looking in general, I'm looking for a specific man, a guy who does construction work here. Since your ex is an electrician here, maybe he knows him. Or even you? Floyd LeBeau."

She leaned back, her eyes focusing on me with a hardness I hadn't seen until now. For one wild moment, I pictured her in a shooting stance, her arms extended, hands gripping a lethal weapon.

"Why?"

Refusing to be cowed by her look or the challenge in her tone, I said, "His wife hasn't heard from him in a while. She's worried."

Her demeanor morphed further, and she leaned forward aggressively, both arms planted on the table, and I saw the part of her that probably hadn't changed since Marney knew her in high school, that awful part that was capable of meanness on many levels, that was able to read people and target their weaknesses.

Right now, I was the target.

In a harsh voice, she said, "Marmaduke's looking for her husband, is she? The ferret lady wants him back? And you're going to find him, I suppose."

I know she expected me to shrink back, to falter and slip into defensive mode. *Oh, no . . . I didn't mean to imply . . . didn't mean to offend . . .*

That would be the natural reaction. Defend myself? I think not.

"She wants me to find him."

"That's hard to believe, unless, of course, money is involved. Or does she just want to shoot him and be done with it?"

Shoot him? I understood that she was exaggerating, but her words still struck me as extreme.

"Do you know where he is?" I asked, all pretense of friendliness gone.

"You a relative?"

"No," I said.

"Who the hell are you?"

She folded her arms, and stared, her eyes boring into me, challenging, demanding. Her attempt to intimidate would have worked on most people. It was wasted on me.

I'd been stared at by the best, cornered in high school stairwells by violent girls looking for a fight in that school I attended in the Bronx, and I had learned quickly to hold my own. Any action that signaled appeasement or backing down—looking away, blinking rapidly, twitching, handing over what they wanted—was a signal that brought on greater consequences.

So I stared back and took my time replying. "She hired me."

Beverly blinked, literally.

"Hired? You're a private investigator?"

"Yes." Technically a lie, but I *was* investigating and privacy *was* involved. Put the two together and what have you got?

Although she was perceptive, I didn't expect her to call me on it. What could she do? Ask for ID? From a woman fresh from the puddle at the bottom of the slopes? I think not.

She was silent for several seconds.

"Are you any good?"

Another surprise. I kept my expression neutral. "I am," I answered, throwing modesty to the winds and stretching the truth on the same currents. "Interested in hiring me?"

Her brows shot up. "You never know."

She finished the last sip of her wine and pushed her glass aside.

Then I went for it. "What do you need a PI for? Lose some money? Maybe a large hunk of cash?"

It was difficult to keep my expression neutral, not let the unease show. I wasn't sure how hard to push. I was not good at this. Definitely. I wondered whether there was a book on the subject. I'd check Amazon.

"What's that supposed to mean?"

Wise or unwise, I continued to push. "I heard you won a lot of money."

She stood so quickly her chair toppled over. Nudging it aside, she fisted her hands and planted them on the table. "I don't know what you're talking about. Where'd you hear this? And what are you after?"

I'd come this far. I realized I had to continue, despite her threatening posture.

"A lottery ticket! I know you and Margaret played the same numbers every week. I know the numbers came in. What happened to the ticket, Beverly?"

"So that's what this is all about? That's why you came up here?"

"Who else knew you played those numbers?"

Anger oozed from every pore. Then she surprised me by answering. "Eddie and Floyd, of course. I don't know who else," she fired. "I also don't have the ticket. It's missing. So get lost."

Without another word, she stormed off.

I watched her go, certain I'd burned a few bridges, but knowing no other way to go. Beverly knew why I had come, knew she was in the crosshairs.

I checked in at the main desk, and asked about Floyd. No one had seen him. I picked up a flyer for an après ski party this evening, signed for a room, and asked about a cleaning service for my jacket and ski pants. Fortunately, they had a special one-hour service I could use. I was willing the pay the extra for it.

Next, I called Mary Fran, who didn't answer, of course. I left a message on her cell phone, told her to pick up the room key at the desk, and dragged my tired and abused body up to take a nap. With all the people expected at this après ski affair, someone would probably know where Floyd was. Maybe I could solve some of this mystery tonight. I hoped so, because so far, nothing.

A few hours later, I suddenly shot up from my nap and threw my feet over the edge of the bed, heart pounding and fists clenched as adrenalin charged through my body. Mary Fran had burst into the room like a creature with a herd of stampeding cattle at her back.

What was wrong with this woman!

After depositing her ski equipment in the closet with enough thunking and clanking to rouse the folks in this entire wing, she stamped her way into the main part of the room like a paso doble dancer, arms raised, fingers snapping, and asked, "Were you sleeping?"

"Seriously? That's your question?"

"I guess you were. Sorry," she said, not sounding the least bit sorry, not altering her dancing stance. "I met a very nice guy. We're meeting for drinks later."

"Oh? He has information about Floyd? Or Beverly?"

The paso doble dance stopped mid-stomp. "You haven't cleared that up yet?"

I just stared at her.

"I guess that's a no," she said, dropping her arms.

"We're going to an après ski social," I said. "We have to be there tonight because people who work here will attend. Someone's got to know something about Floyd. If Beverly knows where he is, she isn't saying, at least not to me. I talked to her. It didn't go well. I think there's more to this than I first thought."

"Maybe we should ask about Floyd at the front desk," Mary Fran suggested.

"I already did that. They know nothing."

"Hmm. Too bad." She paused. "I met a new guy."

"Not interested. Were you listening to me? We're here on business, and that comes first."

Resigned, Mary Fran plunked into a chair by the desk, then suddenly hopped up with a re-burst of energy. "I found out that Beverly's room is at the end of the personnel housing section, a corner unit." She ran to the window, and pointed. "There it is! All the way back there."

I joined her by the window. "Good work. I've got the key, not that I'd go inside. That would be trespassing."

Not that trespassing would stop me, but I could tell Mary Fran was uneasy about it.

I began to pace. "I need a plan. It will involve surveillance," I said. "She and Floyd could be into something together. He might be hiding at her place, or meeting her. I need to hide out near her place and watch for him."

I paused and thought about it. "Or she could be hooking up with someone else. Hard to tell without watching her."

I faced Mary Fran. "This whole mess is like a Beverly sandwich. Margaret on one side, Marney on the other and Beverly in the middle. Money is the dressing."

"You think other people are involved, too?"

"It's possible."

I paced the room, concentrating, impatient to come up with a plan, shushing Mary Fran with a wave of my hand when she interrupted the ebb and flow of my thoughts. Ideas rolled like quicksilver as I visualized one scenario after another. Finally, a plan gelled.

"Okay. Here's what we'll do. First, the après ski party. We'll ask around about Floyd. You'll talk to Beverly."

"About what?"

"I don't know! Hair. Your salon. Anything. Just probe. She might be more forthcoming with you." I paused. "Then again, maybe not. But see what you can find out. Don't let her know we're together, although if she guesses, and she might, don't deny it. You have to appear to be upfront with her. I told her I was here with a friend, but didn't mention a name. I said the friend was interested in meeting someone.

She knows I'm here to look for Floyd."

"My new guy mentioned the après ski party. He'll be there."

"We're here to work. Don't mention that new guy again. I don't want to hear about him."

"Okay, but wait till you see him! To die for."

"Don't make me crazy, Mary Fran. Next, you need to watch Beverly. You need to notice who she talks to. I intend to leave the party ahead of her and go to her place. And your job-"

"Is to call and warn you when she's leaving the party, right?"

"Yes. Good. You need to be super alert without being obvious. Watch her, but don't stare. Can you do that?"

"I was born to do that. I own a hair salon!"

"Right. Your job will be to phone me the minute she heads for the door."

"So you can make your escape. I got it."

"You sure?" I asked.

"Of course. You can count on me." She paused and looked at me, a question behind her eyes.

"What?" I asked.

"I know you have a key. You're going in to look around, right? You're not going to stand around outside and wait for her. It gets really cold here at night, not like this afternoon which was a freakish weather event, the temp going above freezing and all."

"I was going to do surveillance only, but maybe I should go into her place, get it over with."

"Hmmm." Mary Fran mulled that over, then said, "What if you get caught? Breaking and entering is a crime. You could be arrested, you know."

Those words brought on a light bulb moment, and her eyes opened wider. "Could I be arrested as an accomplice?"

I did not know the answer to that one, so I shrugged with an insouciance I didn't feel. "Such a worrywart. I won't get caught."

CHAPTER TEN

I stashed my freshly-laundered jacket and super-traction L.L. Bean boots under a bench by the door that led to the personnel housing units out back, so I could find them quickly when the time came. An unfortunate fashion choice made this necessary. I had to wear my Jimmy Choo leather skimmers to the après ski party, a faux pas on several levels. Not only did they not fit the occasion, but the leather soles offered no traction on snow. Thus, the need for boots under the bench.

In my haste, and there was no excuse for not consulting my list—I assume full blame here—I'd thrown the skimmers into my bag because I truly love them. They were among the items I'd purchased when I was flush with cash back in the days when I'd had an actual job in the City. Had I been thinking, I'd have picked something more appropriate for a ski resort.

"Are you covering the boots so no one will see them, or are you a neatness freak?" Mary Fran asked as she watched me tug my jacket to cover the toes of my boots.

"Neatness," I lied as I got to my feet.

"Hiding them is a good idea," Mary Fran said in contradiction.

When we neared the door of the après ski party, I stopped. "Wait here. I'll go in first. Give me a few minutes before you enter. No need to let Beverly know we're together. Although she'll probably figure that out soon enough."

I showed my room pass and walked in. The large hall

was surprisingly cozy, with a fire crackling in the fireplace, candles set in hurricane lamps on every table, a bar at one end and a buffet at the other. Beverly stood near the bar talking to the T-bar lift guy. We made eye contact and she turned her back.

The lift guy pretended he didn't see me. I could understand that. He probably pictured me knocking over the bar, or crashing into the food table, something big that would destroy his evening.

About thirty or forty people stood around in small groups, talking, laughing, most with a drink in hand. I adjusted the cowl neck on my chunky white wool sweater and made my way to the buffet table. Most people wore low-heeled après ski boots. My Jimmy Choos and I didn't fit, for sure.

I stopped dead in my tracks when I noticed Hazel from the first aid station. Too late. She saw me and yelled, "Yoo-hoo! Over here."

She was with two women from my ski class. If I didn't have to investigate Beverly, I would have ducked out the exit, but there was no ducking this trio.

"We saw the . . . incident. I'm sure you'll get better," the older woman said, shaking her head, sympathy oozing from every pore as she moved close enough for me to smell the clams casino on her breath while she scrutinized my face for evidence of trauma.

I wanted to run and hide, possibly yank a bag over my head.

"None the worse for wear?" the petite woman with the high hairdo asked.

Hazel's eyes widened as her busybody antenna kicked into high gear. "What *else* did he do?" she said before I could answer.

"Someone harmed you? A man? Oh, you poor thing. Is he a stalker or an abuser?" Ms. Clams Casino asked, one hand clutching her throat. "How awful. Can we help? Is he here tonight?" Eyes narrowing, she glanced around.

Looking directly at Hazel, I said firmly, "No man was involved. I fell skiing, as you all know. That's it. No big deal."

"You don't have to be embarrassed," the clams casino eater said as she eyed my fat lip which had puffed up some since the T-bar incident. "We understand. We won't say another word about it."

"Yes, mum's the word," said Ms. High Hair.

Hazel smirked.

We chatted until the theme from the *Lone Ranger* sounded on my cell. Nick to the rescue. Thank heavens. I excused myself, noted Mary Fran poking her head in the door and held my phone up so she could see why I was coming her way.

"Do not get sidetracked with your new guy, if he's here," I whispered as I passed her. "Keep your mind on the mission."

As soon as I was out the door, I said, "Hi, Nick. How's the investigation going?"

"That's why I'm calling. The body's been identified and—"

"Who?" I asked before he finished.

"Floyd LeBeau."

I gasped loud enough for people passing to glance my way.

"It's definitely murder. I need to question Beverly and Eddie since the Binderwig ring was found at the scene. I'll go up in the morning."

Several people heading into the après ski party gave me odd looks, and I realized my mouth was agape. I snapped it shut and turned away.

"Floyd? Murdered!" I exclaimed, making a weak attempt to keep my voice from cracking.

"Three shots, one to the right side, one to the head, one to the heart. All bullets were recovered from the body. One casing was found wedged between the seats. We'll probably find the other two when we examine the wreck more carefully."

"So he was shot at close range?"

"Very close. Probably by someone who got into his truck. Can't figure that one. As near as we can tell he was shot, then set on fire. No other vehicles around."

"There's no question that it was Floyd, I guess."

"None. The teeth were intact. Harold made the identification from x-rays."

"Maybe he trusted the person he let into his truck."

"Can't say."

Another murder. And it affected people I was involved with. I really had to leave Silver Stream. Soon.

I could almost hear my brother going on about how I kept getting involved in murder investigations. Well, not this time, Howie. Nick was in charge. Period.

Of course, I'd have to talk to Marney, see if she still wanted me to investigate the money situation. I didn't want to consider the possibility that the money was related to the murder. Why I had this pesky feeling that it was probably all connected, I didn't know.

As soon as I went back into the party hall, Mary Fran headed in my direction.

"Beverly Sue guessed we were together. I may have lost a customer," Mary Fran said. "Who called?"

"Nick. He said—"

"This is great, isn't it?" she interrupted. "I've met so many people, some new folks, and some I know but haven't seen in years. And Beverly thinks you're investigating her, or Eddie, not Floyd. You'd better watch it with her, and the guy I met on the slopes is here, eyeing me. We haven't talked yet. I'm sure he's getting ready to come over."

Mary Fran took a breath. "I wanted to ask Beverly about her ring to see if she knew where it was, but my lips were zipped on that one." She turned. "Oh, there's my friend, over by the bar munching on a pretzel, talking to some blonde, but I don't think he's really interested in her. Does he look interested?"

I resisted the urge to stamp my foot. "Mary Fran, stop rambling. Tell me more about Beverly."

"Right," she said, her gaze never straying from the guy and the blonde.

"Mary Fran! Focus. Beverly! What did you talk about?"

Startled, she drew her eyes from the new guy and stared at me. "Right. Beverly wasn't very friendly. I don't think she likes me anymore. She probably won't be back to Hot Heads Heaven. Don't know where she'll go for her bleach job. Anyway, she's not dumb. First thing she said was she knew we were together. She doesn't want to get involved in anything you're investigating. She thinks you want to know about . . ." She paused and held up her hand as if she were trying to think.

"Know about what? Floyd?"

"I think he's coming over. Act casual."

I caught myself before I grabbed her arm and shook her. "Mary Fran! What does Beverly think I want to know about?"

"I'm not sure," she whispered. "Something about some group that comes up here every few weeks. Floyd and Eddie were friendly with them at first, and then Eddie backed off."

"What group? Who are you talking about?"

"She figured I knew, and I didn't want to give away the fact that I didn't know."

Mary Fran glanced to her left and smirked, and I noticed her new guy had stopped to talk to someone else.

"I think Beverly plans to meet someone later," she went on. "When I walked over there, she was on her cell, and she tried to whisper, but as you know I have supersonic-slash-bionic hearing."

I rolled my eyes but didn't interrupt.

"I heard her say something about this being the last time. She sounded angry. Maybe she's meeting Floyd."

I shook my head. "Not Floyd. That call I took was from Nick. They identified the body."

Suddenly I had Mary Fran's undivided attention.

"Floyd LeBeau?" she whispered. "Dead?"

"Yes."

"Get outa here!" she said, her voice loud enough to get the attention of several people near us, including her new guy.

"Shhh. Quiet! Do not mention this to a soul."

"Absolutely."

"I'll leave soon, so keep your dialing finger ready."

"Right, boss."

Beverly watched us from her location near the bar. Instead of averting her gaze when I made eye contact, the way most people would when caught staring, aggressive Beverly continued to stare.

Unbidden, Margaret's original claim about stolen reference books appeared front and center in my thoughts. Had Margaret made that up? Or had Beverly Sue actually stolen reference books? I could picture Beverly doing a lot of horrible things, but stealing library books was not among them.

"I'm going to talk to her before I leave. Stay here."

Mary Fran touched my arm, almost like a warning. "For what it's worth, she doesn't like you at all."

"I know."

Curiosity about the person Beverly was going to meet, especially the reason for her anger at that person, floated through my head as I walked over. Her stare mutated into a glare, a look she'd probably perfected the first time she watched *Rapunzel* say the words, 'Mirror, mirror on the wall.' No, that wasn't *Rapunzel*. *Cinderella* or maybe *Snow White*.

"What?" Beverly fired before I'd even spoken.

I could hear Aunt Ida in my head saying you can catch more flies with honey than with vinegar, so I tried the honey approach. "Beverly, I know you don't want to get involved, but please, talk to me for a few minutes. I won't use you as a source, I promise."

"Get involved? I don't know a thing that will help your investigation. Get lost."

Honey wasn't working, but I was not ready to try a different approach yet. The lottery ticket was still a problem. Of course, I had no intention of mentioning that yet. What I did need was to gauge her reaction when I mentioned Floyd.

"I know you have little concern for Marney."

"Little concern? Really? How about none!"

"Regardless, you knew Floyd. He worked here. You must have seen him around. Have you seen him this week?" I paused, waiting for a reply, or even a telling expression, but she remained stone-faced.

"Have you seen him in passing or at a distance recently? Maybe today?"

Determined to let the question hang for as long as I could, I went for several excruciatingly long seconds without speaking. Silence didn't seem to affect her. I was about ready to throw in the towel and leave, when I saw a slight flex of her jaw muscle. Jaw clenching. A good sign. If I hadn't been watching so closely, I never would have noticed.

Beverly was too proud to simply walk away, but she was nervous. My questions were making the Tough One uncomfortable. She knew something. I was sure of it.

Instead of leaving, I pushed on, this time approaching from another angle. "Your ex-husband works with him. Perhaps he mentioned something to you? Something that will help me find Floyd?"

"I don't have anything to do with my ex-husband. I was friends with Floyd, which you probably know about, courtesy of bigmouth Marmaduke. Although I'm sure she thought there was more going on. I'm not interested in either of them now. So the Great Dane can go scratch her fleas on that one. I don't care whether you find Floyd or not."

She edged away as her eyes drifted to Mary Fran, who

was finally talking with her new guy.

I decided to push a little more. "Why did Floyd need money so badly?"

Her eyes flickered in surprise, but she came right back at me. "I guess you know more than I do because I wasn't aware he was in dire straits. Regardless, you're not getting the message. I couldn't care less about anything you're investigating. Floyd can rot in hell for all I care, and his dog-faced wife with him."

With that she turned and headed across the floor. I followed. It's easy to be brave when there's a roomful of people around.

"Did he try to get money from you?"

She swung around, anger oozing around the edges. "Stay away from me, Nora. Keep your distance or you'll regret it."

I mentally glued my feet to the floor. "Or did you ask him for money? Were you in debt?"

Eyes flaring like a demented actor in a cheap horror movie, she took a step toward me, expecting, I'm sure, to intimidate me into taking a step back. She was a hair taller, obviously stronger. I should go to the gym, work on my biceps. My shoulders, my legs. I could wear that cute little workout outfit I bought over a year ago, the black one with the pink and white stripes down the side of the legs.

I didn't move.

Beverly could probably take me in a fight. But she was not going to attack me here. And it was obvious she didn't understand about my feet being glued to the floor.

We were almost nose to nose. Her pores were larger than I'd thought. I had some cream that would do wonders for pores.

"I don't care who hired you. My affairs are none of your business. I'm warning you to back off."

"So this is a threat?"

"More like a promise. You are the last person I ever want to see again. So back off."

Her cell phone rang, and she stormed away to answer it. For a rash moment I considered following, but common sense prevailed, and I rejoined Mary Fran and her new guy.

"Nora, this is Sal Baldino. Sal's a great skier. Nora and I came up together this morning. She's learning to ski."

We shook hands. "How'd it go today?" he asked.

"Wonderful," I lied.

Sal was tall, swarthy and not bad looking. He reminded me of a young Al Pacino. Women were probably attracted to him. I was not, and I didn't know why because I liked Al Pacino. Strange. This Al, I mean Sal, didn't hold the same charm.

His clothes were expensive, very high-end, something I recognized at first glance. When I had that high-paying job as a computer analyst in the City and was heavily into upscale clothing, I'd focused on designers, fashions and fabrics with the enthusiasm some would devote to a hobby.

I had some beautiful pieces, but this guy was out of my league. The last time I'd seen clothes in this price range was at a "casual" cocktail party thrown by my former boss for his daughter who'd gotten a job as assistant to the newly-appointed ambassador to a small country I'd never heard of.

I tried to place the sweater he wore. Six or maybe eight-ply cashmere, crew collar, stone color, Italian designer. Brunello Cucinelli? Yes, maybe.

I wondered what he did for a living. Stocks? Hedge funds? Something illegal? With the Al Pacino reference circling in my head next to Floyd's murder, my thoughts flew straight to the mob-related activities featured in *The Godfather*. Then to *The Sopranos*. Hit man? Could Sal be a hit man? I blinked forcefully and shook my head to clear away such a foolish idea. I reined in my thoughts. My imagination was cranking overtime, probably because I was nervous about venturing out. Snooping made me nervous. I was not a born snoop, for sure.

I selected another crab-stuffed mushroom. These were so good. I loved mushrooms. I loved crab. Put them together, and the result was the perfect food.

I positioned myself so I could watch Beverly across the room as I pretended interest in Mary Fran's narration about a difficult run she'd taken. By nodding my head at appropriate moments and dabbing my mouth with a napkin, I was also able to monitor Al. No, Sal. With my last dab, I noticed his gaze shift to Beverly.

Did she incline her head toward him? Or was I imagining that? Hard to tell.

On impulse, I interrupted Mary Fran's mogul-by-mogul account and turned to Sal. "You don't happen to know a guy named Floyd LeBeau, do you, Al?"

Shock sent Mary Fran's eyebrows skidding into her hairline.

"Excuse me. I mean *Sal*, of course."

He barely reacted. "Does this guy work around here?"

"Yes," I said.

"Name's not ringing any bells." His direct eye contact was close to unnerving. Dark, intense eyes. Al Pacino eyes, *Godfather* eyes.

"Umm. Well, if you'll both excuse me. I have to get up early. Mary Fran, I'm going to head back to the room."

Once clear of the party room, I hurried around to the back door, grabbed the jacket that I'd left under the bench, and gaped at the empty spot. The boots were missing.

Someone had stolen my L.L. Beans? What kind of a place was this? I rushed down the hall, checking under and around every bench and potted plant, hoping some prankster had moved them. Nothing. They were gone.

Going into the cold Maine mountain night wearing these flats was crazy. My feet could freeze. I could slip. On the other hand, if I didn't go, I wouldn't get to see who Beverly was meeting, and that could be important.

Boots or no boots, I had to brave it because once Beverly found out Floyd was dead and she was a suspect, or maybe her ex was, she would set up a wall around herself that would be hard to penetrate.

I felt the key in the pocket of my slacks, unsure of whether I'd have the nerve to use it or not. I'd decide when I got near her place.

I pulled on my gloves and opened the door. There was a thermometer next to the door. It was probably incorrect because it registered five below zero. It couldn't have dropped that much. It had been warm enough this afternoon to create a puddle for a person to tumble into.

I took one step and one deep breath. My nose hairs froze. Okay, so the thermometer was probably correct. That puddle at the base of the hill had probably frozen hours ago. I closed the door behind me and stood for a moment. The shoveled path that led to the employees' housing section was well lit, lined with packed snow. Across the way on the other side of a parking lot was a section of expensive units. People like Sal probably stayed there.

I hesitated before moving.

Designer icicles decorated every tree. It was beautiful. Light from a fat blue-white moon kissed every icy surface from tree limbs to rooftops to lighted pathways, turning this part of the world into fairytale territory.

I could be a princess alighting from her carriage, diamond crown in place, spotlight on me as I surveyed my kingdom.

I took one cautious step onto the path. Concentrating, attentive, I took one more careful step and then another. Then, without warning, my Jimmy Choos and I were airborne. Fortunately, the limb of an evergreen laden with ice hung low enough for me to grab. Scrambling for purchase, my imaginary crown disappearing as quickly as it had come, I swung myself into the snow bank alongside the path and landed feetfirst in a classic dismount maneuver that rated a ten, if anyone had been keeping score. Then I wobbled a bit and threw my hands out for balance. In the next instant, I crashed hands first through the sheen of ice. I connected with the under-layer of hard, crusty snow.

Stunned, frozen, I didn't move for several seconds,

time enough for icy tentacles to snake through my hands
and wrap around my arms, time enough for me to wonder
whether I'd lost my shoes. My feet were that cold.

Desperate, I tried to get up, planting my knees in the
snow for better balance and added oomph. That didn't work.
I fell forward. I tried three more times with the same result.
In the distance, I heard music wafting from the après ski
party. I could be here a long time.

If my toes froze, if they got the dreaded frostbite I'd
heard about over the years, gangrene would set in and some
doctor would give the word: Amputate! I felt tears pressing
behind my eyes, and I forced myself to get control. If they
froze too, I'd be in deeper doo. My lids would become
cemented shut, or worse.

On my next attempt to get to my feet, I heard the
welcome sound of crunching snow behind me. Rescue,
thank God. I tried to stand, and slipped again.

"Hold on. I'll help," a man said.

I recognized the voice immediately, and turned my
head. Oh, no. Anyone but him.

"Oh, it's you," Sal said, putting both his hands under
my arm.

"Someone stole my good boots," I felt compelled to
explain as he helped me to my feet. "Thank you. I'm so glad
you came along when you did."

Sort of glad.

"I'm happy I could be of assistance."

I stepped onto the slippery path with great care, my
mind racing for possible excuses for my presence on the
path to the personnel housing section or possibly the
expensive units. Taking in the sights? Checking the
temperature? Admiring the phase of the moon?

"You all right?"

"Fine."

"You don't have boots on. I thought your room was
upstairs."

"I just stepped out to see . . . the ice formations on the

trees. Certainly is exquisite, isn't it?"

He did not look at the ice formations, not even a glance. He just stared at me. Being the perceptive woman I am, I figured he didn't believe me.

"Well, thank you again. I guess I'll go back inside now." That sounded lame, so I added, "Enough beauty for one night."

"Right."

I expected him to ask where I was headed, so I took a few careful steps and reached for the doorknob. As if it were a timed move, precisely calculated, someone inside also grabbed the knob, turned and pushed. The door flew open, almost knocking me off the step. I wobbled. Sal moved into position behind me. Fortunately for both of us, I managed to stay upright.

"Beverly!"

"Nora?"

The "Eye of the Tiger" blasted from my cell phone, Mary Fran calling to warn me. I didn't bother to answer.

CHAPTER ELEVEN

Since there is no such thing as a cloak of invisibility, I did the next best thing. I looked Beverly right in the eye, smiled my friendliest and said, "Well, good night. It's been a busy day."

I turned to Sal and wished him a good night. I caught the door before it slammed behind Beverly, who stood there staring at my back, I'm sure.

Despite my frozen, aching feet, I hotfooted it up the stairs to my room. So far, my plans had not gone well. Time to re-group. Too bad I was a novice investigator and had no idea how to accomplish that. Once in the room, I switched on the bathroom light, left the others off, grabbed the binoculars and a blanket and dragged a chair to the window. I wrapped the blanket around my feet and watched Beverly wave goodbye to Sal as he headed off the path, presumably to his unit as she continued to her room. I wondered whether they had talked about me.

I rested my elbows on the windowsill and watched her enter the employees' residence. I remained in place until my arms got tired, about ten minutes, then set the binoculars on the windowsill, but continued my stakeout, eyes drooping.

That's what this was, of course. A stakeout. I, Nora Lassiter, computer analyst, member of the Lassiter clan, fake detective, photography hobbyist, was on a stakeout. I should have one of those broad-brimmed hats, a fedora I think they're called. Mine would be white felt with a black band at the base of the crown. I snapped the imaginary brim down in front, and continued to keep my eyes on the target area.

About half an hour later, I needed to go to the

bathroom. I tried not to think about it, which made me think about it more. Finally, I left my post. Less than a minute later I was back on the job.

Someone dressed in dark colors, head down, hood up, hurried from the employees' residence entrance. If he had been in Beverly's room I could have walked in on him if I'd entered to search the place. I snatched up the binoculars and focused, but couldn't make out much. Better binoculars might help, something with night vision, maybe military grade. I watched as the figure dashed from very dim light into the circle of light cast by one of the post lanterns—I thought it was a man—and proceeded up a slight incline toward the cluster of expensive-looking A-frames. He disappeared around a corner. Less than a minute later he reappeared, carrying two large duffel bags. Money, drugs, guns? His ski clothes? I wished I'd been able to see which A-frame he'd gone to. Wished even more I knew what was in those bags.

My heart rate bumped up a notch with every step he took.

This was important. I could feel it.

I needed to follow him, but without boots that would be impossible. My flats were too thin, Mary Fran's boots were too small, and using my ski boots wasn't worth considering.

I kept watch for another hour or so, then gave up and collapsed in a heap on my bed.

* * *

A loud knocking woke me from a sound sleep. Seconds later, I was on my feet, alert, standing in a square of bright morning sun, still fully dressed. Some people are slow to come around in the morning. I am not one of them. I take after my father and hit the ground running. Actually, I should have been running hours ago. The digital clock on the night table beside my bed said ten-oh-four. So late.

Mary Fran was snoring up a storm and didn't stir. I never heard her come in last night.

The knocking continued, and I went to the door, peered through the peephole and smiled as I turned the knob.

"Nick!"

"Hi, sweet stuff. You're up and dressed already?" he said, pulling me into his arms and kissing my neck, which was wonderful but did make me wonder whether he detected my morning breath.

Dressed in a winter bomber uniform jacket the color of his dark brown slacks, his crisp khaki shirt visible at the neck, he looked wonderful.

"I've been up for hours," I lied, taking his campaign hat and tossing it on a chair, wishing I'd brushed my teeth before I'd opened the door.

He laughed. "At the crack of dawn, I'll bet. And you've been on the slopes already."

"How did you know?"

"I'm the sheriff. It's my job to know things."

I brushed my hand over the star on his sleeve. He sat on the edge of the bed, and I sat down beside him.

"When did you get here?" I said, diverting my morning breath as I spoke.

"Just after eight. I've already interviewed Beverly. I'll talk to Eddie in an hour."

"And?"

"She seemed genuinely shocked when I told her about Floyd. About the ring, she claims she returned it to Eddie when they split. Said she threw it at him."

I covered my mouth with tightly closed fingers. "That's probably true. After all, it wasn't a diamond. A woman would hold onto a diamond. Maybe sell it."

As soon as the words were out, I wanted to snatch them back. Crystal the Lovely, with the perfect figure and the long dark hair that flowed like a silk curtain in a summer breeze, may have held onto the diamond he'd given her.

Since she'd broken their engagement, the ring should have been returned. If it hadn't, it might be a sore spot. I waited.

The silence stretched between us, along with my patience and curiosity.

I finally blurted, "Did Crystal return the ring?"

The hint of a smile touched his lips. I suspected he had known what I was thinking. Such a perceptive man.

"Why don't you take a shower, and I'll meet you downstairs in the coffee shop. If I sit on this bed with you another minute, I'll convert the images in my head into reality. Unless you're ready for that—"

I hopped up, knowing he had no intention of discussing his ex-fiancée with me. He was an honorable man, which was annoying sometimes, but which also drew me to him. However, right now I did want to know, which I suppose makes me less than honorable.

"Give me a couple of hours," I said.

"Twenty-five minutes." He stood, put his arms around me and kissed me on my morning-breath mouth. "Dress warmly. It's still below zero. We can take a stroll outside before you go. I love this weather."

He loves below zero? Crazy Maine man.

Forty-five minutes later I met him in the coffee shop, sitting with a man I didn't recognize.

"Nora, this is Eddie Binderwig," Nick said, his expression somber. "Beverly's former husband. He worked with Floyd for years. I just told him about Floyd's death."

I couldn't tell whether Eddie was upset by Floyd's death or not. I wondered whether Beverly had given him a heads-up. Or if he knew before anyone else.

As if divining my thoughts, Nick said, "Eddie said this is the first he's heard of it."

Eddie nodded, his somber expression mirroring Nick's. Whether this was pretense or not, I couldn't tell. Marney had said that Floyd and Eddie had fought over something, she had no idea what, and they were no longer friends. Whether that was true or not, I didn't know.

Eddie glanced at me.

"Sorry to hear about your friend," I said, taking a chair at the small round table.

Eddie gave another nod to acknowledge I'd spoken. I tried to picture him with Beverly. I couldn't. She came across as lively and full of life. I could see her as the town flirt. He seemed sluggish, dull, depressed. The terrible news he'd received could account for some of his world-weary appearance, but if they were not friends, something else was bothering him. Nick had him on the persons of interest list. That might do it.

I wondered whether Eddie had murdered Floyd. He probably thought his wife had an affair with Floyd. Marney believed that. Beverly denied it to me, which may or may not have been the truth.

I also wondered what Beverly had seen in him. She'd married him over twenty years ago. Maybe he was better looking then, young and virile, his face not as weathered, his eyes not as droopy, his hair not as sparse. He had a crew cut, and most of the crew had bailed out.

Perhaps he had a wonderful sense of humor, or possessed attributes so endearing that she couldn't resist.

"Nora knows Marney," Nick said, breaking the silence.

"That so? Never liked that woman much."

Eddie's left brow inched up. He turned my way and angled the right side of his mouth down. It came across as a partial smirk. Odd facial manipulation. Left brow up, right side of mouth down. I had the strongest desire to attempt the maneuver. Later when I was alone, I'd try it.

Beverly couldn't have been attracted to his facial expressions.

"Why didn't you like Marney?" I asked.

Ignoring me, he turned to Nick. "I gotta run. There's an electrical problem with lift four I have to see to. You need to talk again, I'll be around."

As he pushed away from the table, Nick placed a restraining hand on his arm. "Hold up. Just a few more things."

I thought Nick was going to repeat my question.

Wary, Eddie sat forward, his large hands gripping the empty coffee mug. "I know you're looking to find out who done this. I ain't your guy. No sir. Wasn't me. I been here all week."

Nick nodded. "Twenty-four-seven?"

"Yep."

"In view the whole time?"

"Well, I was down sick with some bug for two days, but I didn't leave the mountain."

"Anyone see you those days?"

"I called Bev."

"She come by?"

"Too busy. Besides, she said she hoped I'd vomit my brains out."

Based on the short time I'd known Beverly, that had a ring of truth.

Nick pulled a small item from his shirt pocket and held it out to Eddie. "Found this at the murder site."

Eddie's dull eyes widened and his jaw dropped. "Wow. Haven't seen this in a long time."

He picked up the ring and turned it over in his hand. "She threw this at me when we decided to get a divorce. Pinged me smack in the head. I kept it in my toolbox for years. Don't know why I put it there, or why I kept it as long as I did. Finally, I gave it back to her, told her to take it to a pawnshop. Couldn't say what happened after that. But she was the last person to have it."

His matter-of-fact tone conveyed sincerity, but his words incriminated his ex-wife.

Interesting that he chose to elaborate when there was no need. All he had to say was he hadn't seen it in years. I wondered what Nick was thinking. His poker face revealed nothing, so I couldn't tell whether he believed Eddie or not. He was really good at this.

Eddie scrunched up his lips as he stared at the ring.

The silence stretched. Since Nick had his cop face on, I decided to keep quiet. Finally, Eddie tipped his hand and the ring fell with a clink onto the Formica table. "You're thinking I mighta killed Floyd. I guess I get that."

"Have to be thorough, Eddie, check anyone who might know anything. Anyone who talked to Floyd in the last few days before his death might be important. You remember anyone?"

"People who work here, a 'course. My ex-wife. Maybe a few others." Eddie sat quietly for long minutes, his brow wrinkled. "One of the skiers, some guy Sal something or other. He comes up here a lot. Rich guy. Maybe he had a problem in his unit. Don't know."

Mary Fran's new guy? Huh.

Nick nodded. "Please make a list for me."

"Okay. So, I'm not under arrest?"

"No. But stick around. If anything else comes up, I might want to talk again. Meantime, I'll need that list." He passed Eddie a card. "Call me when you're done."

Without looking at it, Eddie stuffed it in his shirt pocket. "Sure, sure. I ain't going nowhere. I got work to do here."

Looking like a man who had been given a Get out of Jail card, he stood, tipped his head to me and left.

"Do you think he murdered Floyd?" I asked when he was out of earshot.

"Too soon to make that call. He's definitely a person of interest. So's Beverly. Even if neither of them dropped the ring, or planted it, I'd need to check it out. I'll talk to Beverly later today."

"I think he might be guilty."

"That the latest from your crystal ball?"

"No, it's in the shop. But I don't like him."

"Well, that settles it. He's guilty. I should arrest him."

Smiling, I elbowed him, then picked up the ring and turned it over. The trace of an EKG was carved around the outside of the silver band. The EKG met at a heart symbol where Beverly and Eddie's initials were engraved in fancy script. It was an inexpensive ring. Yet the beauty, no, the sentiment, spoke of love in a way few other rings did. They must have loved each other very much. No wonder Eddie didn't want to throw it out.

A feeling of sadness gripped me with unexpected intensity as I thought of the ring I once owned, an exquisite diamond worth thousands. In a heartbeat I would have taken this if it came from a good and faithful man.

I set the ring on the table and fiddled with my purse to hide a rush of emotion I didn't want Nick to see.

"Are you going to cry?"

"Over a silly, sentimental ring?" I replied with a huff. "Don't be ridiculous!"

I took a quick deep breath and stood. "I'm going to buy a cranberry-walnut muffin. I've been thinking about it since I got up. Hours ago." I gave a tight smile and said flippantly, "Save my seat."

"Whatever you want, Nora. Always," he spoke so softly I stopped dead in my tracks and turned. His voice was a lover's voice, husky, warm. More devastating, his aspect mirrored his tone. His penetrating gaze held mine in thrall for long seconds, holding me like no other man ever had. "I'll always save a place for you," he said.

Sheriff Nick Renzo was a man of surprises.

Whatever you want, Nora. Always.

How was it possible that so few words could take my breath away? I had to stop reacting to him like this. Had-to, had-to. The unexpected warmth in his tone made me want to run to him and throw my arms around his neck and kiss his face about a million times. To counter the impulse, I forced my expression into neutral and clamped my mouth shut. For a few awful seconds I wondered why I was standing here. Then my stomach growled, and I remembered the cranberry muffin.

I broke eye contact, gathered my aplomb and my handbag and headed for the muffin counter, reminding

myself that I would not be in Maine much longer. Soon I'd
be headed back to New York and the job hunt. Besides,
Nick had Crystal and her little gift boxes with the stupid
little bows that he kept on the seat of his official sheriff's
SUV.

Nick Renzo was not the man for me, and I had to
remember that. He was a Maine man who wanted a Maine
life. I was a New York City woman who needed city life, a
steady job and a decent salary.

Somewhere on this planet there was a man who would
give me a ring as expressive as the heartbeat ring and would
be faithful to me forever and a day.

When I returned with my muffin, he watched me eat
for several nerve-wracking minutes, then said, "What's
bothering you?"

"Nothing." I broke off a piece of muffin. "This is
delicious. You should try it."

As I lifted my hand, his fingers closed around my wrist
and held it, preventing further muffin movement as he
leaned forward, his gaze locking me up with the force of a
tether. In that instant, I saw him in a new light. I could
picture him interrogating a suspect, and I realized that
despite the rural background, he was tough, and likely on a
par with the most seasoned detectives in any big city.

From that realization my next thought flowed
naturally. If he were that good, he should know what was
wrong. He was back with Crystal, or at least accepting gifts
from her. He was not telling me about dinner with his
mother. He always told me about dinner with her. So why
the silence now, unless there was something to hide.

Still, I couldn't bring myself to ask him what I wanted
to know. It would sound petty. Make me seem like a jealous
woman. I did not want to be either of those things. I had the
sudden feeling I was going to cry. Foolish woman.

Finally, I pulled back slightly, indicating he should
release me. In response, he flipped my hand over, kissed the
back of it, and then let go, which made me drop my muffin,

which missed the plate, which hit the table, and rolled onto the floor.

As he bent to retrieve it, I blurted, "How was dinner with your mother?"

CHAPTER TWELVE

"Tense," he said, nodding, signaling that he understood my concern. With that, he got right to the point. "Crystal was there. My mom hadn't bothered to inform me until just before I saw you in town. The word that fits best is *blindsided.*"

My heart did a joyful flip, but I carefully kept my expression neutral, a skill I'd honed since working as a detective. No joy bubbled up to touch this face.

I pushed a little harder. "So, are you getting back together?"

Why was I asking this? I shouldn't. Really. None of my business. But I wanted to hear more, wanted to keep this conversation going, wanted to clarify what was in his head and his heart. Even though we were not a couple, he was fond of kissing me, and I didn't want to continue that unless he was completely free. I would not be the other woman in any man's life.

He gave me his flinty look. I love his flinty look. I wanted to smile, but of course, I didn't. My newly-acquired neutral expression skill was at work.

"You think I'd be kissing you if I were getting back with Crystal?"

Relief mingled with joy. This man was who I thought he was. My doubts had been colored by my experience with Whatshisname, the ex-fiancé, and a few other double-dealers I'd met along the way.

"I would hope not," I said quietly, my tone implying

I'd known that all along.

He took my hand. "Not what I asked, but good enough. Let's go for a walk."

I liked this warm spot, surrounded by the delicious smell of baking breads and pastries, but I left the half-eaten muffin, grabbed my jacket and bag and went with him. He was better than comforting aromas.

Rather than head for the bedroom, which would have been risky considering how I felt about him at this moment, we went out to the deck that overlooked the base of the mountain. It was a beautiful day, polar cold, sunny.

"I didn't tell you because there was no point," he said. "It was an uncomfortable evening, awkward. I was happy when it was over."

My happiness quotient soared.

His gaze on the mountain, he said, "I was happy I could see you before I went home."

My heartbeat kicked up another notch, and I wanted to jump up and down. The phrase *jump for joy* raced around my thoughts like it was on wheels. What was the matter with me, breaking all my rules. I made an effort to still my heart, my thoughts, my pulse.

Since I didn't know what to say to him, I chose to be wise and keep silent.

A few seconds later, he said, "You saw the box on the seat?"

This I could deal with. "I did."

"How did you know who—?"

"Hah! I'm a *hotshot New York detective*, or have you forgotten, Sheriff Renzo?"

We both laughed, and he put his arm around me and hugged me. It felt so good to be close to him, touching. I almost made the mistake of telling him that, but again, wisdom prevailed as it does every now and again, and I kept my thoughts to myself as we headed down the deck.

"I'm so glad you're happy. I love to see joy on your face."

Joy? Couldn't I keep anything from this guy! I got defensive. "You're mistaken. Reading me wrong. This is my neutral expression."

"My mistake. So, are you going to tell me how you did on the slopes yesterday?"

"No."

"You fell a few times?"

"Maybe."

"Is that how you got the bump on your lip?"

"I don't know what you're talking about. There is no bump on my lip."

"Forgive me. I'm mistaken, again," he said, eyeing the bump on my upper lip.

I could get used to this man.

Pulling the scarf high enough to cover my nose, I walked the length of the deck beside him, our conversation centering around the murder. I told him Beverly's reaction to my questions. He told me about giving the news to Marney.

"Marney cried. Told me Floyd was the love of her life, even if he did stray. She just wanted to see him again. Talk to him. Get him to tell her why he took the money. No mention of Beverly."

"I'm not sure from your tone, but do you think this was honest grief?"

"You mean, is she a suspect?"

"Is she?"

"Person of interest. I intend to look into everyone who had any connection to Floyd and that includes Marney, Eddie and Beverly. I'll also check out other people around here who knew him."

"That was it? That's all she said?"

He stopped walking and stood with arms folded. "If you know something more about this, now would be a good time to tell me."

I rested my hand on the deck railing and faced him. "Since she hired me, I feel like there's some code I should be following." I paused and waited for him to tell me all the reasons I should tell him what I knew. In typical Nick Renzo fashion, he said nothing. He simply waited for me to speak.

So I decided, without his input, that murder negated the code.

"I think she wanted revenge."

Think, Nora? Did you say *think?*

Nick waited patiently for me to continue.

"Let me rephrase that. She wanted revenge, period. That's what my investigation was about. She asked me to find out why he needed the money because she figured he was into something illegal, and she wanted to get him on that, see him sent to jail. She was a very angry woman, Nick, angry at a husband who had betrayed her, stolen from her, left her without a financial safety net."

He leaned down and kissed me on the cheek. "Thank you for telling me." He took my hand, and we continued walking.

"Something illegal? She never mentioned that when I spoke to her. If that's true, I need to find out what Floyd was mixed up in. Find people he may have crossed. Eddie has to know more. Beverly, too. Looks like I'll be here most of the day, possibly overnight."

My thoughts flew to Beverly's room. Not that I'd be able to get in there during the day, but I would have given it a try, possibly wearing the smelly ski boots. I shivered at the thought, relieved that Nick's presence made that impossible.

I'd come back in a few days.

Or maybe Nick would be able to access her computer and in turn let me have access. Slim chance. That probable cause requirement in the Fourth Amendment was sometimes a wall too high to scale.

I turned my thoughts to the murder scene and asked about the burned-out truck, and what else they'd learned.

"Like I said, he was shot three times, once in the right side, another in the heart, a third in the head. Not sure which shot was fired first. I'm guessing the side. The M.E. may know."

"You think he planned to meet someone?"

"Probably. He was off the main road, and that wasn't the shortest way to either his house or the mountain."

I thought about that, then asked, "So no other physical clues?"

Nick nodded. "One that might be important. Floyd had two broken fingers on his left hand, thumb and index finger. Besides that, we have very little. Gasoline accelerant. The M.E. said Floyd was dead when the fire started. We have all the bullets."

"The truck was definitely Floyd's truck?"

"Pretty sure. The Major Crime Unit will report back. They may find something else. We'll see. Right now the only tracks are those left by the truck the body was in. They were pretty deep. The kids who found the body were on skimobiles, and they crisscrossed the area. Pretty much destroyed any other tracks that might have been there. The only footprints belong to the kids."

"Mary Fran wants to stop at the scene on the way home. Snoop around. She wanted to see the truck, too. She'll be disappointed that it's gone."

"No harm looking around. We finished up. Tape's down. Forensics took everything. Those guys do a thorough job, so I doubt you'll find anything."

Nick watched a group of skiers heading for the lift.

"That guy with Mary Fran? Do you know him?"

I followed his gaze. "That's Al or Sal. Something like that. She met him yesterday."

Mary Fran noticed us and waved.

Shading his eyes, the man in question turned our way as Nick and I waved back. Mary Fran yelled, "Nick, Nora! Hi-ya."

"Baldino. Sal Baldino," Nick said, his expression unreadable, as it was at times.

"Where do you know him from?"

"He's with the movie crew at the station house. Not sure what he does. Met him a few days ago."

Mary Fran spotted us and skied over with Sal.

"Hi, sheriff," Sal said. "Great day for skiing. You here on business?"

Nick nodded a yes and said hello to Mary Fran without answering Sal specifically.

Sal looked at me, the memory of last night's snow episode evident in his smile. I did not like that smile. Smarmy.

"And Nora. Hello again," Sal said. "We met twice last night," he said to Mary Fran and Nick. Then to me, "Do you two work together?" He looked from me to Nick several times.

Nick said, "No," while I was still trying to decide.

"Well, then there's no comparison to the Nick and Nora Charles duo from the *Thin Man* series who solved murder mysteries in those old movies." He smiled his smarmy smile again. Mary Fran probably found it enchanting. "I'm a movie buff."

I told Mary Fran we'd be leaving in a few hours. She did not look happy.

CHAPTER THIRTEEN

"I gave Sal my number. Do you think he'll call? He liked me. We got along. I asked him if he liked kids, and he said sure. That's a good sign, right?"

Mary Fran had not stopped talking about *saint* Sal since we left the mountain. If I heard much more, I might gag.

"When's the engagement?" I asked.

Her concentration took a hit. "What!"

She swerved, and I banged my shoulder against the door.

"Did he say something to you about getting engaged? So soon!"

"Mary Fran, back to earth, ple-eease. This minute."

She slowed and stopped on the side of the road. "You're right. I'm a little nuts at the moment. It's just . . . he's so . . . sexy, so charming. Classy. I never met a man like him, so different from Percy."

"Maybe we should skip the turnoff at the switchback," I said to shift her attention because I didn't want to talk about the men in her life.

She sat up straighter in her seat. "No. We have to go. The switchback is only a few miles ahead."

"I should be getting back home. When I called Ida earlier she said they were all in a *tizzy* about something. I'm not sure what the tizzy is and decided not to ask until I was on the scene."

Besides, I didn't want to get out in this cold weather. The thermometer still hovered around zero, and this vehicle was warm.

"I know I'm being foolish about Sal. I won't say another word. Promise. I'm back down to earth. Ready to work."

Right. And pigs could fly.

"All right," I said finally. "We'll stop."

We took off again and headed for the crime scene. When we arrived, I hopped out of the SUV, determined to get this over as quickly as possible. We circled the burned-out area where the truck had been.

Thank God, Floyd was dead when the truck had been set on fire.

I went back to the Sorento and grabbed my camera from the back seat. Being a camera fanatic, I was seldom without my Canon. With a fresh, super-size disk inserted, I moved the camera slowly as I fired from every possible angle.

Then, despite the extreme cold, I switched to a macro lens.

"What are you doing?" Mary Fran asked when I got down on my knees to shoot close-ups. "I mean, there's nothing on the ground except black, charred dirt and rocks. And you just had those pants and jacket cleaned."

She was right. I continued anyway. After shooting every possible spot, I changed lenses again, this time to a powerful telephoto, a favorite of mine that took incredibly clear distant photos. I panned the area, then sighted far beyond the section where the trucks had been and angled up into the trees, thinking this was probably a waste of time.

Mary Fran watched with a critical eye. "You're taking pictures of the trees, too? Isn't that a little over the top?"

"I want to be thorough. Please walk around. See if they missed anything," I said as I got down on my knees and set my elbows in the crusty snow for a second time so I could get odd angles of surrounding trees, thinking as my right elbow connected with a rock that I was a little nutty for doing this. But I was a cameraperson to the bone, addicted to taking photos, to being thorough.

Besides, I felt I had to do something because I sure hadn't been able to help Marney. I had to give back most of the money she had given me.

* * *

"Ya got company," Mary Fran said as she pulled into Ida's driveway an hour later behind a car I didn't recognize. On the porch, three women who looked like they were going on an Artic expedition with their thick no-nonsense boots, wooly-looking scarfs, and coats that might be effective to minus fifty below, were heading down the steps, their gloved hands gripping the railing. I recognized them from the senior citizens' group.

Behind the storm door Ida and Hannah waved goodbye to them.

"Hi, Nora. Ida told us you went skiing," the woman in the violet down coat said. "Did you enjoy it?"

"Absolutely," I lied. "Wonderful sport. How was your day?"

"We had a good practice," the shortest declared as she opened the car door. "We've got the ball rolling. Those young ones can't count us out now."

I nodded and smiled. "Good." I had no idea what she was talking about, but I was sure it was related to the tizzy.

The third grumpy-looking woman limped to the car. "Too much. Way too much" she said. "Even dangerous, if you ask me."

What on earth!

Ida's face brightened when she saw me, and she braved the cold to hold the door open and yell, "Yoohoo, Nora. Glad you're home."

Home. Now there was a word with a warm sound. As I got closer, I saw that she was wearing slacks. Slacks! Since when did Ida wear anything but a skirt? I hurried up the steps to give her a hug and insist she close the door on the biting cold.

"Oh, phooey on that," Hannah said behind her. "Come give me a hug, too."

Hannah also wore slacks, but not regular slacks. These were geometric print pants, heavy on the reds and purples with added greens and golds. After a warm hug, I stood back to admire her red tee shirt. *Come On Inner Peace, I Don't Have All Day.*

"Love the tee. It's perfect. So you!"

Completing the Aunt trio, Agnes appeared in the hall wearing bright splatter-print pants with black banded cuffs at the ankles, and a white tee shirt that said *Yoga Chick* in flowing script with the outline of a little yellow chick below it.

Agnes turned so I could get a 360° view of her in her new outfit. "These duds are the latest. Hannah's granddaughter helped us order them. And she was kind enough to go pick them up for us."

Hannah twirled around in her smart-looking outfit.

Ida took center stage next, pointed her foot and swung left, then right, to show off her camouflage print pants, same slim cut as the others. Her tee shirt—bless her, Ida actually had a tee shirt on, probably her first ever—said *Love, Peace, Yoga,* and below that was a stick figure in a yoga pose. "Do you think they're too tight in the seat?"

"Nah. They're perfect," I said, as I studied the colorful outfits.

Out front, Mary Fran tooted her horn.

"Be right back," I told them, relieved by the reprieve.

I hurried out, grabbed my bag and smelly boots and said goodbye to Mary Fran, who sat in the driver's seat shaking her head.

"What?" I said, although I figured I knew what she was thinking.

"How would they react if you left Silver Stream for a year or more?" She put her hand up like a traffic cop. "No need to answer. See ya."

"Thanks for driving," I said, thinking about how the aunts would react when I finally returned to the City.

"Did you meet up with Nick?" Ida asked as I walked in. "Anything new with you two?" Her tone was casual, too casual, but I was wise to her.

"Don't you dare keep us waiting," Hannah said as I reached for a cracker and some Edam cheese on the tray. "No delaying tactics! We'll get you cocoa in a minute. Come sit with us."

If anyone else ordered me around like this, I'd resent it. From Hannah, I simply accepted with quiet joy.

My thoughts flew back to an incident from my teen years. I'd come home one evening from a first date with a guy I had the biggest crush on. My mother was aware of my feelings, and I was eager to tell her how wonderful he was and what a great time we had. Even though she didn't seem interested very often, she had her moments, and I figured this would be one of them.

I floated in the door on a cloud reserved for teenage girls madly in love for the first time. Before I got a word out, she said, "Finally, you're home. Now, get to bed. I've waited up long enough. There was nothing worth watching on this television tonight. I've been bored out of my mind."

And that was that.

So the aunts could pester me all they wanted.

But teasing was part of the fun, so I went back at them. "That wasn't the purpose of the trip, Aunt Ida. It was business. I told you that. And there's been a big development. Huge. Floyd LeBeau's been murdered. So I won't be looking for Marney's husband any more."

"Yes. We heard he met his maker," Agnes said, tugging at the slacks, rearranging the fabric folds that draped her upper thighs like a blanket.

"We're more interested in you," Hannah said, "Ida's inquiry is based on our order of interest. We want to hear all about your investigation, of course, but Nick first, please. Ida told us you seemed troubled when you left, and she suspected it had to do with him. Ida's pretty sharp about things like that."

Hannah and Agnes nodded in unison as they regarded Ida who was obviously pleased by the compliment, but attempting to look humble at the same time. Hannah continued, "Is something off between you and Nick?"

I didn't answer immediately. In reaction to the stares, I finally said, "It was. It's been . . . fixed. Everything is a-okay. Now can I get something to eat?"

They accepted that and being Mainers, didn't pry further. Ida got up. "Cocoa? Coffee?"

We all followed her down the hall, a slow conga line, three 80-year-olds and me.

Ida said, "I know you're not a tea drinker, but you really should consider it, Nora. Green tea especially. It's good for you."

"I'll take cocoa." I stopped short, hands up, before I entered the kitchen. "Hold everything. When is someone going to tell me what on earth is going on here? Why the slacks? You guys skipped that part."

"Yoga clothes for the movie," Ida said as she took down my favorite cup, the bone china one with the little violets on it, while Hannah and Agnes sat at the table and focused their attention on me with laser intensity.

"First you must tell us more about Nick," Hannah said. "How was your visit with him when you were up at the mountain?"

And I thought that discussion was over. Some trade-off.

I took a deep breath and began. "I saw him today. We had coffee together. And I had part of a muffin. Cranberry with walnuts. I didn't finish it, but it tasted—"

"Enough!" Hannah declared in her no-nonsense voice. "We do not care about the menu unless it has a direct bearing on the situation. Does it?"

"Not exactly." I grinned.

Seeing this, Ida and Agnes smiled back. Hannah

reserved judgment.

Ida poured the cocoa, and I added a bit of milk to cool it. Purposely stalling while I decided how much to tell them, I stirred, and stirred some more. Finally, giving a mental what-the-heck shrug, I said, "Crystal and Nick had dinner together at his mother's house. He didn't tell me, even when the opportunity presented itself. I deduced it from certain clues." I pursed my lips. "It should not have bothered me, but it did, mostly because he kept it secret."

"Was he cool to you?" Hannah asked, as if everything I had just said was irrelevant.

My smile gave me away before I answered. "No," I said, thinking, absolutely not cool. Just the opposite.

"Well, that settles it. Everything is fine with Nick and our Nora. Thank heavens," Agnes said. "Now, let's set out the apple crisp that's warming in the oven. I like mine with a dollop of cream on top. Do you have cream, Ida?"

"Nothing is settled," Ida announced as she opened the refrigerator. "Did you hear what Nora said, Agnes? Crystal is moving into her territory."

"No!" I raised a hand in protest. I had to stop this discussion before it went further. "No territory! Nick and I are friends. We have not made *any* commitments to each other. We enjoy each other's company, period. But he intends to stay in Maine, and I need to return to New York, so if he wants to get back with Crystal, he should."

Saying this aloud deepened a chasm that existed somewhere in the region of my heart. Separation by time and distance would sound a death knell for our relationship. The aunts seemed to be waiting for me to say more, but I needed to end this discussion.

I said, "It was a mistake to give it a second thought, but he came directly here after their dinner and said nothing about it."

"Ah!" Hannah said, raising her fork as well as her eyebrows. "You thought *secret*; he thought *the less said the better*. Men are like that. Okay, then, on to other things. The murder! What do you know about it?"

I noticed they ignored the fact that I'd mentioned moving back to New York City.

"Wild stories are circulating all over the place. The whole town's buzzing," Agnes said as she scooped cream onto her apple crisp. "We depend on you for the true lowdown."

"Yes," said Ida. "What did you find out?"

"Did you meet Beverly's ex? Is he a suspect?" Hannah asked.

"Oh, and did the ski boots fit? Were they comfortable? I know you didn't have time to try them on before you left," Ida said.

"Did you actually ski?" Hannah asked, brows raised.

"Is that how you got the bump on your lip?" Agnes asked.

It was like being a celebrity at a news conference with reporters lobbing questions from all directions. "Whoa!" I said. "One at time."

The questions slowed, and I gave them an abbreviated version of the last two days. When I finished, I turned the spotlight on them and asked about the exercise clothes and the meeting they had with the senior citizens who had been leaving when we drove up.

Eyes brightened around the table. Agnes put her fork down, Hannah rested her elbows on the table and Ida leaned forward. All three looked from one to the other, and I realized they were deciding who should tell me the story. Finally, Hannah gave Ida the nod.

"The senior citizens are going to be in a short scene," Ida said slowly, too slowly for Hannah who stood up and cut in before Ida finished speaking.

"We'll be participating in the senior yoga group in the church basement when the perp comes charging through. To show he means business, he'll shoot one of us!" Hannah grabbed her arm and staggered around the kitchen before flopping into her chair. "Someone else will be a hostage."

Ida and Agnes clapped. "Oh, Hannah, you are the one," Ida said. "You'll be perfect in either role."

"I want to be the hostage," Agnes said. "I can make frightened faces like nobody's business." She demonstrated a few.

"The yoga group will be enough for me," Ida said. "I have no desire to pursue an acting career."

"Yoga?" *Participating in a yoga class*? The mental images that flashed in my head were not pretty. "But none of you are in a yoga class. You've never done any yoga. Have you?"

"We're in yoga class now," Hannah said proudly. "We signed up. Our first public session is day after tomorrow. We have to get ready. We thought you might help."

Help? No, I couldn't do this. I really could not.

"Me? I've never done yoga."

"We've already begun. We got a DVD from the library and tried a few moves today," Ida said.

"The girls you saw leaving have joined, too. We had a little practice here so we'd know what to expect at the real session in the church basement. Right now only the young sixty and seventy-year-olds do senior yoga. They'll soon meet their competition," Hannah informed me, a note of pride in her voice.

Agnes stood, extended both arms, and bent a few inches to one side. She immediately returned to an upright position. "That was the Triangle Pose. It's my best one. It's supposed to be good for flat feet. I've got those." She looked down. "I'm wondering how soon that'll clear up. I may like this yoga business."

Although it bore no resemblance to anything triangular, I decided not to ask about the name. "Nice," I said, unable to think of anything else.

"It needs work," Hannah said, picking up a book on yoga from the table and flipping through the pages. "We've only done standing and some sitting poses on a chair. We're hoping they mostly do those. Then there are the floor poses."

"The floor?" Agnes plopped her hands on her hips. "If you ever find me on the floor, call an ambulance. The only reason I'd be there is if I fell. My aim in life is to keep myself *off* the floor."

Everyone nodded their understanding.

Ida said, "You're right, Agnes. Of course. Floor positions are foolish for many. We will just use chairs."

"Why would they use the *stairs* instead of the floor?" Agnes asked.

"Chairs, I said chairs," Ida repeated.

"Then some folks are smart," Agnes commented.

"Enough about positions," Hannah said. "More important, one person, a resident of Silver Stream, will be selected for a speaking role. In the scene, Josh Rockford will come rushing up the steps of the sheriff's office and ask if the sheriff is in. One lucky person will reply: "He's been here all morning."

Tension ratcheted up around the table.

"He's *been* here all morning," Hannah said with a flourish.

"He's been *here* all morning," Agnes said as if she were imparting insider information.

"He's been here *all* morning," Ida said firmly.

They waited expectantly. I was not sure what I was supposed to do. Finally, Hannah said, "Well, which one did you like best?"

I bit my bottom lip. "Hard to say. All were good."

"Ever the diplomat. She's not going to choose," Ida said. "So, let's move on." She paused dramatically. "There is one more part they have to fill. It's for a young, attractive woman."

They all stared at me, smiling.

I sat back in my chair and shook my head. "No," I said before anyone pursued the matter. "I will not."

"Let Ida finish," Hannah said. "You need to hear this."

With my mouth clamped shut, I continued to shake my

head.

Ida went on. "We have some inside information from a very good source."

She took a deep breath. Hannah nodded, urging her to continue.

"For one scene, they need a hotsy-totsy woman to walk into the sheriff's office, hand him some papers, and kiss him. When she notices Josh is also in the room, she pretends to be embarrassed and leaves."

Hotsy-totsy?

"That's it?" I said. "One question. Is this what the *tizzy* was about?"

"It's a major part of it," Hannah said. "Because Crystal has submitted her name for consideration."

"And the sheriff will be playing himself," Agnes said with an anxious nod. "The two of them . . . co-starring. Together for rehearsals. For luncheons. For possibly dozens of retakes of the scene. Kissing and more kissing."

"He's not a lump of coal. He's a man. How could he not be affected by all that . . . closeness?" Ida said, with a worried expression that touched my heart. "So maybe you should try out for the part."

"Thank you for being concerned about my feelings, but I don't want to be in the movie. And if Crystal gets the part and Nick is affected? So be it."

Such brave words from a woman who had lost a night's sleep over a plastic box on a passenger seat.

CHAPTER FOURTEEN

A feeling of déjà vu swept through me like a fierce storm, chilling me to the bone, as I pulled into Marney's driveway and saw her sitting on the porch, again, on this cold day, wearing that puffy red coat with the hood pulled so tightly that only a small portion of her face was visible. It was clear she didn't want me to see the inside of her house which, of course, triggered a need to do exactly that. What was the woman hiding? Ferrets? A big fat mess? Bodies? Gold?

She took a puff on her cigar and sent a swirl of blue smoke eddying around her head, where it mixed with her steamy breaths. Briefly, her face was enveloped by a mist that rivaled the one in my head when I thought of her reaction to Nick's revelation about her husband's murder.

That reaction confused me. Totally.

When I first spoke to her, anger and resentment were evident. Revenge was her objective, and Floyd was the target. She wanted me to check his computer, investigate his bank records, his emails and any other evidence that would show him guilty of a crime that could result in jail time. She specifically mentioned jail.

I thought her heart was a solid wall of hatred with no trace of love, or any feeling remotely resembling it.

I had misread her.

How could I have been so wrong?

Nick was good at reading people, and he said she was upset when she heard the news of Floyd's murder. No rejoicing like I would have expected. I had to accept that. Pushing doubts aside, I trekked through the cleared path toward the porch.

Marney gave a wave of recognition, and I nodded hello as I approached the house. No friendly shout-out this time.

"The sheriff told me he gave you the news of Floyd's death," I said as I climbed the rickety steps to the porch.

I waited for her to speak, but she merely nodded. I think I heard a small sniffle. Not sure.

"He said you were very upset. I'm sorry for your loss, Marney." It was a customary phrase to the bereaved that had a hollow ring in this instance.

"I was upset. Still am." She eyed me intently. "It's true I wanted to get back at the two-timing jackass. But someone murdered my Floyd and burned his body!" She gave a sniffle that I heard clearly, and wiped at her eyes with one open-fingered gloved hand. Her lip quivered. "That's shameful, don't ya think? What kinda monster would do such a thing to my Floyd?"

My Floyd?

Though I was prepared for this reaction, the emotion that accompanied her words was beyond the expected. This was a different Marney than the one I'd met over a week ago. If I were a psychologist or a psychiatrist I'd probably have a better grasp of what was going on in her head. As just plain Nora Lassiter, a pretend detective and computer analyst, I was out of my depth.

The curtain, actually the sheet, fluttered in the window. I heard a crash inside. This time I didn't react since I knew about the lively ferrets Marney favored.

I took out the envelope with the cash she had given me and held it close to my chest. I needed to return most of it today because I probably would not be back. I did have to ask if she wanted me to do anything else.

Despite my unwillingness to cause further pain, I realized I also had to ask about her one-eighty course correction.

As tactfully as possible, I said, "Marney, I can see you're upset, and I don't want to add to it, but when we spoke before, the love you now seem to feel for Floyd didn't come across. Just the opposite. You wanted him in jail."

I paused and waited for a reaction. Nothing. Not even a change of expression. I continued, "I need to know if you still want me to look into his records. Follow the money trail. Find your money."

The smoke from her cigar swirled around in the silence between us, and I turned my head away for a breath of smokeless air. Seeing her expression, I realized I'd made a huge mistake. A grieving woman didn't need this. What was wrong with me?

I was about to beg her pardon when she squinted at me, took another puff on her cigar, and said in a gravelly voice, "Scare tactic. I never would have gone through with it. I wanted to threaten him. Make him grovel. Make him see I could send him to jail. I didn't want him to have my money to spend on that bitch."

That made sense, but something was still off.

"So, you didn't want him to go to jail?"

She shook her head. "Oh, no. No. Not actually. All I needed was the evidence. Having that would get me the result I wanted."

I remembered the conversation well: *"Serious snooping. I want to hold all the cards. I'll be able to send him to jail."*

I misunderstood?

She had continued. *"I know him real good, and I know he's up to something fishy. He can't be put in jail for gettin' ahold of my money, but he can be put in jail for something illegal."*

I gave a mental shrug. I had no choice but to accept her feelings. Only one question remained. "Do you want me to find your money?"

"I'm guessin' it's most likely gone. Besides, the life insurance'll tide me over. It's not much, but it'll do."

Really? I almost said. Instead, I opted for tact. "I don't think I could be that kind."

She sniffled, and her chin quivered.

Shut up, Nora Big-mouth. Evidently her husband's brutal death had stamped out her anger.

I wondered whether telling her that Beverly had stopped seeing or dating Floyd a while back would make her feel better. It took mere seconds for me to decide not to risk another word. Time to leave.

I handed her the envelope of cash she'd given me originally, minus my fee and expenses.

She took a few bills and handed the envelope back. "You keep this."

Shaking my head in protest, I said, "But, Marney—"

She stepped toward the front door. "You done what I asked you to do. You earned it. We have finished our business."

That wasn't entirely true, and we both knew it, but I also heard the finality in her voice. I thanked her, stuffed the envelope in my pocket, wished her well and headed down the rickety steps, one hand on the rail with a light touch.

At the bottom, I stopped and turned. "Marney, do you have any friends to keep you company? It'd be better than being alone right now."

"Nope. I pretty much keep to myself these days. Got my ferrets. I'll be fine. Thanks for askin'. Now you go on with your other business. No need to come back. Cross me off your list."

* * *

Marney held front and center in my thoughts most of the way back to town. Obviously, I'd misread her determination to seal her husband's fate. She had loved her husband, and wanted to scare him into returning to her.

Based on the condition of the outside of her house, I had figured she desperately needed money. Wrong again.

Perhaps I was using my standards when I should be using hers, whatever they were.

Marney was a woman willing to forgive in the face of brutality, a woman not as focused on money as most of us would be. Suddenly, my thoughts took an unappealing detour into Whatshisname territory, and I realized my feelings regarding my ex-fiancé's betrayal colored my judgment when it came to assessing Marney's reactions. I had to be careful about that.

When Main Street came into view, my jaw dropped and I stopped. What on earth! As far as I could see from this section of the incline that lead into town, cars, trucks and SUVs formed a conga line of vehicles in both directions, all seeming to slow near the sheriff's office. Deputies Miller and Trimble were out front directing traffic, looking harried, shouting orders, especially skinny Trimble who reminded me of that nervous deputy—what was his name?—on some show Aunt Ida watched that was set in an idyllic town called Mayberry.

I was witnessing a genuine traffic jam, probably the first in the whole history of Silver Stream.

Prime parking spaces in front of the sheriff's office were occupied, and one large vehicle was unloading camera equipment. Some of these vehicles should have parked around back in the police parking lot.

Despite Trimble's frantic arm-waving, traffic was at a complete stop. Chaos ensued. Horns beeped. People yelled. Fists gestured. Before someone blocked me in back, I put Ce-ce into reverse and backed up with enough trepidation to make my hands shake. With what I thought of as a deft maneuver, I swung around and cut down the street that led to the library.

* * *

Margaret stood on the front step, a black jacket pulled tightly around her shoulders, a plaid scarf covering her nose, and Harold standing beside her, bundled up like he was heading for a trek to the North Pole. His round head was encased in a fur-trimmed, olive green mad bomber hat. I'd seen one like it in the L.L. Bean catalog and had wondered who on earth would wear such a thing. The earflaps were down, but not secured. I suppose he was roughing it.

Looking a bit panicky, Margaret waved at me. I was not sure whether she was waving me off or not. No matter. I would not give her secret away. She should know that.

With no place to park in the small lot, I pulled in front of the step and got out.

"You must be here to see the movie stars. I heard they'll be at Winterfest, too," Margaret said quickly before I had a chance to speak. This woman was taking no chances.

"Hello, Margaret, Harold. Yes, absolutely. I was afraid to tackle Main Street. I hoped I'd find a space here."

"Everyone's excited. Hollywood has come to Silver Stream."

Harold pursed his lips and made a huffing sound. "Speak for yourself, Margie. I could care less about these Hollywood types. Bunch of phonies, if you ask me."

Margie? Interesting.

"Well, much as I hate to leave you, I do have to get back to work. I have a patient coming in shortly. One of those Hollywood hotshots lost a cap. I think someone popped him in the mouth. 'Course I couldn't say for sure. None of my business."

Margaret's brows shot up as she looked at Harold. "What! You never mentioned that. Who?"

Harold removed his rugged gloves—probably weather-tested to minus 100 below—tucked them under his arms, and tied the strings that dangled from his earflaps in a neat bow under his chin.

"I don't recall his name."

"Perhaps I can drop by for a few minutes and meet him," Margaret said.

Harold was shaking his head before she even finished.

"Inappropriate. Out of the question."

"Certainly. What was I thinking," Margaret said as the dentist pulled his gloves back on.

Margaret's sincere look bothered me. Or, was I reading her wrong, too? That bothered me even more as we watched Harold walk to his office.

When he was out of earshot, I gave her an update about the lottery ticket.

"So I'll have to go back there," I said finally. "In a few days. I'll keep you posted."

She watched the dentist disappear among the trees near his office. "Okay. Thanks, Nora."

"I'm going over to the Sheriff's Office. Want to join me?"

She sighed. "No."

"Or we could spy on the guy with the cap problem."

"Of course not! If Harold ever—"

"Never mind, Margaret." I'd spy by myself. "Can I park in back of your car? I'll be back before you're ready to leave for the day and move it so you can get out."

At her nod, I parked the truck.

"See you later, Margaret."

"Wait," she called as I went to open the door. "Be honest with me. Is there any chance you'll be able to get my lottery winnings from Beverly Sue?"

I didn't want to tell her that on a scale of one to ten with one being the least likely, my chance of recovering her lottery winnings fell between one and zero. "Too soon to tell," I said. "Give it time."

Lying to Margaret increased my determination to try harder to succeed, even if it meant threatening the horrible Beverly Sue.

As I headed for the police station, I tried to think of ways to threaten Beverly.

Nothing came.

I was a flop at threatening.

CHAPTER FIFTEEN

The chaos in the police station brought memories of New York City. People scurried this way and that, some shouting, others positioning equipment, a few arguing, all trying to look important. Off to the side, watching with arms folded and gaze narrowed unpleasantly as he took it all in, was the sheriff of Silver Stream, handsome Nick Renzo. It wasn't hard to read his thoughts. I smiled. Waved at him across the room. I didn't expect him to see me right away, but he looked at me immediately.

For long moments neither of us moved. We held each other's gaze, as if temporarily disconnected from the turmoil swirling around. Or was I imagining that? Being a romantic? Hard to say. But I was humming "Some Enchanted Evening" in my head, a song from the movie *South Pacific* that Ida had watched on a DVD last week. I began to sway. Crazy woman.

Nick smiled. Caught again!

I smiled back and wended my way through the crowd.

Nick put his arm around my shoulder. "Hi, sweet stuff. Welcome to the set."

"Getting impatient with all this?"

"Absolutely not. I love every freaking minute. How could I not?" His lips tightened. "Messing up my station house, pulling my deputies away from what they're supposed to be doing, knocking over a stack of reports I was working on. How special! Next time I see the head of the town council, he'll get my laundry list. He's owes me. Ayah. Big-time. And I mean to collect."

I waited an appropriate four seconds, then asked, "Anything new on Floyd's case? Any suspects?"

"What were you humming?"

I shot him my mystified look. "What on earth are you talking about?"

"Promise that someday you'll tell me."

I redid the mystified look. "I was standing quietly, not moving, not humming."

He gave me his doubting look.

"Crazy man," I said.

He nodded, smiled. "Only when it comes to you."

Since I didn't know what to say to that, I remained mute.

"Lots of dead ends," he said. "I interviewed everyone on the mountain with any connection to Floyd. Nothing. Actually, one lead, but not much help. Someone was in his room before we searched it, someone who evidently knew about the monitor in the hall. Guy wore a hoodie and kept his face averted. Can't tell what was taken, if anything. Whoever it was left in under three minutes."

"So he knew what and where."

Brows raised, Nick looked at me in question.

I shrugged. "The guy went in for something specific, something small, and knew where it was, right?"

"Yeah. But the tech people took longer to come to that conclusion. Could be that he came out with nothing."

"Nah. I don't think so." I shook my head, then said, "Want to hear about my visit to the widow?"

"Let's talk in my office."

Once inside, he closed the door and walked to his desk. So it was to be a business visit. He really did want to talk. I masked my disappointment and pasted on a pleasant expression.

He leaned his hips on the edge of the desk, pulled me between his legs, drew me into his arms and kissed me.

My handbag landed with a thump and a rattle on his

foot, then toppled to the floor. When he lifted his head and smiled down at me, my arms encircled his waist. His dark eyes, warm and wanting, drew me in, and he bent his head to kiss me again. As his mouth covered mine, I melted into him, felt his hands press my back. He pulled me closer and slowly, ever so slowly, his tongue eased between my lips on a journey of re-acquaintance.

"Missed you," he whispered, leaving a trail of fluttery kisses along my neck and ear.

A sudden frantic pounding on the door made me jump back. Nick stepped behind his desk and yelled, "Come in."

Skinny Trimble looked desperate. "You'd better come out front, boss. It's getting ugly. We got a three-car crash and hot tempers. Old lady Brooks drove into town wearing her new glasses and plowed into some guy's truck."

"Coming," Nick said, grabbing his jacket.

As they headed out, Trimble continued. "Truck driver tapped some guy's classy Land Rover. Seems odd, but that guy doesn't seem to care. Said he's in a hurry to leave, and there was no damage. But the truck guy's mad as hell at old lady Brooks. She's a mess."

I followed Nick and Trimble through the station house, which had emptied quickly, as if someone had yelled, "Fire!"

But not everyone had left.

Standing near the hall that led to the cells, I saw Sal talking with another man. They glanced our way, but neither acknowledged us.

Outside, pandemonium reigned. Miller stepped aside as Nick took over, first, by stepping between the new eyeglass wearer, who was flush against the passenger side of her car, and the truck driver guy who'd been screaming at her. Nick took the woman's arm, leaned close and talked calmly as he led her around to the other side. When he coaxed her into her car, I saw her smile at him. I'd have to ask him later what he said to elicit a smile from someone so obviously upset.

Next, he confronted the obnoxious truck owner. I was impressed with his ability to take charge and soothe people without causing a bigger scene as some might have done.

I enjoyed watching him. I would have been content to remain that way all day, but a nagging feeling about the two guys back in the station house pulled my attention in that direction. Most people are drawn to the scene of an accident. Rubberneckers. Evidently Al, no, Sal and the guy he was talking with weren't rubberneckers. Unusual. Could be nothing.

I might have dismissed those thoughts if Eddie Binderwig had never mentioned Sal talking to Floyd shortly before his disappearance and murder. I suppose it was possible Sal didn't know Floyd by name when I mentioned Floyd at the après ski party. Possible, but not probable.

"You don't happen to know a guy named Floyd LeBeau, do you, Al?"

He barely reacted. "Does this guy work around here?"

"Yes," I said.

"Name's not ringing any bells."

No. He knew. I could feel it. Floyd was not an ordinary name. He would have remembered it.

Common sense prompted me to ignore what I suspected below the surface. Not only was it not my investigation any longer, but the people involved were not friends or family. I should stay out of this.

Churning inside was a strong desire to find the truth, and ultimately, that is what impelled me to move.

With the accident the cynosure of all eyes, I slipped around to the side of the building and peered in a window. The men were still talking, or at least Al Pacino's doppelganger was. The other guy with bushy hair that looked like someone had plopped a dust mop on his head midway back, kept nodding. I wished I could hear. I had a strong feeling this had nothing to do with the movie. But I was guessing. I couldn't see either face clearly through the dirty window.

Bushy head was taller and heavier than Sal, but took a step back when Sal poked him in the chest with a hostile jab. I needed a better vantage point. I dashed around back to the rear station house entrance. I'd never been back here before. I tested the door. Unlocked. Careless cops leaving their door open.

In stealth mode, I slipped inside and closed the door, whisper-quiet. I skulked past a fire extinguisher that someone had left on the bottom step, then continued up the stairs, past a collection of department pictures, past a memento box. I'd like to look at that later. When I wasn't so busy.

Only someone with supersonic hearing, maybe someone from the planet Krypton—the thought made me smile—would know I was here. I was that quiet. At the top, I headed left toward the main room. The cells to the right were empty. Amazing that no one was around.

"A stupid thing to do. Damn stupid," I heard Sal say as I approached the end of the short corridor, his voice threatening enough to scare me. Mary Fran could really pick 'em.

"I gave you a chance. You blew it. You've got twenty-four hours to fix this mess."

"But my job. First I have to handle—"

"I need to repeat myself, Lucca? Do I? Huh? Do I? You want to lose another cap? Or maybe I should just remind you about what happened to the last person who crossed me? No one gets in my way."

His words sent chills racing through me. The hairs on my neck stood up.

I heard shuffling steps. I figured Lucca was backing up, maybe being poked in the chest again. With extreme caution, I risked a peek around the corner. Bad timing. Lucca's gaze shot in my direction. Even scared as I was, my fashion-conscious nature registered his eyebrows. They almost met in the middle like two dark caterpillars.

Sal must have caught the eye shift because he turned. That was enough to activate my fight-or-flight response. Flight won out, and I took off like I was shot from a canon.

Escape my only thought, I flew down the short hall and bounded down the stairs like a woman training for a decathlon. I was so caught up in that image that I vaulted over the last step in an attempt to reach the door as quickly as possible.

Suddenly, I was under attack. A maniacal snake hissed and spun, weaseled inside my aqua jacket and caused it to inflate like a huge helium balloon in the Macy's Thanksgiving parade. Oh, dear God, help!

Panicked, fighting back, I swung my handbag, lost my balance and smacked into the wall. White powder erupted all over the place, almost blinding me, coating the walls, the floor, the stairs, and filling the air with a dense white mist.

I could barely breathe. What was happening? I had to get away.

Then the fire extinguisher hit the floor, ricocheted off the wall and rolled over my foot, spewing more white powder all over. Faster than Wonder Woman, I gathered my wits, sidestepped the canister, ignoring my injured foot, and pushed the door, leaving mayhem to continue without me.

Once outside, instead of heading around front, I took the shortest route and hurried—limping and wobbling—straight to the police parking lot, which contained several rows of vehicles. If Sal followed me . . .

I crouched behind a patrol vehicle, grabbed my cell phone and hit Mary Fran's number.

"Don't ask any questions," I said as soon as she answered. "Just listen. Do you have an extra jacket handy?"

"Of course."

"How about slacks? A sweater?" I asked, brushing the powder off my clothes as I scanned the parking lot, my gaze shifting from side to side, wary, on the lookout for a hiding place while keeping an eye on the door for anyone who looked like a member of the Corleone family.

"Yeah, I keep extra stuff on hand. You know that. For those days I come in and maybe I got soaked in the rain just running into the building. Take last week as a case in point—"

"Mary Fran!"

"Okay, okay. Where are you? Do you want me to meet you?"

I spotted a Ford pickup truck in the second row with EVIDENCE painted on the windshield in big white letters.

"I'll call you back," I interrupted, hanging up as plan C replaced plan B, and I headed for the truck. I had to get out of sight, fast. I couldn't wait for Mary Fran, or anyone. Too dangerous. I couldn't let Sal see me. Even if he did nothing now . . .

His words resounded in my head. *"Nothing, no one gets in my way."*

I tested the door handle on the truck, found it open and slipped in. Cat-quick, I removed my jacket and shook it out. Powder flew everywhere. Next, I brushed off my jeans, swatting at them with my gloves until the inside of the cab looked like a fierce nor'easter at its peak.

I began to sneeze. Three in a row. I coughed to clear my throat and sneezed six more times. To filter some of the particles, I pulled my sweater up over my nose, which was now running like a faucet.

I may be a record-holder when it comes to sneezing. When my allergies get a whiff of animal dander, dust, pollen or similar material—I could now add fire extinguisher dust to the list— they take off. I sneezed four more times. Just before I narrowed my eyes on the last sneeze, I saw the hunter at the station house back door scanning the parking lot.

Panicked, I jammed myself between the bucket seats and squirmed into the back where I rolled onto the floor with a painful thud. Plumes of white dust puffed around me, triggering another sneeze, a real whopper on the seismic scale. That one must have been waiting in the wings.

I was on top of a dirty blanket that smelled like an animal with severe body odor had called it home for a year or two. Fighting revulsion, I yanked it from beneath me, twisted it over me for cover, twisted too far and got stuck, then wrestled to unravel myself.

Oh, God, please help.

It felt like my feet were tied and my right arm was encased in a cast. I struggled. I twisted. I grappled until I loosened, then freed, my left hand. I felt for the cell phone under my elbow and managed to reach it. Shaking in my boots, I brought it close enough to see, and hit Nick's private number on speed dial.

No answer.

I hit it again, my heart palpitating like a long-distance runner nearing the finish line. Still no answer. Next, I hit Mary Fran's number. Before it rang, I heard a sound outside, a vibration, as if someone had touched the truck. Lightning-quick, I turned the phone off. If my heart pounded any faster it would explode out of my chest. I held as still as I could, taking controlled, shallow breaths to keep the dirty blanket from rising and falling too obviously.

Minutes later, something slammed against the front fender. He'd found me. I waited for the execution I knew was coming. A bullet to the back of the head? A knife in the heart? After my execution, maybe he'd set this car on fire, and I'd be reduced to a pile of ashes. Like Floyd.

Something evil was going on, and Mary Fran's new guy was involved. Sal must have killed Floyd, too.

What was wrong with me? My last moments on the planet, and I was thinking about a murder case.

Tempus fugit.

I squeezed my eyes shut and hoped my murder wouldn't hurt too much. Then I turned my final thoughts away from anything regarding this murder mystery and toward things that really mattered, the people in my life.

My brother Howie. I should have followed his advice and returned to New York City. I'd never get to tell him he was right. He would have loved to hear that. I'd never talk to Howie again. A tear slipped out.

I'd never talk to Ida . . . Or Hannah . . . Or Agnes . . .

I wiped my runny nose on the smelly blanket, gagged, and past caring, sneezed three more times before closing tear-filled eyes and waiting for the end.

Nick. Oh, Nick. I should have told you . . .

Another slam on the truck. More tears leaked out. I trembled. I could not control the shaking.

The end was near.

CHAPTER SIXTEEN

Hope has wings.

The slam against the front fender had sounded like a death knell, yet the minutes ticked by, and I was still here. No gunshot, no knife had laid me low. Was I actually safe? Was it possible?

For reasons unknown, the monster had not acted. Whether he'd given up or was just cautious, I didn't know. Maybe I could sneak out. Slip around front and take cover in the crowd.

I unraveled myself from the malodorous blanket and raised my head to window level. Peered out. Coast was clear. I eased up high enough to scan a 360-degree area. No sign of anyone. If he wasn't in the parking lot, he must have returned to the station house.

Unchecked, joy moved through me like a whirlwind. The monster had disappeared. I had been given a reprieve.

I forced myself to remain calm, to resist the impulse to jump out of the truck and run. Sal might be watching from a back window of the station house. Maybe he'd seen a flash of color, the bright aqua of my jacket or the color of my hair, dark blonde with frosted highlights. I had a feeling he would definitely notice that. All he had to do was identify me, and he could get me whenever he wanted.

I squirmed back into the front seat, conscious of the visual range of station house windows, grateful I'd selected a vehicle at the end of the second row that might not be seen easily. I grabbed the smelly blanket and sneezed four times, whether from the blanket or the white powder I'd disturbed, was hard to say.

I opened the passenger door, slid out, and hit the ground, right knee first. I broke the forward momentum with my hands, then closed the door as quietly as possible. Fortunately, daylight made the overhead light less visible from a distance.

Hunkering down next to the truck, I wrapped myself in the blanket, including my head, and gagged. I massaged my sore knee. Maybe it was bleeding, but I couldn't stop to check now. I took a quick inventory of my other damaged body parts. Besides the knee, my right foot throbbed from the blow of the heavy fire extinguisher. Maybe I had a broken toe. Both of my palms hurt and had blood on them. I gently wiped them on the blanket.

Instead of heading to the front of the building where the crowd gathered, I opted for the shorter but trickier trek through the wooded area that abutted the back of the buildings along Main Street.

If Sal saw me, and he might, the trees and this awful blanket would make it impossible for him to identify me. I realized he would not have to be an ace tracker to follow me in this snow, but I was moving fast despite the limp and would be among the crowd shortly.

Just before Hot Heads Heaven salon, I dropped the blanket, removed my jacket and turned it inside out. The quilted lining was dark blue, generic in this crowd, except for the aqua seams. It was not a reversible jacket. To camouflage further, I pulled up the hood and tied the string beneath my chin, sort of like Marney. I felt silly, but silly beat dead, so I limped on, hoping I didn't run into anyone I knew before I got hold of Mary Fran.

As I merged with the rubberneckers on Maine Street, I was relieved to see strangers, more relieved to finally spot Mary Fran near the station house close to the action.

This was going well.

I tried to call her on my cell phone, but the noise level

made it difficult for her to hear. She should have it on vibrate. I waved to get her attention, but that was useless.

Frustrated, I hurried along, with a lurch here and there due to the pain in my knee and foot, wondering whether I had the torn meniscus problem Aunt Agnes talked about. I didn't even know what a meniscus was. I should pay more attention. Of course, I could also have a broken toe.

I focused on Mary Fran instead of my knee and foot. Not only did I have to get a different coat from her, but I had to warn her about Sal. I saw her hand go up in a wave and was about to wave back when I realized the object of her attention was on the front steps of the station house. It was like a kick in the gut.

Sal!

I grabbed my cell phone and hit Mary Fran's number on speed dial again, hoping, hoping, hoping . . .

Still no answer.

From his lofty vantage point, Sal surveyed the crowd, ignoring Mary Fran while he searched for the woman in the bright aqua jacket.

Mary Fran waved to him like a maniac.

I had to get out of here, fast. Heedless of the folks around me, I lurched in the opposite direction.

Right into Nick's former fiancée, Crystal, who was heading toward the heart of the action. Beside her, Nick's mother Arianna, who assigned me to a toxic category along with artificial food preservatives and MSG, was beside her, and gave a surprised yelp when I jostled The Lovely One.

"Sorry," I muttered, head down, sidestepping, hoping to escape scrutiny.

No such luck.

"Nora," Crystal said, her voice dripping with false concern, her lovely brows forming two pronounced vees as they shot up. "Are you all right? You look a little," she paused and treated me to a full, slow perusal.

"Disheveled," she said finally. "That inside-out look, is it some new fashion statement that city women favor?"

Arianna fixed a pleasant expression on her face. "Hello, Nora."

"Arianna," I said with a polite nod, followed by a big, fat lie. "Good to see you."

To Crystal I replied, "Yes. You should try it."

"And the white powder in your hair?" Crystal questioned.

Ieyee.

I'd forgotten about my hair.

The compartment of my brain that comes up with excuses shut down temporarily, and I hesitated. A reason? A reason? What could I say?

Finally, I opted for the outrageous. "It's supposed to resemble snow. I thought I'd try for a part in the movie. I was going for an authentic look. Does it work? What do you think?"

I twirled a strand around my finger.

Nora, Nora, Nora. What are you doing?

Arianna looked from me to Crystal. I could tell she was unsure of what to say. Without a doubt she felt the situation called for her input, but since her son had shown an interest in me, outright rudeness was off the table. She chose neutrality.

"Crystal, perhaps we should move on."

When Crystal didn't respond, Arianna shifted out of neutral. "Nick will be ready for you shortly."

I could tell from Crystal's expression that Arianna's last comment was a partial success. She tossed her dark, silken mane over her shoulder and smiled her viper smile. "Stick with it, Nora. You'll be a shoe-in." She laughed in derision.

I shot Crystal the I-don't-give-a-damn smile I'd perfected as a teenager and watched them move on, realizing they posed an additional threat. If they mentioned the white powder to anyone, and Sal heard about it, I was toast.

He probably had powder on him after moving through

the blizzard I'd created.

Nick will be ready for us shortly.

Really, Arianna? Choosing sides so obviously?

I didn't have time to wonder about what Nick was ready for. One thing at a time. I had to get out of town, fast, without help from Mary Fran who now stood next to the evil one.

Keeping to the edge of the crowd, I made my way to the Country Store. I'd cut through to the back door and head for Ce-ce in the library parking lot.

I was on the top step to the Country Store, reaching for the door, when I spotted a man entering Harold's office. It wasn't much of a leap to figure he was the broken cap guy Harold had mentioned earlier. As I watched, he opened the door, turning just enough for me to see his face.

Lucca!

No big surprise there.

"*. . . should I just remind you about what happened to the last person who crossed me? No one gets in my way.*"

"*. . . You want to lose another cap?*"

Something bad was going down, and Sal was involved. Lucca too.

I went into the Country Store, stood behind the jars of baked beans near the window, and focused on Sal across the street. I wondered for the second time that day if he'd murdered Floyd. Beyond that, I wondered what else he was involved in, and what his connection to Lucca was. And to the dentist, if any.

So many possibilities.

I needed to talk to Nick. And Mary Fran. And the aunts.

But first things first. I was a mess, I smelled like an unwashed animal bed, and I needed to ditch the aqua jacket that I'd grown really fond of.

Without wasting another second, I hurried past a collection of magazines I wanted to read, a glass barrel of hard candies I wanted to taste, and the fresh fruit I should be eating more of. I paused by the wine section and grabbed a bottle of merlot. I quickly pulled out a few bills and stuffed them in Alice's apron pocket as she stood by a back table taking an order. I held up the bottle to indicate what I'd taken, and kept going.

CHAPTER SEVENTEEN

Deep shadows were merging with purples when I finally pulled into Ida's driveway.

Ida let out a yelp and pushed up from her favorite chair as soon as I walked into the front room. "Oh, Nora! What happened? Were you in an accident? Are you all right?"

She hugged me and stepped back quickly, her nose wrinkled. "Oh, my. That's a strong odor."

"Aunt Ida, I'm fine now, but I have to shower and change. Then I'll tell you about my day—the good, the bad, and the super ugly."

"Just toss those clothes down here. I'll throw them in the washing machine straight away."

When I entered the kitchen about an hour later, Great-Aunts Hannah and Agnes were at the table with Ida, and a place had been set for me. Ida had heated up her chicken noodle soup, a thick and hearty meal, unrivaled, I think, in the world of soups. It was loaded with enough chunky vegetables and chicken to sustain a team of Olympians.

Ida had changed clothes. Her other clothes probably smelled from our hug and had joined mine in the wash.

After hugs all around, Ida filled the blue and white ceramic tureen that had been in the Lassiter family since Great-Grandma Evie was a bride; Agnes placed warm, chunky rolls in a basket and brought them to the table; and Hannah filled the water glasses.

"Tell us," Agnes said as soon as we were all seated. "We didn't want to badger you when you first came down, but we've got to know."

"Yes. Don't keep us in suspense a moment longer," Hannah said, reaching for a roll. "Ida told us about your appearance and your reeking clothing."

"Well, the day started with a visit to Marney," I began. I recounted our conversation almost verbatim.

"So she wants you to back off the investigation," Hannah said, her eyes narrowed in suspicion.

"And now she's madly in love with the cheating Floyd?" Ida said. "Sounds like she's got something to hide."

"That occurred to me, too."

Next I told them about the library stop and meeting Margaret and Harold, without revealing Margaret's secret, which I felt honor-bound to keep.

"So she's still interested in the missing books?" Ida asked as she ladled more soup.

"Seems a little thin to me," Hannah said. "You holding back on us, Nora? I thought that might be the case last time you mentioned Margaret."

Hannah was sharp. I released a deep sigh. "It's personal to Margaret, not connected with anything much, and I promised to keep it private. Let's leave it at that."

"As long as she didn't murder anyone, or rob a bank," Ida said as she dipped the crusty edge of her roll into her soup.

"Someone's robbed a bank? When did this happen?" Agnes said with a gasp as a noodle slipped off her spoon and landed with a soft plop in her bowl. "What's happening to this town?"

"Where are your hearing aids, Agnes? You promised to wear them," Hannah said.

"So, what did she say?" Agnes asked, ignoring Hannah.

"No bank was robbed," I assured Agnes. "But I need to keep Margaret's secret. It's nothing criminal, just private."

"Where?" Hannah persisted, looking at Agnes. "You had it on when you left the house."

Agnes flopped her arms on the table, angled her chin up and said, "If you must know, the batteries went dead and I didn't have replacements. We'll need to go to the County Store soon."

Hannah nodded. "Tomorrow. When we go to our first yoga session we'll stop there." To Nora she said, "The yoga scene won't be shot until next week, so we must be part of the group before then."

"How's the yoga coming?" I asked, hoping to deflect attention from my situation.

"No, you don't! No sidetracking. We haven't heard the most important part of your day," Hannah said. "Like what happened to *you*."

"Yes," Agnes said. "Ida told us you had a huge problem in town. You looked like you'd been attacked by a moose, or worse."

What could be worse? Just the thought of one of those huge animals coming at me rattled my nerves like few other threats.

"Do they attack in winter?" I asked.

"Only if there's been a lot of snow and food is hard to find," Ida said.

Like this winter, I thought.

I was reluctant to tell them about what happened in town. I'd thought about it the whole time I was in the shower, which, granted, wasn't that long, considering the water traveled from hot to lukewarm to definitely cold in record time today. The hot water guy had come to fix the tank and burner a few weeks ago, and the fix lasted two glorious days. When I called him back I got his answering machine. No return call yet.

Bottom line, I didn't know how much to tell them. Didn't want them scared and worrying about my safety. Didn't want them looking at Sal as if he were a Mafia don.

Despite all that, I decided to confide. While I detailed my harrowing experience, the chicken soup remained untouched.

I ended by saying, "Sal was angry at the guy on the movie crew named Lucca. He told him: "I gave you a chance. You blew it. Now fix this mess. The guy tried to make an excuse by saying he had something he had to handle first, but Sal didn't want to hear any of it. I think Sal's a nasty guy."

I refrained from mentioning how much of a threat I considered Sal.

I told them about my dash from the building when I thought I might have been seen, the attack of the fire extinguisher, my stint in the truck under the smelly blanket, and the slight injury to my knee and foot, making light of it all as if my actions had been an unnecessary and foolish precaution.

From the expressions on their faces, I realized my attempts to minimize the danger were not working, not for a nanosecond. These were bright women. Beyond that, naiveté was a quality they had left by the wayside years ago.

"You played it smart, Nora," Hannah said with a nod of acknowledgment.

"Absolutely," Agnes said, getting back to her soup.

"Indeed. Our Nora is a smart one, that's for sure," Ida said, beaming. Then her expression turned somber. "I hope you told Nick about all this."

"I haven't had time."

"As soon as we've finished eating, you make time," Hannah said in a tone that brooked no argument. "And maybe you should see a doctor about your injuries."

"Even though you handled it smart," Agnes said as she buttered her roll, "what you did was dangerous. You shouldn't be doing stuff like that alone. You don't even carry a gun."

"We don't want to lose you, Nora, honey," Ida said, a catch in her voice.

Hannah reached for my hand and nodded her agreement. Agnes sniffled. Next thing, all of us were holding hands around the table, eyes misting.

* * *

After eating, I phoned Nick. When I finished telling him what had happened behind the station house after I'd left him at the scene of the multi-car fender bender, he was silent for so long I finally asked if he were still there.

"Still here," he said. "Processing your actions and wondering when you're going to retire from the detective career you have no training for. And no license for. And wondering if you realize how dangerous your actions were."

"I realize, so let's move on. What should we do now?"

"*We?*"

"Oh, Nick. Come on! The guy's into something shady. Criminal. You know it."

"My dear Nora, let's meet for breakfast. We'll talk about it then."

I wanted to ask a few questions about the movie, about Crystal and her possible part in it, and a few more things, but I kept it all to myself. Maybe I'd keep the part about Crystal to myself forever.

Or at least until tomorrow.

"Okay. Breakfast it is.

* * *

The aroma of coffee and bacon competed with the mixed scents of aftershave and cologne in the Country Store when Nick and I arrived for breakfast. Many of the movie crew had crowded in. Some looked impatient as they waited for attention, others seemed to take in the ambience, perhaps absorbing local color for the sake of authenticity in the movie. Hard to tell.

I wore an old jacket that belonged to Ida. Black, roomy, with a hood. In an attempt to make it look better, I'd belted it. The attempt wasn't all that successful, but for now it would do.

Alice, the waitress with the tight, bobbing curls and quick smile, looked like a woman besieged. I stepped forward to help her. Nick's hand on my arm stopped me.

"Several other folks have been called in to work while this crew is here." He tipped his head toward the back room where the old guys sat around the potbelly stove. I saw Uncle Walter back there and smiled at him.

"See the folks putting on aprons in the back room," Nick said. "Two of those folks are cooks, the others will wait on customers. Alice'll have help soon. You join in and they won't get their tips."

"I didn't think of that," I said, stepping back.

"There's coffee at the station house." Nick took out a pen and a pad. "Want eggs? Pancakes? What?" he asked.

I narrowed my eyes. "You cooking?"

"Ordering."

"Blueberry pancakes and bacon."

Nick wrote, ripped off the paper and handed it to Alice. "Take your time," he said to her. "No hurry."

We were a few feet from the exit when I gasped and stopped so abruptly I stumbled on my shadow. He was here. Framed and mounted in the bubble glass that topped the Country Store door, clear enough to see, distorted enough to frighten, my nightmare come to life.

Without a word, Nick touched my back and opened the door.

CHAPTER EIGHTEEN

Startled by the sudden appearance of the hunter who would probably give a small fortune to get me in the crosshairs, I gathered my composure, lifted my head, and walked with purpose, Nick's hand on my back steading me. Sal, assuming the role of gentleman, stepped aside on the broad top step and, smiling, held the door so I could pass. The big phony.

I offered the facsimile of a smile and gave a cheery, "'Morning" to the possible murderer of Floyd LeBeau, who might or might not know I was on to him.

Nick gave his noncommittal sheriff's nod.

Once outside, we remained silent until we were well out of hearing range.

"Nora, you have to calm down. From what you told me, he probably didn't see your face. If you don't ease up around him, he'll get suspicious. I don't think he misses much. In any case, he knows I'll protect you so he won't chance anything that could be traced back to him."

My voice was clipped as I said, "You're right. I'm on it. Be friendly to Sal. And his friends. Even though he might remember that I have a fashionable aqua jacket."

Nick rolled his eyes. I ignored him.

Once we were in his office, I said, "I haven't told Mary Fran yet. I was going to call her last night. I changed my mind. If she acted squirrelly around him, that would really tip him off."

"Squirrelly. You mean like you at the door of the Country Store? Good thinking." Nick handed me some papers. "Read these. I ran a check on him. Guy's an expeditor for a shipping company in New Jersey. Makes decent money. An ex-wife's mentioned, two kids, three siblings and parents."

"I think that's what he told Mary Fran. She went on about him. I didn't listen too closely. I mentally shut down after a half hour of gushing. Maybe less. I can't stand gushing."

Nick poured two cups of coffee, added milk, set one on his desk for me, then sat behind the desk.

"Did Beverly say anything interesting when you interviewed her? You never said."

"She contradicted Eddie about the ring. Said he never gave it back to her."

"Oh, gosh. Are they both pointing fingers at the other?"

"Don't know yet."

His cell phone sounded with the ring of an old-fashioned phone. He glanced at the caller ID and let it ring. Less than a minute later, it began again. Same ringtone. Another glance and this time he answered, listened for a few seconds, his face expressionless, and said, "Tell them I'm busy. I'll let them know when I'm ready."

I didn't know whether he had the same awful ring for everyone. Wouldn't ask, of course. He knew I had different rings for different people. If he had a special ring for me, I wondered what it would be. I was tempted to call his phone, check it out.

When our breakfast arrived, I put the papers aside and moved closer to the desk. I topped the pancakes with butter and maple syrup and arranged the bacon around the stack. Neatly.

"I love blueberry pancakes," I said, after my first bite.

"I can see," he said, indicating a drop of syrup on my chin.

Nick's cell phone rang again, same boring traditional telephone ring. When he answered, I was close enough to hear a woman's voice, but it was impossible to make out what she was saying, or who she was.

"No," he said. "He didn't make it up. I told him that. I'm busy. You'll have to wait." Polite but firm, brooking no argument.

The woman's voice again. The words were still too low to hear. However, I suspected Crystal.

I took a sip of my coffee, wishing I had one of Aunt Agnes's hearing aids to amplify the sound. In lieu of that, I leaned in to reposition the cup. First here, then there, searching for the perfect spot. Sometimes I am a foolish woman. He'd notice.

He hung up. Smiled at me. I smiled back. He knew that I knew that he knew. No words needed.

We ate in silence for a few minutes, me wondering if that had been Crystal calling, him enjoying his scrambled eggs and the fact that I was curious about his caller.

Finally, nodding toward the papers, he said, "What do you think?"

"Sal sounds like a paragon. No charges against him, not so much as a traffic ticket. Even the church he attends is mentioned. How'd that get in the report?"

"He's godfather to a nephew. I think the notice was in a local paper."

Because it was the last thing I needed, a scene from *The Godfather* cut through my head with horrible clarity. Corleone at the baptismal font peacefully holding a nephew while his crew, on his orders, went on a murderous rampage.

I blocked the images in my head and asked, "What's he doing on this movie set? Nothing mentioned here about any connection to Hollywood."

Nick reached in his desk drawer and pulled out a copy of the script. "See the name listed way down at the bottom, second assistant director?

"Lucca Baldino? Sal's relative?"

"Older brother."

I chewed on that idea as I took the last bite of bacon.

"Sal's got nothing to do with the movie?"

"Far as I know he's just visiting. I'll check on that later."

I need to repeat myself, Lucca? Do I? Huh? Do I?

"So Sal was threatening his brother. Wonder what that was all about."

A gentle knock on the door was accompanied by a sweet voice. "Nick. It's me."

Good thing I'd swallowed my bacon, or I might have gagged.

"Come in, Mom."

Nick got up and went over to give Arianna a kiss on the cheek.

I did not get squirrelly.

"Oh, you have company." Arianna's pleasant smile belied what must be a host of unpleasant thoughts in her head. I wondered whether Nick suspected that, too. "Hello, Nora."

I smiled graciously at the woman who'd buy me a ticket to New York or to Hong Kong if she thought I'd go, and stay there.

"Arianna. Good morning."

She gave me the smallest nod possible.

"What's up, Mom?"

"When Crystal said you were busy, I was sure it involved important police business."

So it *was* Crystal on the phone.

"It does, Mom. It's important that the chief eat breakfast. You always said it was the most important meal of the day, and I agree."

"Well, I don't want to rush you, but we *are* waiting. The audition is scheduled, and they won't change the time. Crystal is a bundle of nerves as you might imagine."

"I don't see why I have to be involved in this. My presence isn't necessary. She can audition with anyone. I'll be there for the filming."

"You need to rehearse, too. You'll be in the actual

scene, so she wants you there for the audition. Will you do this for me, if not for her?"

There it was! The mother-loyalty hook. Gag me with a spoon!

"We'll see. Depends on my schedule."

When the Wicked Witch closed the door from the other side, I asked, "Is this the kissing scene I've heard about?" knowing the answer before he replied.

Which he didn't. He looked at me. No expression. No words. He expected me to understand a look. Personally, I preferred words. Men can be so annoying at times.

But I let it slide when he gently cupped my face with both hands and said, "I hate to let you out of my sight today, and I'm not just talking about your *detective* career. I wish we could spend the day together."

He kissed me softly on the lips, then slid his arms around me, making me feel cherished in that way that was so dear to my heart. I kissed him back, not caring about any kissing scene he had in the movie because I knew it didn't matter.

Of course, I really had understood his look.

* * *

On the off chance that Harold had mentioned something to Margaret about Lucca and his chipped tooth, or that she knew anything about him that I didn't know, I headed over to the library.

Unlike yesterday, Margaret was alone today. She took me to the back room immediately.

"We can talk here. No one's around, but I need to get these finished," she said, pointing to a stack of uncovered books. "Cover and paste and then paste the card holder in back."

I suspected if I worked with her on this, she'd talk more freely, so I offered. "I can paste the card holders in." How difficult could that be?

She explained what to do. "Just be careful with the glue. I use gorilla super glue."

"Got it."

All was going well. We were chit-chatting about this and that, mostly library stuff, when I finally asked, "Margaret, did Harold tell you anything about the patient he saw yesterday? The one who needed the cap?"

"I'm not supposed to discuss it."

I tipped the glue bottle and let a drop fall on the inside back cover of the book. "But you know something?"

"Ummm."

"You don't have to share. I understand. I'm just curious about folks in the movie business. They lead such glamorous lives, don't they?" I pressed the card holder in place on the glue.

Margaret sighed. "I suppose it wouldn't hurt to share. It's not such a big deal. His name is Lucca. He's some sort of director's helper, and he got punched in the mouth."

I tried for an aghast sound, which fell a little short of the mark, somewhere between a huff and a tsk. I should practice that. "Punched! My goodness. Why? What did he do?"

"He told Harold it was a misunderstanding."

I made another strange sound, going for disbelief this time—the tsk first, then the huff. It came out a little better.

"I don't believe that, do you?"

"No." She paused and bit her lower lip. "I felt sorry for that guy Lucca. But maybe I shouldn't. I think he's up to something."

"What?"

"I know it was wrong for me to leave the library unattended, but . . . I did. I watched that guy when he was on the police station steps the day after Harold treated him."

"And?" It was like pulling teeth. She and Harold were made for each other.

"He did an odd thing. He was talking to some people, and the owner of that fancy Land Rover, the one in the little fender-bender, drove by and stopped right in the middle of the street. I think Lucca signaled him. I doubt anyone noticed. It was subtle. Like this."

Margaret narrowed her eyes, then angled her head in a quick motion.

"Like he was telling the guy to move on down the road. I got the feeling they were going to meet."

"Did they?"

"Maybe. The whole thing was very fast. Over in a blink. Of course, he could have been brushing lint off his jacket. But I don't think so because the Land Rover guy took off."

I stopped working, stared at her. Just to be sure, I asked, "And? Did Lucca follow?"

Margaret shrugged, "I don't know. But he left the folks he was talking to and walked off that way. So maybe they met up. I went back to the library. I'd been away too long."

Oh, geeze.

Nick and I had never discussed the accident. My experience took center stage. I had to let him know about this. I could call, or—

"Margaret, I've got to be going."

"Wait. I haven't been totally honest with you. It's not too important," Margaret said, stopping me before I grabbed my handbag, "but my conscience demands I tell you anyway. A few books *were* stolen from the library and a few DVDs. Like I told you originally."

Conscience. I wished she hadn't used that word. I should clear my conscience and tell her about the book on Lincoln I'd checked out of the library when I was ten years old, before the family moved to New York City. I'd found that book in an old box this past year. In a way, I was a library thief. I should confess. I should at least return the twenty-year overdue Lincoln book. Clear my conscience.

"What about them?"

I forced myself to stay put. I'd listen to her. Instead of the handbag, I picked up the glue bottle and the last card holder. No glue came out, so I held the bottle upside down while she went on about the pilfered items.

"I'd actually like you to look into it. Even though I told you not to."

Ieee. I didn't want to bother with such nonsense. What were library items compared to a murder case? Of course, I wasn't involved in a murder case, per se.

Since I'd had no luck so far finding her lottery winnings, I decided to do this. I suppose some of the missing items might be related to my cases. They bore looking into. I remembered what Nick had said. *When you're tracking a killer, no detail is unimportant.*

Maybe there was some cockamamie connection. Who knew!

"Okay, Margaret. I'll do that. What subjects? Titles? Can you get me a list?" I asked, needing to ease her conscience and mine, needing to feel I was doing something to help her.

"I've been carrying the list in my pocket."

Margaret handed me her list, then nodded, started to go, then stopped again. "Do you think you'll ever find out what happened to my lottery ticket? Please be totally honest. Is there a chance I'll get it back?"

I swallowed hard. She'd asked for honesty. I thought her chances of getting the money were slim. After all, she'd never signed an agreement with Beverly Sue. Worse, Beverly Sue denied it outright—*I have no winning ticket. Anyone who tells you different is a liar, for sh-ur*—definitely not a good sign.

"Margaret, there's always a chance. It's a large amount of money. Difficult to hide. I won't give up. I promise you that, but that's all I can promise."

Not really an answer, but the best I could do. I thought her eyes had misted over as I spoke.

"Oh, I hope Harold doesn't find out about my gambling."

"Stand up to him! You didn't murder anyone. No one

is perfect. Tell him that."

"I don't think I could do that. I'm not strong like you."

When she left, I scanned the list. Books on skiing, snowshoeing, first aid, and guns. Most interesting were the books and DVDs on computer usage that ranged from beginning to advanced. I wondered who would be interested in those topics.

I picked up my phone and was about to hit Nick's number when I decided to do a thorough job with the card holders. It was the least I could do. I like to finish a job once I've started it, so I set the phone on the table next to the book and went at it.

Stupid glue wasn't coming out even after I'd been holding it upside down all this time. Impatient, I gave a simultaneous squeeze and a shake. A huge glob splattered out. Good grief!

As if on cue, the cell phone sounded with Nick's ringtone. I grabbed it, answered and put it to my ear.

"Nora, if you're still in town, stop by before you leave."

"Okay. I was just going to call you. I have something else to tell you."

I heard a loud noise in the background.

"I've been at the library talking to Margaret, and she told me something interesting about Lucca."

"It's hard to hear."

I repeated what I'd said over the loud cacophony in the background.

"It's no use. See you later. Gotta run."

He ended the call.

I did not. Could not. My day had suddenly taken an unexpected turn.

CHAPTER NINETEEN

My cell phone played "Ida, Sweet as Apple Cider," and since the phone was now glued to my ear, it was convenient to answer. Although I would not advocate this as a method of easy access, in this instance, it was handy.

"Hi, Ida. What's up?" I asked as I headed for the police station to see why Nick had asked me to stop by, but more important, hoping he knew a thing or two about removing gorilla super glue.

To lessen the tug on my ear caused by walking, I pressed the roomy hood tighter. I never realized I was such a bouncy walker. Step, bounce, step, bounce. Despite my efforts, it felt as if the skin on my ear was tearing, so I tried another stride. Glide and step, glide and step. Since skaters glided, I hummed a waltz I'd heard at Rockefeller Center skating rink when I'd taken a lesson there many years ago, not something I should be thinking about now. But of course, unbidden, the scene of me crashing into three little kids flashed in my head. Their mother was so upset. She yelled that I should be banned from the skating rink forever. She wanted to sue my mother, who apologized profusely and promised I would never return.

Although that had been a mini catastrophe, I remembered the skating music, "Lara's Theme" from *Doctor Zhivago*. "Somewhere, my love, there will be songs to sing. La-la-la, la-la-la."

I continued to hum until Ida's voice jolted me back to the present.

"Will you be able to come?" Ida asked,

"What? Say that again. I didn't hear you."

"We'll be in the church basement for our first yoga practice. Thought you might like to come by and watch the class."

"I'd love that. Right now I have a small problem."

"Anything I can help with?"

Step and glide, step and glide. Glide, glide, glide.

"Do you know how to remove super glue?"

"Sure. A little nail polish remover. I think it's the acetone that does the trick. If you don't have that, white vinegar can work, too. Uncle Walter uses that to remove hardened glue from wood furniture."

"Thanks. You've been a help. I'll stop by later to watch your class, if I have time."

I changed direction and glided toward Hot Heads Heaven. Just as well. I'd made a decision about Mary Fran, and I might as well handle it now.

The beauty salon was busier than I'd ever seen it. Evidently, every woman in town felt the need to put her best hairdo forward today. Mary Fran looked like she might burst into song as she flitted through the silver and magenta themed room to work on a customer.

"I need nail polish remover and your help for a minute or two," I said to Mary Fran, interrupting the woman in the chair who was showing her a photo of a hairdo she wanted. "Nice choice," I said to her. "A lot of stars are choosing that look." She beamed at me.

"In a minute, Nora. Take your jacket off and sit by the nail seat. I'll have the girl do you next. You may have to deal with about twenty angry customers though." She gave a quick laugh.

"No." I shook my head, which in hindsight was a mistake. My hand went to my sore ear. "Oww. In back, Mary Fran. Now."

She shot me a questioning look, her gaze going to the unlikely hood I wore.

Still clasping the hood tightly, I stared back with an expression meant to communicate distress. "I'll meet you there."

"What's up?" she said minutes later as she closed the door to the back room.

I pushed back the hood, and her eyes widened as she stared at the hanging phone.

"How the heck—"

"Don't ask how. It's a glue problem," I said before she had a chance to ask. "Acetone will work. That's what Aunt Ida said. Besides that, there's something we have to talk about."

"Why do I get the feeling I won't like the talking part?"

"I don't like this part," I said, pointing to my ear. "Let's get this phone off first. Acetone. Nail polish remover."

She took down a bottle from the supply shelf, grabbed cotton balls and set to work. "Talk to me as I do this. I have to know."

Mary Fran could get jittery at times, and I didn't want her to jerk the bottle and accidently splash nail polish remover near my eyes. "Finish this first, then I'll tell you."

"Uh-oh. It must be really bad. Does it have to do with Sal?" she asked as she tipped the bottle and drenched the cotton ball again.

"Maybe a little," I said after she set the bottle down. "Tell me!"

Someone banged on the door. "Mary Fran, your next customer is in the chair waving a picture and asking when you'll be back. What shall I tell her?"

"Something obscene comes to mind," she yelled, "so you decide. Be polite, of course. Make my excuses."

"Sit," I said, pointing to a stool as I grabbed the wet cotton puff from her. Normally, I would have nodded instead of pointing, but I'd learned nodding wasn't a good choice. "I'll work on this for a bit."

I wiggled the phone back and forth slightly, pausing frequently as I dabbed more remover on my ear. While I worked, I filled her in, starting with the station house discussion between Sal and Lucca. From there, I touched on the fire extinguisher episode, the smelly blanket event, and finally the escape.

I was prepared for the explosion I suspected was coming.

But life and people are full of surprises. Mary Fran's body language spoke volumes. She was one of the most unpredictable, and often volatile, women I knew. The fireworks never erupted. She was calm, and it was not a case of anger held in check. I doubt she possessed that ability. Instead she seemed wistful.

She understood, without my verbalizing it, that Sal might be a killer. At the very least he was involved in something criminal.

"I wasn't going to tell you," I said. "But I was afraid when you were with him, you'd give yourself, or me, away. I have to trust you to act . . . professionally."

She got up and took a fresh cotton ball, drenched it and pushed my hand aside.

"The glue is in your hair, too. I'll have to trim it out. It'll be short in spots."

That conjured up pictures of some of the hairdos I'd seen come out of this shop. Mary Fran was a hairspray enthusiast. A person leaving here could go through a typhoon that would send them sailing down the street, but their coiffure, usually an extremely high one, would remain secure.

"Short *spots*?" I said. "How short?"

"Trust me. Hair styling. It's what I do. I'll make it look okay."

I'd argue about this when the phone came off my ear. I still waited for her response about what I'd just told her. I thought that would come immediately.

Finally, she folded her arms and took a deep, sad breath.

"I'm glad you trusted me enough to tell me. You

know, I thought I could care about him. Maybe I wanted that so much that I saw things in him that weren't really there. That's a mistake I made with Percy. Now that he's in prison, I see my soon-to-be ex-husband as the lousy rat scumbag he really is."

I nodded, as much in relief as acceptance.

This was the first time she'd mentioned Percy to me, and although I wondered if she thought about him much, maybe even missed him, I never asked, considering it a matter of privacy.

"I'll be alert next time I'm with Sal."

"Good," was all I said in reply.

"Or do you think I shouldn't see him anymore?"

"Ending the relationship too abruptly would probably signal something was wrong. You can't do anything to make him suspicious. Can you act normal around him?"

"Definitely."

I hoped so.

CHAPTER TWENTY

"Sorry I had you stop back again," Nick said, staring at my new hairdo, which was sticking out at odd angles. Mary Fran had shown me pictures of stars with their hair this way. I should have brought them to show Nick.

"I didn't want to talk on the phone, but I wanted you to see some info I obtained, and with all these people roaming around—"

"You're not one bit sorry," I interrupted, smiling. "At least I hope not."

His all-business cop persona remained. Startled by the absence of a smile, I stared at him, unsure, until his hand cupped my neck, and he gently pulled me toward him and kissed me.

"So perceptive, Ms. Lassiter," he said, still in cop-mode.

"It's one of the qualities of a good private detective."

"Don't push it."

He reached into his bottom desk drawer for a manila envelope and handed it to me. When I read the name and the first few bits of information, I looked up.

"Wow. Lucca has a record. Served time for DUI and cocaine possession in California. So how did he break into movies? And get a job as second assistant director, forheavensakes?"

"Can't say for sure, but his cellmate was Josh Rockford's grandson."

"Well, gee whiz. That couldn't possibly have anything to do with it, could it?"

He smirked.

I read a little more, then asked, "Does Sal have any connection to the movie industry?"

"I checked. I can't find any connection. Doesn't mean there isn't one. I don't have a list of his investments. Maybe this is just a family thing. Could be as simple as him holding this jail time over his brother's head."

"Could be."

"Don't say anything," he said. "The guy served his time. He wouldn't want this spread around."

Nick put the report back in his desk and locked the drawer.

"I heard from Marney," he said. "Seems that Floyd's remains have been released. She's having them cremated tomorrow and buried the following day. There'll be a short service in the church. She asked me to tell you."

"Why didn't she call me herself? Did she say?"

"Didn't say. But she also asked me to call Eddie and Beverly Sue. I just got off the phone with Eddie."

"Humph. He coming?"

"Eddie definitely. Beverly, I doubt. They were all in high school together."

"I know about that. But it doesn't make sense. Why would she want Beverly Sue around? She hates her. At least that's what she led me to believe. And Beverly Sue is not too fond of her, either."

"You never know what makes people tick."

"I'm pretty sure Beverly won't come. Margaret will probably be there. No way Beverly wants a confrontation with either woman."

"Margaret?" he said.

"Can't talk about that."

"Okay. For now."

So Eddie wouldn't be at the mountain. A possibility flitted through my head, and just as quickly I banished it.

Never.

Too foolish.

"I don't want to know what you're thinking," Nick

said.

Smiling now, he took my hand. "I take back what I said about being sorry I had you stop by again. I won't be able to see you for a few days, unless you come to the funeral." He shook his head. "I'm not even sure about that. I have to be here every day with this movie crew around. And I have meetings every night this week.

"Town board tonight, about Winterfest, and then another meeting with the Winterfest committee tomorrow. It's a big deal this year because the movie crew will use some of the activities for background shots."

"And there's also *your* scene in the movie. The famous kissing scene." I paused. "Here." I gestured with a wide sweep of my arms. "In this very office."

His brows shot up. "Do you think I should practice? Here?" He paused. "Now?"

"Well, I'm not sure," I said slowly, my drama-filled demeanor communicating an insouciance that was diametrically opposed to my feelings. "Rehearsals *are* important, I suppose."

He stepped away and locked the door, something I'd never seen him do before. The look he gave me sent butterflies dancing in my stomach.

He took my hand, led me to the chair behind his desk, and pulled me onto his lap. He didn't kiss me immediately, like I expected. He just touched my face gently, framed it with his hands, loved me with his eyes. If it were possible to freeze a moment in time to hold and savor whenever I wanted, this moment would be one of my choices.

His gaze was intense, so passionate that I could hardly breathe. My heart beat a rapid rhythm that sent the blood surging through me. My thoughts spiraled like crazy, and for that moment I felt I had been blessed with a brief glimpse of paradise. I was so incredibly happy I almost cried. My eyes filled with moisture as he held my gaze. He kissed me then, sweet and warm. Kissed my eyes, my neck, my face.

When his lips caressed my mouth, I kissed him back. His hands splayed on my hips, then moved up my back, and he pulled me securely into his arms, hugged me close. We stayed like that for long minutes.

Breathless, I said, "In your brief scene . . . your kissing scene . . . are you . . . "

I paused, sorry I'd begun to say what I was saying. He pulled back and regarded me. I was pretty sure I detected a hint of amusement behind his eyes. He said nothing. I let the silence linger, figuring he'd wade into the opening I'd left. He didn't. Annoying man.

Embarrassed that I'd said anything about his upcoming scene with his former fiancée, I bit my lip.

He waited for me to stammer out the rest of my comment. I could back off. But it was not in me to back away from the difficult, so I marshaled forces and plunged on.

"I was just wondering whether you were looking forward to the kissing scene. And, of course, how much oomph you planned to put into it?"

Finally, he smiled. Then he laughed outright.

"You know the answer to that, don't you?"

I smiled. Let a few seconds elapse, and then leaned forward and kissed him.

"I think I do, Sheriff Renzo," I mumbled, my lips on his mouth. "Yes, I believe I do."

* * *

With my new chopped hairdo flying around my face, I headed down to the church to watch the aunts in their first session of the senior yoga class. My thoughts ricocheted all over the place. Visions of Nick competed with the idea that I should go up to the mountain tomorrow when Eddie wasn't there. The added bonus might be Beverly's absence, if she decided to attend the funeral, that is. I'd never returned the master key Marney had given me.

As soon as I stepped in the door of the church, I heard the voice of the yoga instructor. In order not to disturb the class, I walked downstairs quietly and sat on the bottom step to observe. Ida spotted me and gave a little wave. I waved back.

"Next we'll do the Mountain Pose."

"Oh, good," I heard Aunt Agnes say. "That's my favorite pose. I used to like the Triangle Pose best, but now I like the Mountain Pose."

"Find your length. Big toes together, heels touching," the instructor said.

"I got my heels together, but my toes refuse to touch. That happens sometimes." Agnes again.

"Draw your core in and up."

"Will this help my toes? I have a bunion," Agnes said. "I don't see how this could help, but I could be wrong."

"Let's get past the toe problem. Your core," the yoga instructor repeated. "Concentrate on your core."

Agnes, dressed in her new splatter pants and white Yoga Chick tee shirt, tried to pull in her belly.

"Core. My belly, right? In and up isn't happening today. For sh-ure," Agnes said. "It's still out there."

The yoga instructor, obviously a woman of tremendous patience, said pleasantly, "Let's not distract others with our comments."

"I'm all for that," Agnes agreed.

"Then you should shut up," one of the sixty-year-olds said. "You're disrupting the flow. My concentration's off. And you've been doing that since we started."

"She shouldn't be in this class," one of the others said.

"Well, of all the—" Hannah began.

"Ladies. Concentrate on the pose, please."

Hannah, wearing her new multicolored yoga outfit, kept the intended rebuke to herself, but I saw her laser focus remain on the one who had expressed the outrageous condemnation. This wasn't over. I had a feeling that woman would hear from Hannah later.

Despite the undercurrent of hostility toward the interlopers, the group listened to the instructor and resumed the session with quiet attention.

I watched Aunt Ida. She looked good in her new yoga outfit.

Occasionally she tugged on her tee, communicating her unease with dressing outside her comfort zone.

My thoughts shifted to tomorrow. I decided I definitely had to go back to the mountain. Either Beverly or Eddie had lied about who had possession of the ring. Either one could have the lottery ticket. That ticket was worth millions. Either one, or both, could have been involved in Floyd's murder. All three were aware of the numbers, and, I suspected, had a fair idea of where they could find Margaret's agreement with Beverly.

I didn't see how all this connected, but there was so much I was not seeing. I knew I could definitely check Eddie's room tomorrow. Maybe something would turn up.

I'd drive alone. Mary Fran had to attend the funeral. It might set off alarm bells if we both missed it. I wished I didn't have to go, but I knew I did. It was unlikely I'd get this opportunity again.

"Peace. We strive for peace," the instructor said.

After a few moments of silence, she said. "The correctly executed mountain pose will use every muscle in the body. It will improve posture and balance. It will encourage healthy digestion and elimination."

"Oh, I got healthy elimination, so that's no plus. Why, just this morning I had a bout of—"

"No one wants to hear about your diarrhea," Ida said politely to Agnes.

"I know. I'm distracting again." Agnes made the universal lip-zipping motion. "Not another word from me."

"Dare we hope," one of the seventy-year-olds said.

Peace. With the lines so sharply drawn, the antagonism so open, I figured peace had little chance in this yoga class. The sixty and seventy-year-olds versus the new eighty-year-olds. The Hatfields versus the McCoys. And all for a chance to be in a movie with the formerly famous Josh Rockford.

"They're not here for the exercise. They just want to be in the movie with Big Josh," another seventy-year-old whispered loud enough for everyone to hear, except Agnes, who was concentrating on her pose, and fortunately, in this instance, was hard of hearing.

CHAPTER TWENTY-ONE

I skipped my shower. At 4:30 on a Maine winter morning no one with any sense should take a shower, especially in Aunt Ida's house where the water goes from hot to warm to cool in record time.

Yesterday, before I left town, I had Mary Fran draw me a map to the mountain. She scribbled a few notations to help. I studied it last night and taped it on Ce-ce's dashboard for easy reference.

I'd also tossed in the bulky, black garbage bag with my equipment for the day—pillows, bungee cords, Aunt Agnes's old jumbo-sized jacket and the grotesque gray wig.

My handbag held the essentials I always carried—cell phone, makeup bag, L.L. Bean red Swiss pocketknife with a few thousand tools, multi-interface micro SD card reader, tissues, safety pins, mints. I also had an insulated lunch tote patterned in black and white with hot pink trim, very attractive, designer even. It contained one apple, two thermoses, one with milk so I could eat my cookies properly, and the other for coffee. It was essential that Oreo cookies be dunked. The timing of the dunk was an art I'd mastered over the years. My cookies were never over or under dunked. I also packed a tuna sandwich and two hard-boiled eggs that Ida had made for me yesterday.

I was prepared.

Only the aunts and Mary Fran knew where I was headed, and they understood the need for secrecy. Nick had no need to know. He'd only worry.

Ce-ce needed a little coaxing to get started. I was glad

I had a trickle charger for the battery, or I'd be sitting here forever. I finally took off around five, a truly ungodly hour. It was still dark, which wasn't too bad because I remembered the first part of the trip. I only made a few wrong turns and was at the mountain by nine. When Mary Fran drove, it had taken about two hours, so I figured four hours was about right for me.

Relieved to have arrived, I drove into the employees' parking lot behind their housing unit, zipped into an open space, then grabbed my cell phone and hit Mary Fran's number.

"What's happening?" I asked as soon as she answered. "Who's at the funeral?"

"Hold it." When she came back on, she said, "Had to get away from the crowd. Everyone's going into the church now. Marney's been shaking hands with the whole town, like she's the grieving widow. Or the star of a reality show."

"Is Eddie there? Beverly Sue?"

"Eddie's with a bunch of guys from the mountain. Haven't seen Beverly. She won't come here."

I remembered Beverly's few choice words about Marney when I met her.

"Marmaduke's looking for her husband, is she? The ferret lady wants him back? That's hard to believe, unless, of course, money is involved. Or does she just want to shoot him and be done with it?"

"Did you get there yet, or are you lost?" Mary Fran asked.

"For your information, I'm sitting here. In the parking lot."

"You planning to get out of your truck?"

"Why would I do that? The scenery's so nice, I think I'll just sit here."

"Okay. Dumb question."

"Time to get busy. Talk later."

I grabbed my binoculars and scanned the short row of resident units that angled off the main part of the lodge to the right. Nothing much visible. I swung the binoculars around and glimpsed a few cabins nestled among the trees. Off to the left the mountain rose up. With stronger binoculars I might be able to make out skiers and snowboarders on the trails.

I set the binoculars on the passenger seat, removed my jacket, and shoved my seat back as far as I could. For a few desperate moments, I considered getting out and walking around to the other side, but that would leave me too exposed, so I struggled over, banging one knee on the steering wheel, the other on the shift.

Once positioned in the passenger seat, I grabbed both pillows and began the process. Stuffing pillows beneath two sets of suspenders is no easy task, especially while sitting.

Aunt Agnes's old jacket was next. Another struggle to get that on over the pillows.

Breaking and entering was a criminal offense. If caught, I'd be in double-doo, subject to jail time. So, I'd do what I had to do in order not to get caught. Actually, I had the note Marney had given me when she gave me the key, granting me permission to enter her husband's room. Although I suspected that was no longer valid. Besides, I wasn't interested in Floyd's old room. The cops had been in there after they identified the body.

Ten minutes later my disguise was in place.

My phone played "Bad Boys," announcing my brother Howie calling. I answered. If I didn't, he'd know something was up.

"Hi, Howie. Don't say it. I know I should have called before now, but I've been super busy."

"Are you sorry you're not keeping in touch with your only brother?"

"Absolutely. How is life for Miami-Dade's super cop?"

"You can call me sergeant, if you don't mind."

"Oh, my goodness. Congratulations! Mom must be proud of you. I forgot you'd taken the test. I'm so happy for you, Howie."

"Thank you."

"I'd send you a bouquet of flowers if I thought you'd appreciate it."

"Skip the gushy business. What's going on with you? When are you leaving Maine?"

Silence followed as I looked around the parking lot. Then I said, "Well."

And he said, "So you're involved with this latest murder, and you're not going back. Just yet, that is?"

The sarcasm zipped across the ether and landed with his words in my phone.

"Could we talk about something else, Howie? Your new girlfriend maybe?"

"Sure. Tell me what's going on in Silver Stream, and then I'll fill you in about my new girlfriend."

I decided to count this as a reprieve and told him about Sal and his brother Lucca and the movie business. I kept it short because I had to get moving.

I knew he'd laugh when I told him about hiding in the truck in back of the station house. And he did. But when I finished he was silent.

"What?" I finally said.

"Is Nick investigating further?"

"Absolutely. He's checking things out."

"Sal might be into some racket. Maybe stolen cars, fake designer goods, money laundering, gambling. Stay away from him."

"I intend to."

We talked a bit longer and ended promising to keep in touch more frequently.

I patted my pillows and struggled out of the truck. Off balance, I tilted slightly, but managed to right myself before I toppled. I suppose I should have tested this gear before I used it. Being a private detective is definitely a learning process.

Most of the people who worked on the mountain were

busy at this time of morning, and several were in Silver
Stream for the funeral of one of their own, which meant the
area was almost clear. Good thing.

I didn't see anyone until I waddled into the community
room of the employees' residence where a guy was zipping
up his jacket. He gave me a friendly nod which I returned as
I lifted a gloved hand to toy with a lock of gray hair
dangling in front of my post-surgery, all-encompassing
sunglasses, a contribution from Ida that she'd used after
cataract surgery last year.

"Morning, Ma'am."

"Ummm."

The hood of Agnes's jumbo black thermal jacket was
pulled tightly around my face as I shuffled across the room,
unsure of exactly where I was going. I spotted a bulletin
board and pretended interest as the guy left, and my
breathing returned to normal. Almost normal. My heart still
beat a raucous rhythm in my chest.

I removed both gloves and fingered the items in my
right pocket, the black thermal ski mask with eyeholes and
the plastic gloves. My left pocket held the master key.

Remembering the video cam that tracked the unknown
visitor who entered Floyd's room after the murder, I was
prepared for my trek down that same hall. They wouldn't
see my face. Wouldn't recognize my walk or my rotund
shape.

With plastic gloves on, I used the key and opened
Eddie's door. Once inside, I scanned the room. It was
incredibly small, not much bigger than a jail cell, with room
for a bed, small dresser, and end table. I shifted the pillows
wrapped around my middle and tackled the narrow, linen-
sized closet first.

When I spotted the toolbox, I flopped down and sat
cross-legged in front of it while visions of Pandora's Box
danced in my head.

On top of the tools was a square white box. I pulled
out a smoke detector, then returned it to its box and set it

aside. I rummaged through hammers, screwdrivers, pliers, tape measure, wrenches, and other items. Nothing qualified as incriminating as far as I could tell, so I replaced the smoke detector box and closed the toolbox.

Other boxes of smoke detectors were piled against the back wall, all labeled. I opened one. It was exactly like the picture on the box.

I checked all drawers, under the bed, the small lamp, the box on his dresser, then stood in the middle of the room, wondering whether I might be seeing something incriminating and not even know it. Suddenly the feeling of inadequacy that took hold made me angry.

What. Was. I. Missing.

My cell phone played the theme from the *Lone Ranger*, aka "The William Tell Overture." Nick calling. I didn't answer. He would ask where I was.

♪ *Dum,da-dum,da,dum,dum,dum* ♪

I turned the phone off to keep it silent. I should have done that sooner.

I had to leave before I was discovered. Disappointed almost beyond bearing, I toed the toolbox back into the closet. The thought that I was missing something made me turn and scan the room item by item.

I kept coming back to the toolbox. Once before Eddie had placed something special in there, that wedding ring with the heartbeat lines. People are creatures of habit. The thought wasn't fully formed before I crawled back into the closet and reopened the toolbox. I removed the white box with the smoke detector. Unlike the labeled smoke detector boxes piled by the wall, this box was plain white. Odd, maybe.

I took the detector out and examined it. Nothing hit me. I stared at it. I was about to put it back when I decided *What the heck*, grabbed a small screwdriver and pried the unit open.

Was I being a crazy woman?

Probably.

But as I stared at the contents, I realized what I was looking at. Being a camera buff, the slot for the SanDisk was a dead giveaway. The disk, of course, was AWOL.

Using my cell phone camera, I took photos of this from all angles. I was pretty sure I was looking at a spy camera. To compare it to a regular smoke detector, I opened one of the labeled boxes and popped the detector open. Yes. This was the real thing.

The question was, Who was Eddie spying on, and why? Floyd? Beverly Sue, another worker?

There must have been a disk in here, so what had happened to it? He could have tossed it, but that seemed unlikely. I put everything back and looked around again, this time with an eye to the specific. Where would he hide a small disk?

I rummaged through the drawers again, the tiny closet, the jeans' pockets. Nothing.

With each minute that passed, the possibility of discovery increased. Time's up, I thought. I needed to get out of here, needed to go to Floyd's room, possibly Beverly's, too, if I had time.

I adjusted the pillows around my middle—which had a way of shifting in the stretchy suspender harness and bungee cords—and dug into my pocket for the ski mask, which I yanked over my gray wig. I peeked into the hallway. The coast was clear. I was about to slip out the door when I took one last desperate look around. It had to be here. Had to.

When I glanced at the air vent, I remembered the mystery show Ida had watched where the bad guy hid something, I think it was a camera, in an air vent.

Without wasting another second, I closed the door and dragged the plastic chair beneath the vent. I selected the screwdriver from my handy L.L. Bean red pocketknife, one of my best purchases, and heaved myself onto the chair. Once steady, I unscrewed the vent and felt around inside. Nothing. So disappointing.

Raising my shoulders, I gushed a heavy sigh, which in hindsight was a mistake. It affected my balance. Teetering resulted. I counteracted by holding my arms out for better balance. Tottering happened. I tried again. Tipping took place. Next thing, I was looking at the ceiling, from the floor.

I twisted and tried to roll onto my belly so I could get up. Pictures of turtles on their backs, four little feet kicking up a storm, flew through my head. I started to laugh.

Then I spotted the SanDisk taped to the underside of the toppled chair. Lo and behold! I rolled to my belly and pried the disk loose.

Minutes later, using the lightning connector on the micro SD card reader, I downloaded the contents of the disk, then re-taped the disk under the chair and returned the chair to its original position. Less than a minute later, I was on my way down the hall. Checking Floyd's room was imperative, Beverly's, too. I had to see if there was a spy camera in either room. It might have been removed, but traces of its installation might remain.

I was unlocking Floyd's former room when I heard people enter the community room. Quick as a shot I slipped inside, heart pounding a wild tattoo in my chest. The condition of the room was a shock—ski pants on the bed, shirts on a chair, a knapsack on the floor, and worst of all an open laptop on the dresser with its green light aglow indicating I was on camera.

I was being watched at this very moment.

CHAPTER TWENTY-TWO

Mask and hood still in place, I tossed a shirt over the computer to block the camera and quickly surveyed the room, paying particular attention to the smoke detector. Knowing I might have been seen on camera, live, possibly recorded somewhere, I scanned the room and took video with my cell phone, with special focus on the smoke detector. It might have been my imagination, but I thought there was a larger imprint or shadow surrounding this detector. The spy camera could have been here. Enlarging the photo would help.

I heard voices again.

People in the hall.

My heartbeat kicked into high gear.

I shoved the cell phone in my pocket. I had to get out of here. I checked the window and decided the drop was too high. If I were a stunt person I could probably manage it, but I was a woman who almost broke her neck falling off a chair, forheavensakes.

Laughter in the hall. At least two people.

"Richie! You in there? It's Hank."

Someone banged on the door.

My heartbeat picked up speed like an out-of-control downhill racer. What to do! What to do? Evidently they did not have access to the camera in the room, thank heavens, but still I had to think of a way out.

Appearing with a ski mask was out of the question.

Think, Nora, think.

Desperate, I went with the only possibility I could think of. I yanked off the ski mask and dug out Ida's post-cataract surgery wraparound sunglasses.

More banging. "Hey Rich! Is Jessica in there with you? She was looking for you before."

Male laughter. At least two guys.

I flipped the hood off. Using the bathroom mirror, I adjusted the wig, artfully trailing large hanks of the gray messy wig over the glasses and across my face. The effect was scary. I wouldn't look out of place pushing a shopping cart full of garbage around a city street. With care not to alter the effect, I pulled the hood back in place and tied it under my chin. To justify my slow response to the laughing duo at the door, I flushed the toilet.

That was greeted by rolling-on-the-floor laughter. These guys were easily entertained. I had to act fast.

"Did she find you?" Same male voice. "Come-on, Richie. We want to meet her. We know you're in there. We heard the toilet flush."

To accumulate saliva, I popped a Life Saver in my mouth and sucked it furiously. Next, I put a small plug of tissue in each nostril to simulate a stuffed nose. Finally, I pulled on my fat gloves and said in a raspy, saliva-filled, nose-stuffed voice, "Not Jessica. His Aunt . . . Babs."

Caught off guard, the laughing ones fell silent.

That was my cue. I opened the door, and nodding to the two giants in ski outfits who thought they were so funny, passed between them. Despite the sunglasses, I kept my head down to keep my face as unclear as possible and pretended to sneeze, careful not to dislodge the tissue.

When they stepped back to let the rotund old lady with the bad cold pass, I cleared my throat loudly. "Ah, aach, aaach." It was a definite gagging sound that signaled the presence of mucus. I repeated the noise. "Ah, aach, aaach."

Both took another step back to avoid contamination, and I lumbered between them, teetered a bit because I couldn't resist the added dramatics, and headed for the door before they caught on and decided to tackle me, or maybe shoot me. You never knew about people these days. Some are crazy.

* * *

Safely ensconced in my truck, squished behind the wheel, motor running for a quick getaway, I pushed the hood back and lifted a lock of the gray wig off my face.

I called Nick.

"Where are you?" he asked, bypassing hello. "You ignored my call before. I expected you at the funeral."

"Hello, Nick. And how are you?" I said in reproach.

He waited a beat, and repeated his question.

In reply, I asked, "What was in Eddie's toolbox when you examined it?"

A pregnant pause followed. Then, "Oh, Nora! Don't tell me. Please. You're not—"

"The toolbox," I cut in before he finished.

"Tools!" he shouted, a note of panic in his voice. "Nothing else. You know, I may have to arrest you if you're up to something illegal. And telling me about it, no less? You're confessing to an officer sworn to uphold the law! Have you ever heard of the Miranda warning? You know, the part about anything you say can and will be used against you in a court of law."

I cut to the chase. "How about a spy camera in a smoke detector? Huh! What would you say about that? I mean, why would Eddie have that?"

Another pause.

"Quiet, Nora. Not another word."

I complied. Sometimes I do things just to make him happy. I could picture him wrestling with the possibilities such an item suggested.

Then, "I suppose you touched it and your fingerprints are all over it. So, offhand, I'd say it's worthless."

I recognized the question in his statement, and his acceptance of the value of my find.

"Give me more credit than to touch it without gloves.

My dad was a cop. I watch police shows with Aunt Ida, for goodness sakes. So offhand, I'd say you should get up here and seize it before it disappears, the way the ring disappeared from the same toolbox, however that happened. Nick, I know it's not worthless, and I think you do, too."

Silence.

I continued, "I know you consider Eddie a person of interest because Floyd took up with his ex-wife. Eddie said he hated Floyd for a time, but he got over it. You believe him? What if he didn't get over it?"

"You honestly think I haven't considered that?"

"Okay. What if he were spying on Floyd or Beverly? Wouldn't that be important?"

Across the parking lot, I saw the two guys who'd been banging on Floyd's door looking around. It would not be a stretch to say they were looking for me.

I spoke quickly. "A SanDisk is involved. It might have vital information on it. Photos, videos. I guess it would help if you had that."

I eased the hood back up, my gaze following the guys who were now in the parking lot, actively searching.

"I don't want to hear it. Understand? Don't tell me another thing."

"About the disk, you mean?"

"Of course. Aren't you listening?"

"But I was thinking—"

"Don't go anywhere else up there. Don't *do* anything else. I mean it, Nora. And stop talking about this. Not another word. Tell me exactly where you are, now."

I ducked low in my seat so the guys couldn't see me, which was awkward considering I had two bed pillows harnessed around my middle. I considered rolling onto the floor, but changed my mind, realizing how difficult it would be to get up.

"I'm in the parking lot behind the resident housing."

Peeking out the window, I saw the guys split up. One headed in my direction. "But leaving now," I said quickly.

"Why? Where are you going?" he demanded in his cop voice.

I tossed the phone, thankful I'd turned the motor on as soon as I'd hopped in the truck. Like a speed demon, I headed out of the parking lot at a reckless twenty miles per hour—ten miles above my usual snowy parking lot speed— all the while listening to Nick call my name from the seat next to me.

Continuing in reckless mode, I risked a look in the rearview mirror. My pursuers persisted.

Ce-ce and I skidded around a corner and headed in the direction of the ski rental shack. I had actually skidded. Like one of those speed demons I can't stand. I had to be more careful. With a death grip on the steering wheel, I slowed and focused on the road ahead. Once I hit a straight section, I risked a backward glance. The chasers were nowhere in sight.

I swerved.

Even though I had taken my eyes off the road for mere seconds, I had swerved. It must have been the equivalent of texting while driving. It was the tiniest swerve. To counteract it, I yanked the wheel in the opposite direction.

Wrong maneuver.

Ce-ce veered into a section of snow mounded by a plow at the side of the road, and got stuck. Shifting into reverse seemed to make it worse. I tried Drive again. After several more tries that involved spinning wheels, I gave up. I was jammed in. I'd have to get out and push. Or wait for help.

"Nora, answer me. Are you all right?" Nick yelled from the passenger seat. "Why aren't you answering me?"

I finally picked up the phone. "Things could be better. Which is to say they are not perfect at the moment."

"What happened?"

"Nothing too unusual. I had a run-in with some piled snow."

"You're stuck? Are you hurt?"

"Nothing I can't handle," I said, not sure of how true that was.

"What does that mean?"

"A little push would help. It shouldn't take much. I can do it myself."

"Oh, for heaven sakes! Don't try that. You'll break your neck. If you're near the lodge, get out and walk or else phone them and ask for help."

Yeah. That would work. They'd send one of the red jacket guys, and I'd be toast. "Good plan," I answered.

"Okay. I'll leave it up to you. Call me back. Let me know how you're doing."

"I will."

"I'm at my place now. Throwing a few things in a duffle bag. Won't have a search warrant, of course, but I'll be able to question a few more people. If you meet me at the lodge, we can have lunch together. Or, stay in your truck, and I'll find you. Whichever is easier. What do you say?"

"Good idea," I answered. Then asked, "How about Eddie? Did you talk to him at the funeral?"

"He left immediately after the service with the folks from the mountain."

Well, I felt good about the rest of the day. Everything would be fine here. The worst that could happen, had happened.

Shifting the annoying pillows, I twisted in my seat, and opened the door. "See you in a bit."

I ended the call and stepped out to analyze the stuck truck situation. A firm push would solve this. I scaled the little snow pile—only two feet or so high at most—figuring if I leaned forward from the high point, I would get better leverage, more oomph into the push. I might not need anyone's help. First, I'd remove these cumbersome pillows.

That's when the second worse thing happened.

From my vantage point, I spotted a lone figure in a red jacket suddenly appear on the road heading in this direction. Startled, I pitched backwards. To counteract, I threw myself forward. A back and forth motion developed as I tried to achieve balance.

In the process, I made three wild grabs at the hood, but had no luck with that slippery thing. The seesaw motion caused my boots to sink, which should have helped. It did not.

Unfortunately, they were not sinking far enough to prevent the third worst thing, a backwards tumble with enough energy to send me rolling down the hill like a giant snowball.

Well, this trip was not going well at all.

Over and over I went. Feet twisting in the air. Hands flailing. Pillows doing their shifting and rolling. I should have removed them as soon and I got out. Too late.

How long was this stupid hill, anyway?

I felt my face getting scratched, and tried to shield it, but was only partially successful, what with the rolling snowball action in effect.

They say a rolling stone gathers no moss. No one ever mentioned gathering snow. No one considered that, did they!

This was packing snow. Good for making snowballs. Maybe good for skiing. I'd never know about that because I was never going skiing on this mountain again. Ever!

My hood fell back. My wig caught on something, and I continued on without it. Rolling, rolling, rolling.

My jacket inched up until it was above my waist. That's when it happened. One elastic suspender snagged on a thick protruding twig or branch.

Like a tethered object, similar to a ball on an elastic cord, I bounced up and down, and around, the words *boing, boing, boing* running through my head like a musical refrain.

Finally, I heard a decisive snap, and I came to a stop. Thank you, God.

Not only was I dizzy from all the rolling and spinning, but my girth had increased a bit with the addition of packed snow. Some snow had slipped down into my pants. Caught as I was, I had trouble sitting up. I made three attempts, the turtle image running through my head again like a video clip. I did not, however, have trouble seeing the guy looking down at me from the top of the hill. A red blur.

I recognized him.

CHAPTER TWENTY-THREE

Hands on hips, he stood on the top of the snow pile at the side of the road. "This is unexpected," he called down mildly.

Lying in an ungainly heap, the back part of my suspender harness still caught on the protruding branch, I forced a tepid smile and a weak, "Hello."

"Unexpected, I'd have to say."

"I can explain," I called up, desperate, wondering what I could possibly say.

"I'm sure you'll think of something, *Aunt Babs*," the guy said as he made his way down the hill.

Fifteen minutes later I was seated behind the wheel of my truck, de-pillowed and un-wigged, with the red coat guy, who said his name was Sean, sitting beside me, staring, as I checked in the mirror for facial damage. Ce-ce's front wheels were still stuck in the snow.

"You're bleeding. You'll need to go to the first aid station."

A few scuffs and scrapes marked my forehead, chin and both cheeks, leaving little blood trails that looked worse than they were.

"I'll fix these myself."

He grunted.

Using a tissue from the box on the floor—I believe in being prepared and always travel with tissues, largely due to my allergies, which cause ridiculous amounts of sneezing— I dabbed at the scratches.

"First, thank you for helping me. Again. I really appreciate it," I said, alternately dabbing and checking for blood evidence. "Believe me, I was not snooping in your friend's room on purpose." At the look on his face, I put my free hand up. "I know, I know. Don't say it." I paused, mid-dab. "But I thought it was the room of the guy who was murdered, and I was looking for clues the police might have missed."

He stared at me, silent, his mouth slightly ajar, his expression shouting *Liar*.

Finally, he said, "You're asking me to believe . . . you're telling me . . . you mean . . . "

It didn't take a keen investigator to see the man was truly flummoxed.

"You're some sort of private investigator?" he finished, his voice filled with incredulity.

I went back to blotting. "Some sort, yes."

"And if I mentioned this to security they'd be okay with it?" he said, controlling the laugher he held in check.

I blotted faster. "Are you going to do that?"

"Not sure."

"You planning to tell Richie?"

"Not sure."

"All I did was take photos of the ceiling."

"The ceiling," he said, nodding as if he accepted that. Then he cocked his head to the side. "Of course. What else would you do in someone's room that you broke into? In disguise." He checked his watch. "I have to be at work soon. Catch people who cause chaos on the lifts and the mountains."

"Hummph," I said as if I didn't know what he referred to.

"A few days ago I heard about some woman who caused a stoppage at the T-bar. Later the same woman skied backwards down the bunny hill. Wish I'd seen that. It was the talk of the whole crew."

"Interesting," I said, setting my tissues aside.

"If you'd be so kind as to give me a push out of this snow pile, that would be good."

"I'll do that," he said, opening the door.

"I'll drive you back."

Silence. He did not jump at the chance. Finally, he said, "I'm not sure I should risk it."

Without another word, he went around front and pushed Ce-ce out of the snow bank. It seemed easy for him.

"Let's go," he said when he hopped into the passenger seat, buckled his seatbelt and braced himself like a man who expected a possible crash.

I drove him to the main part of the lodge, unsure about whether he'd keep my secret. As he was getting out, I thanked him one last time, and asked, "You're not going to—"

Before I could finish, he interrupted, "Still haven't decided whether to mention this or not. However," he paused, "if you promise to stay off the ski slopes, there's a chance."

"Absolutely. No more skiing for me."

"You should go to the first aid station. Get a dozen band aids or so."

"I don't want to."

"Really? You intend to go around looking like a battered woman? And here I am getting out of your truck?"

"Okay. Point taken."

Nurse Hazel was on duty when I walked in. Of course, she remembered me.

"Oh, no! What did the brute do now?" she asked, hands planted on her broad hips.

"I fell."

Her expression skeptical, she brushed a speck of invisible lint off her starched white uniform. "That's what they all say, honey. Now you just come sit over here on the table, and I'll tend to those scrapes. And you tell Hazel all about it."

I got on the table. "I don't want to talk. But I'll listen,"

I said as the paper crinkled beneath me.

Instead of interrupting her lecture, which she clearly wanted to deliver, I let her continue, occasionally making sounds like, "Um-huum," in agreement as I wrinkled my nose at the antiseptic smell.

When she finished, I thanked her and assured her I'd think about everything she'd said.

Hazel shook her head in dismay. "I'm in a quandary here. Do you want me to report this? Report him?"

"Report? What do you mean?" I asked, feeling the panic gauge inside me inch into the danger zone.

"Someone should protect you. I can handle it, if you want."

"No! I do not want. Absolutely not. Promise me you won't report this to anyone."

After a little back and forth, she gave her word.

* * *

I sat by the broad window in the lodge, my hands warming around a cup of hot chocolate, watching skiers come down the trails while I waited for Nick. Spectacular view. Any other time I might have enjoyed it.

I ducked back slightly when I spotted Beverly walking toward her ski group. No surprise that she hadn't attended the funeral.

I knew she'd be busy for the next hour, at least, and her room would be unattended. As soon as the thought popped into my head, I kicked it out. No more snooping today. I'd leave Beverly for another day.

Nick arrived about half an hour and two cups of hot chocolate later. With a look of alarm I'd only seen on his face in rare moments of stress, he gazed at my bandaged face.

His hand beneath my chin, he turned my face this way and that, inspecting the damage before he bent and kissed me.

"Oh, Nora. My sweet Nora. So many bumps and bruises. What happened? Every detail. And don't sugar-coat it."

"I rolled down a hill," I said as if that covered the situation.

"I think that's the definition of sugar-coating," he said, pulling out the chair opposite me.

"Will you be able to get the search warrant soon? I'm afraid he'll get rid of the evidence, and you won't be able to prove he ever had it."

He shook his head as he sat. "I told you I don't have probable cause. Whether I'll get it remains to be seen. I need a legitimate reason."

"That means waiting. I hate waiting."

"So you've got Eddie convicted already?"

"Tell me you don't find this suspicious? A spy camera!"

Nick took a sip of my now cold hot chocolate and pushed it aside.

"Yes, it's suspicious," he said. "But it's certainly not evidence of murder."

"Really! Did you hear me say the words *spy camera*, forheavensakes! He's up to no good. It's obvious." I moved the cup to the side. "Do you know if he's back from the funeral yet?"

"Probably. But it doesn't matter. I'm not here to question him. What I need to do is check company purchase records. They should be willing to give those to me without a warrant. I also intend to interview more people."

We ordered lunch—grilled cheese sandwiches with pickles and chips on the side—and while we ate I showed him the photos I'd taken in Eddie's and Floyd's rooms. The line around the smoke detector in Floyd's old room was barely visible, even when enlarged.

"Maybe," was all he said as he flipped through the photos.

"I guess it would help if you knew exactly what was

on his spy disk."

He gave me a stony stare. His voice was even stonier when he asked, "And how would I find that out?"

"Just asking if it would help."

"And I'm just saying you committed a crime. B & E, maybe? You broke into Eddie's room."

I made a huffy noise. "I did not break in. I had a key. From Marney. And she came by it legitimately."

"Just tell me you didn't take the disk."

I gave another huff, this one more melodramatic. "Of course not! That would be stealing."

The waitress came with our sandwiches. When she left, I rummaged through my bag and pulled out the multi-interface micro SD card reader and handed it to him without explanation. From his expression, I realized he didn't know what it was.

"It can copy data from one place to another. Like from a disk to a phone. Or to any computer, Apple or PC. It's more versatile than a single flash drive, which only utilizes a USB port."

"Since the information was obtained illegally, I can't use it. I cannot download it to any computer in my department."

I smiled at him as I picked up a pickle. "Fortunately, I have a computer. At home."

"Did you make another copy?"

"Of course. I used the hotel computer and a second drive I brought with me, but made sure no one could track me."

He slipped the disk into his top pocket, nodding. "Let me know what you find. I'll check this out on my home computer. We'll compare notes."

Our conversation from that point on was strictly impersonal. He told me about the movie situation, and the upset it was causing at the station house, the plans for Winterfest, and lastly, Floyd's funeral.

"Marney cried at the funeral. She looked genuinely

upset. The men he worked with were there. She spoke to everyone, I think."

After lunch Nick checked my truck to make sure it was okay to drive back to Silver Stream.

"You need new snow tires," he said, his manner impersonal.

When I opened the driver's side door, he didn't move in my direction, not even a mini step. I wondered whether he was even going to kiss me goodbye. I didn't like this, didn't understand why he seemed distant. Unless . . .

I closed the door and folded my arms. Without preamble, I said, "What?"

He said nothing, just looked at me.

One of the things I liked about Nick was that he understood me. He often knew where my thoughts were focused. The word 'What?' was enough for him. He didn't do a mental dance and pretend not to know what I meant.

He raised his brows.

I answered, "I had to," before he asked the question.

"Go on," he said.

"I took the money from Marney and never did what she asked me to do. When I tried to return it after Floyd's death, she insisted I keep it. Besides that, she didn't want me to look further. She said she had enough money with his insurance and didn't need more. What insurance? It must be a lot." I shrugged my shoulders. "It didn't seem right. She overpaid me and got nothing in return." I paused. "I owe her something."

He gave a huge sigh and leaned against Ce-ce's front fender. I still hadn't reached him.

"What are you holding back?" he asked.

I just stared at him, unable to say more.

Until he said, "Lack of trust, Nora?"

My mouth dropped. "How could you think that?"

He said nothing. The ball was clearly in my court.

I felt tears pressing behind my eyes. Before they made their debut, I had to tell him, had to break a confidence.

"Coincidence. The biggest factor of all," I said. "Coincidence. I know you can't possibly see that because you don't know the full story about Margaret. She is somehow part of this although she doesn't realize it herself.

"But Nick, without a doubt, I know this is all connected. The people all intersect. Margaret with Beverly Sue. Beverly with Eddie, Eddie and Beverly with Floyd. All with Marney. Too big a coincidence. Unacceptable, actually. And Sal, too. He's in the mix."

His expression showed interest, so I continued.

"I don't want to talk about this strong feeling I have. You'll laugh."

"You had me at coincidence. I'm not laughing, Nora. Keep going."

"I'm still working on Margaret's case. Although I haven't tackled the list of missing library items she gave me, there's something more important. I think this is all tired into that in some way. She may be the linchpin. Not sure. If I told you about Margaret's dilemma, you might understand where I'm coming from. So I'm going to break a promise I made to her. It's personal to her, top secret. She doesn't want anyone to know, and I promised to keep it that way. So I want your word that this will stay between us."

"Is it illegal?"

I huffed. "Absolutely not."

"Okay. You've got my word."

"Margaret felt her future happiness depended on my not revealing her secret venture into the world of gambling. The dentist wouldn't approve. So foolish. But I shouldn't judge. She said she signed a no-gambling pledge."

"Gambling? Margaret?"

"A lottery ticket," I said. "She and Beverly went in on a lottery ticket every week. Same numbers. Those numbers finally came in and Beverly, who has the ticket, seems to have no intention of paying up. And, what's worse, Margaret already spent a bundle on a new car."

The expression on his face was priceless. I wanted to

take a picture of him looking like this, but I continued.

"*Follow the money.* That's the mantra here. That's the key. Maybe the biggest part. I checked online, and the ticket has not been turned in yet. The holder is waiting. For what? Maybe he or she intends to cash it and disappear. Maybe buy an island. Who knows?"

"A lottery ticket?" he said in disbelief.

I nodded. "Yes. And I'm sure Floyd and Eddie knew Beverly bought lottery tickets every week, probably even knew the numbers because she'd been playing the same numbers for years. Maybe even Marney knew. Do you know how much this ticket is worth? A few million. But where is the ticket now? AWOL, that's where!"

Nick had listened intently without interrupting. Finally, pushing away from the fender and coming to stand in front of me, he said, "Money is definitely a motive for murder. You may be onto something."

Leaning forward, his hands moved to my face. "With this much money involved, the whole picture changes. I wish you'd told me sooner, but I understand why you didn't."

His fingers trailed down my cheek with a gossamer touch.

"You're going right home now, aren't you?"

"Straight to Aunt Ida's."

His drew me to him and we kissed, softly, mouth to mouth, tongue to tongue. Intimately, warmly, lovingly. For long moments. I'd be content to stay in his arms for the rest of the day. Longer, if honesty were an issue.

He finally stepped back. "Go now, so you're home before dark. Will you be in town tomorrow?"

"I'm not sure."

"Winterfest begins."

"Oh, right. How could I forget that. The aunts mentioned it several hundred times, and there are about a thousand signs all over the place. So yes, I'll be in town."

He smiled down and kissed the spot beside the

bandage on my chin.

"And the following day is my movie debut. After the scene, I plan to go home. To cook."

I raised my brows at this bit of information but refrained from making a comment.

"I think it's time you tasted the Nick Renzo special. Something my dad used to make. You interested?"

"Give me a clue."

"Spaghetti and meatballs."

Another brow raise on my part. He'd never mentioned his father before, other than to tell me he died several years ago. "Your dad cooked?"

"Not much."

I caught myself before I blurted *I'm surprised your mom let him.* Yet, when I thought about it, I realized that no one pushed Nick around, not even the domineering Arianna whose recipe for garbanzo beans gave Aunt Agnes nightmares. Chances were, no one pushed his father around, either.

"Do you take after your father?"

He smiled in a way that made me wonder whether he'd read my thoughts. Impossible. I was not that transparent.

"Don't smile like that!"

"Is that an order, Nora Lassiter?"

"Yes, sheriff."

"Coming to dinner?"

"You using the good china?"

"Depends. How good are you at pretending?"

"It's one of my strong points."

"Fine." He kissed me lightly. "Picture fine china. After we eat, we'll talk about what's on the disk you copied."

"I hope it contains something we can use."

"There's that *we* again."

"Picky, picky."

"Keep in mind, to act on anything, I, not *we*, need probable cause or my hands are tied. Just seeing something incriminating on this video is not enough because of the way you gained it. It's not admissible."

"I know, I know! But it will help, right?"

"Probably."

CHAPTER TWENTY-FOUR

I arrived home just before the sun dipped behind the trees, had a quick supper that Ida had saved for me—fish chowder and crusty rolls—and listened to the latest yoga class news. While I ate, she told me about 'those young, pushy sixty-year-olds who had invaded the group.'

I refrained from pointing out the obvious, that she, Hannah and Agnes were pushy eighty-year-olds who had done the same.

Too tired to discuss my day, I promised to tell all about it when we all went to Winterfest by the Lake. I had memories of Winterfest, some of them best forgotten. Like the snowball incident when I was about nine years old.

I was having a friendly snowball fight with kids in my class when Mary Fran approached. As usual, I panicked. No time to run. No place to hide. Then I figured, erroneously as it turned out, no way would I become cannon fodder this time. I was safe among friends. Next thing I knew her snowball came hurtling at me with the accuracy of a heat-seeking missile. I howled when it connected with its target, which just happened to be my right ear.

Surprise! It had a rock in the middle. In tears, I ran to my mother, who inspected the damage and declared me a big baby for carrying on.

". . . and I'm really eager to see the sleigh," Ida was saying when I realized I was rubbing my ear.

"Thank you for heating up the chowder. It hit the spot," I said as I carried my bowl to the sink and rinsed it out.

"Leave that. Go get some sleep. You look exhausted."

"I was surprised when Agnes mentioned that you were all going for a sleigh ride at Winterfest," I said on my way up the stairs. "It'll be so cold. I heard it's supposed to be in the single digits tomorrow. I figured you'd all sit in the car with the motor running and the heat blasting."

"Not in Maine." Ida chuckled. "No one sits in an auto with the motor running to pollute the area. Our days of spending time outside without extra protection in this weather are long past. But we are Mainers, after all. And we've never missed a Winterfest. We'll be in a covered sleigh. Bundled up, of course. We love our ride around the lake. We get to see many of the activities from there."

"I don't suppose it's heated?"

Aunt Ida laughed. "Oh, Nora. You are the one!"

"And there's room for me?"

"For you, there's always room, honey. Actually, it's a four-seater. Uncle Walter's in charge."

The following morning I was on the computer before I even showered. Ida stopped by my room several times to offer coffee or toast, but I didn't want to take the time. This was too important. Not only did I need to look at the video from the spy camera, but I also wanted to find out more about Sal and his brother, as well as the movie company. I'd never get to all of it this morning, but I wanted to be able to compare notes with Nick when I saw him.

Nick was looking into Sal's activities, too, but I was going deeper. I used tools that supported a wide set of protocols that enabled me to look into emails and company databases that were protected by the latest firewalls.

The computer skills I'd honed over the past ten years were put to good use. I knew I shouldn't be investigating some of these accounts. But I also knew that the folks who worked for most police departments didn't have the expertise I had. So I thought of it as . . . helping them.

Computer science started out as a hobby for me, but by

the time I entered college, it had morphed into a passion. It opened worlds I never knew existed. I became part of a like-minded group of geeks who explored the endless possibilities. I still kept in touch with most of the group via a secret app we'd developed. Last night I had contacted them and given a brief sketch of what I was looking for without revealing specifics. This morning I received updates on some new cutting edge strategies that I would use after I'd reviewed the disk from Eddie's room. So much to do.

I still hadn't finished examining the photos I'd taken at the crime scene. I needed to do that soon. The ones I'd seen so far hadn't revealed a thing.

Many from the movie crew would be at Winterfest today, taking background footage, and I intended to take every opportunity to watch them, Lucca and Sal, in particular. Perhaps they were involved in criminal activities, or someone associated with them was involved. Whatever it was, I suspected it circled back to Floyd, and if so, it could be related to his murder. Why else would Sal deny knowing him?

Although I wasn't keen on going today—I had an aversion to frigid temperatures—I was looking forward to spending time with the aunts, seeing Nick and definitely watching the movie people.

By the time Hannah and Agnes arrived to pick us up, I had learned more than I'd bargained for from the disk. I was startled. It was not at all what I expected. I wondered whether Nick had been able to view it yet.

The decision I had to make was whether to reveal any of this new information to the aunts.

Bundled up in my only other jacket, a white down with a faux-fur trimmed hood, and wearing flannel-lined jeans that I'd ordered from Ida's L.L. Bean catalogue, something I thought I'd never do, I carried the wool blanket that Ida handed me, and climbed into Hannah's new Honda Pilot, a big four-wheel drive. Sturdy vehicle. I felt safe. The great-aunts were all aglow, ready for the day as if it were a wonderful adventure, which I guess it was.

"So tell me about Winterfest," I asked. "What can I expect? It's been many years since I was here last."

Ignoring my question, Agnes said, "How did the disguise work out?"

I should have known. The aunts had a way of zeroing in on what they considered important.

"It was great. It was a wonderful idea, and I thank all of you for helping me pull it together. Agnes's jacket and the pillows clinched it."

"Go on! What happened on the mountain? Don't keep us waiting," Hannah interrupted as she drove down the driveway, sideswiping the low-hanging branch of a snow-laden pine tree, putting me on instant alert.

"You must tell us everything you found out," Ida said as she fastened her seatbelt. "You always tell us the best stuff. Ay-uh. We love being kept in the loop."

Clearly, talk about Winterfest had to wait, so I began. "Remember, what I have to say is for your ears only. Understood?"

"Of course, Nora. You don't even have to mention it. Mums the word," Aunt Agnes said, making her lip-zipping motion.

They listened intently, smiling and nodding with each revelation. When I mentioned finding the spy camera in Eddie's toolbox, they gasped in unison.

"Probably had to do with Beverly," Ida said. "I bet he wanted to catch her with Floyd."

"For sh-ur," Agnes agreed. "Maybe he thought Floyd and Beverly Sue were hatching a plot."

"Oh, Agnes," Ida said. "I doubt that."

Hannah said. "She might be right. Men resent anyone messing with their wives. They're suspicious."

Everyone nodded.

"But they were divorced. Or separated. She could go with anyone she wanted to," I said.

"Doesn't matter," Hannah said, her foot heavier on the

gas pedal than I thought it should be. "There were stories about Eddie, years back when he was in high school, I think it was. Very territorial boy."

"What stories? Tell me what you know. It might be important."

"Oh, that was so long ago. Something about a football player who dated Beverly. Can't recall the details," Hannah said.

"Didn't he do something to the guy's truck?" Aunt Ida asked as we all leaned to the right when the Pilot skidded on a curve. "Smashed the fellow's windshield? Something like that."

"Was he arrested?" I asked, double-checking my seatbelt, then gripping the armrest between myself and Ida as snow-covered trees blurred by.

No one knew whether he had been arrested. I moved on, skipping what I'd found on the disk and making a mental note to ask Nick about Eddie's possible arrest in high school.

"The guy Sal was talking to in the station house was his brother Lucca. Lucca's the second assistant director. Sal threatened him."

This caused another gasp all around, which might have been the result of the SUV going airborne as Hannah drove over a snow ridge in the road, or might have been surprise at my news. Hard to tell.

My grip on the armrest tightened, my heartbeat kicked up a notch, and I checked for evidence of airbags.

"You think Sal's involved in Floyd's murder?" Hannah asked, her hand pressed to her heart, instead of on the wheel where it clearly belonged.

"I don't know," I said.

"Tell us more. We will not say a word to anyone. You know that," Ida said.

"Okay."

I began with Sal's words of denial.

"The first time I met Sal I asked if he knew Floyd and

he said '*Name's not ringing any bells.*' That was a lie. Eddie told me the opposite, said Floyd had talked to '*some guy Sal something-or-other.*'"

Ida said, "It's hard to know who to believe."

"Movie guy's lying," Agnes said with a nod firm enough to make her second chin wobble.

"Agreed," Hannah added as she took another curve too fast. "Keep going, Nora."

"Sal owns a shipping container business at a Jersey port. He's also a major investor in the movie. He put up a lot of money." I paused, unsure whether I should mention what else I found out.

In for a dime, in for a dollar, I thought, and added, "The studio is in financial trouble, big trouble." I skipped the financial details I'd uncovered this morning.

This information was met by stunned silence.

Slowing to a more manageable speed, but still not all that cautious in my estimation, Hannah said, "Will they finish the movie?"

Hannah slowed even more. All three looked at me in expectation. Alarmed at the sight of Hannah's head turned away from the road, even at this slower speed, I answered quickly, "I don't see why they wouldn't."

Their relief was palpable, and so was mine, which was directly connected to Hannah's slowing down.

However, my relief met an abrupt end. With a pedal-to-the-metal action that caused my head to thump against the headrest, and my fists to clench, we were hurtling down the road again.

I continued, hoping my added information would cause Hannah to slow again. "According to Margaret, Sal punched Lucca in the mouth. He went into the dentist's office to get a new cap."

Agnes gasped. "The nerve of these movie people! Going into Harold's office to take a crap!"

"Cap! C-a-p," I said.

Hannah never slowed, not even to ask Agnes about her

hearing aid.

By the time we reached the lake, my heart was racing like a snare drum on steroids. It amazed me that no one else had the same reaction. Lots of smiles in the car. A mystery to consider at a later time.

"Whoa! There it is," Agnes shouted, pointing to her right.

"Oh, wonderful," Ida said, clasping her hands as if she had clapped.

I, on the other hand, was too busy controlling my racing breath as Hannah skidded into a parking space next to a large pickup. I almost said something. But my determination not to be a backseat driver prevailed.

Once the engine was off, I calmed and looked in the direction the others were looking. I spotted the covered sleigh, large, elegant, shiny black with red curlicues painted around the top edge. Harnessed in front were two large white horses, stamping their hooves and snorting out twin white puffs of steam, looking regal and eager to get moving.

"We're riding in that?" I asked, just to be sure.

"Absolutely," Ida said. "Wild Walter's in charge. He bought that from old man Wakefield years back, and repaired and repainted it. Keeps it behind his Sherman tank under a tarp.

Uncle Walter had built a small ordnance museum on property I'd sold him last fall, and he lived in a back room. He did chainsaw wood sculptures and sold them at the museum.

"When we told him you'd be coming, he promised us an extra turn around our end of the lake," Hannah said, adjusting the red wool scarf around her neck.

That's all it took for my thinking to do a one-eighty about the day. "It's beautiful," I said, opening the door, grinning.

"Oh, yes, it does look grand," Agnes said as she maneuvered her feet out the door. "All that fancy red trim is just perfect. What a wonderful restoration job Walter did.

He's a little nutty sometimes, but we like him just fine. He does a lot of good work."

I went around to assist Agnes the rest of the way out.

"Lots of folks will want a ride in that bob sled," Hannah predicted as she joined Great-Aunts Ida and Agnes. "Good investment for him." She took Agnes's arm.

"I can't wait," I said, meaning it.

Linking arms, the four of us headed for the sleigh, walking the broad path in this winter wonderland where the trees were clothed in snow.

If it had been snowy in Cinderella-land, Cinderella might have had a carriage like this to whisk her away to the ball. Just for an instant, certainly no longer, I pictured myself in a blue flowing gown and a white fluffy shoulder wrap, a sprinkle of stars swirling overhead as I alighted from my carriage.

I burst into song.

A dream is a wish your heart makes.
Da-da dum, da-da dum, de dum

The aunts smiled. But they did not join in, so I stopped.

* * *

Next to the sleigh, the spotted menace named Zeus, Uncle Walter's enormous demon dog, hopped and pranced with the impatience of a caged tiger. Since a charge in my direction was not out of the question, I slowed, stopped and braced. Seeing me, Uncle Walter came forward, a smile on his lips. Some might call it a tiny lift at the right corner of his mouth. I thought of it as the Walter-smile.

"Good to see you, Nora." He shook my hand. "You here to participate in some of the activities?"

Still braced, my eyes following Zeus, who was prancing around me like a puppy—which he was not—I said, "Just the one that involves a sleigh ride. Your carriage is beautiful. The aunts told me you restored it."

Zeus circled us as we headed for the sleigh.

Up close, the sleigh was more beautiful that I expected. I ran my hand over the plush red leather seats that matched the decorative red scrolling on the carriage. "Spectacular job, Walter."

"Umm," he said in acknowledgement.

Uncle Walter, a former Marine, was a taciturn guy in his late fifties, definitely not given to chitchat.

After hellos all around, Walter assisted Aunts Ida and Hannah into the carriage with the help of a small stepstool. When it was Agnes's turn, Walter signaled one of the men standing nearby. Together they gave a one-two-three count and Agnes went up. The carriage tilted, springs responded, bounced, then settled.

Next, it was my turn. I could have hopped up unassisted, but I did not. Some things are not meant to be rushed. Uncle Walter extended his hand, and I rested mine lightly upon it, like a princess. Overhead, that sprinkle of stars was back, swirling in an arc as the strains of "A Dream is a Wish Your Heart Makes" played through my head. I took my time getting in. Drew out the moment. Sometimes I am a foolish woman.

Walter gave us two wool throws, and we covered our knees as he took the reins and started out at a slow clip-clop.

The lake was alive with activity. Skaters at one end, a milk jug curling race near the center, people off to the sides preparing for other events.

"It looks like the whole town turned out," I said as I watched a group of folks with dogs near the far end of the lake.

"You can let the Maine winter conquer you, or you can conquer it," Hannah said. "We get into the cold weather spirit around here. We're a hearty bunch." She pointed to the milk jug curling contest. "I used to do that. I stopped one year when I had the flu. Never went back to it."

"You won several years in a row," Ida said, a note of pride in her voice.

I looked at the aunts, and smiled.

Life gifts us with a few perfect moments here and there, fleeting moments when we want nothing more, when we experience a rare feeling of true peace of heart. It never lasts long, so it is up to us to seize and cherish these halcyon moments. As I took in my surroundings, absorbed the sights and sounds of this Maine Winterfest with people I loved, I counted it as one of these perfect moments—the aunts shouting greetings to friends, the clip-clop of hoofs, the creak of the sleigh, the rugged beauty of the lake area with its towering pines and its rocks and boulders lining one side of the hill, people laughing, talking, playing, the scent of hot chocolate and marshmallows, of wood smoke.

I wanted it to last.

I sat next to Aunt Ida, tucked in the shared blanket that covered our knees, and enjoyed.

"This is wonderful," I said.

"Oh, indeed," Hannah said.

Then the sleigh rounded the bend.

Across the lake I saw Sal talking to a woman who looked a little like . . .

I strained to see. Could that be?

"Is that Marney?" I asked.

CHAPTER TWENTY-FIVE

"Oh, look. The hot chocolate and grilled cheese bar is open." Ida said. "Let's go after our sleigh ride. Maybe Josh will stop there."

Well," Agnes said, pointing in a different direction. "The hot chocolate and s'mores bar is also open. That would be my first choice. Nora? Any preference?"

"Yes," I mumbled, my attention focused on the woman standing beyond the bales of hay that were used to prevent the cardboard sled racers from veering off course. She was talking to Sal.

"I don't see who you're looking at," Ida said, gazing across the lake.

"Why would Marney, if it is Marney, be talking to Sal? How does she know him? I always thought she kept to herself."

"Maybe she met him at Floyd's funeral," Hannah said. "Lots of folks were there."

The camera crew, flanked by Sal and his brother Lucca, had a prime spot on a slight rise overlooking the sled racers. Lucca waved his hand and backed away from Sal, who smoked a cigar. Folks jockeyed for position around them. Everyone wanted to be in the movie.

No, not everyone. Not the woman talking to Sal. She had her back to the camera.

"Do you see who I'm talking about?"

"No," said Ida, straining to see.

"Is this important to your investigation?" Agnes asked. "Could be."

Hannah said, "The woman I think you're looking at has blonde hair. I see a bunch of curls sticking out of her hood. Marney is gray. No curls."

"She just dropped her snowshoes on the ground and stepped into them. Easily. She's wearing a light colored jacket, maybe white or cream, not the puffy red down coat I've seen her in."

"I wish I had my binoculars," Agnes said.

"I have binoculars," Walter said. "Military grade. Under my seat." This was the first time he'd spoken since we'd started.

"Is that Marney over that way? By the sled race?" I asked him, pointing across the lake. "Talking to Sal?"

"Don't know no Sal. But I know Marney." Walter grabbed his binoculars and looked across the lake. "Yep. That's Marney talking to some young fella puffing a cigar."

He passed me his binoculars. "Have a look."

"Son of a gun!" I muttered. "Marney."

"Can't help with that," Walter said. "Don't read lips."

I handed Agnes the binoculars and dug in my purse for my cell phone. I hit Nick's number on speed dial and waited while it rang. And rang. And finally went to voice mail.

"Nick, call as soon as you get this," I said.

"What's happening?" Hannah asked. "An emergency? Why are you calling Nick? Because of Marney?"

Although I didn't mind telling the aunts about an event after it happened, I didn't want to involve them in the actual event. Also, Walter was within hearing range. No need to broadcast my alarm to him.

"Just wanted to tell him Marney's here. He wanted to talk to her."

Hannah nodded, but I could see questions piling up in her head, could tell by her keen expression that she knew I was holding back. Ida and Agnes looked puzzled, but said nothing. For the most part, the aunts believed in minding their own business. That philosophy, of course, did not extend to my personal life, especially my relationship with

Nick. That was open season.

Looking through the binoculars, Agnes said, "These are great binoculars. You can see everything so close. I should get some for bird watching. Did I mention I saw a purple finch today?"

As Walter approached our starting point, the cell phone played the *Lone Ranger* theme, and I answered immediately.

"Hi, Nick."

"Good morning, Ms. Lassiter. I'll spring for a hot cocoa, if you meet me at the west end of the lake by the stand?"

"If I knew which way was west, I might consider it."

He laughed and hung up.

Within half an hour Nick and I were seated in his SUV, our conversation interrupted only by sips of hot cocoa and the static-filled communications on his police scanner.

"I saw Marney and Sal talking before. I can't imagine what connection they have."

"Don't go snooping. You've done enough. I'll take it from here."

"Certainly. I wouldn't dream of meddling," I said as I placed my cup in his cup holder.

He smiled the way one does when someone has said something humorous.

"Did you get to view any of the video?"

"Some. I fell asleep watching it last night. I'll watch more today."

"It's a bombshell. Eddie stealing from Floyd," I said as I reached into my pocket for the notes I'd taken. "I was only able to view it once, most at fast-forward speed, and I skipped through some of it. Did you see Floyd stashing a big duffle bag in his room, then later, when Floyd left, Eddie going in and stealing the bag? I wrote down the relevant times."

"Stealing! I didn't get to that," he said, clearly startled.

I handed him my notes. "This will make it easier for

you to do a quick run-through and see what I'm talking about. I'm surprised Eddie didn't erase that incriminating section of the tape. I suppose he figured no one would see it."

"Don't know. Anyway, I didn't fast-forward. I figured I'd miss something, or possibly erase something. I'll watch it whenever I'm home. Then we'll watch it again together with you at the controls."

"Don't worry about erasing anything. I made two extra copies and also downloaded it to my hard drive."

"Good. I wish we could do this tonight, but I have to postpone our dinner for a few days. I've got two meetings tonight, another tomorrow. This movie and the murder investigation are time-consuming."

"I understand." I took a sip of hot chocolate.

"Tell me more about the bombshell. Did you see what was in the bag?"

I shook my head. "No. I thought it might be money, but maybe not. He took one small box out and looked at it, but his back was to the camera, and I couldn't tell what he was looking at."

"Small items? Big bag?"

"Yes. Even though I couldn't see, that was a great camera. It has this wide-angle lens for great scope of view. Takes in the whole room. Too bad it couldn't see though Floyd. See what he had in his hands."

I sipped cocoa in silence for a few minutes. The scent of his coffee mingled with the cocoa, creating a pleasant aroma.

"Do you think Eddie may have murdered Floyd?"

"He's a person of interest. Definitely. I've got to interview him again. See if he'll tell me about the bag in Floyd's room."

"I took pictures of the smoke detector camera and then looked it up. It's designed for long-term covert surveillance. So it could have been there a while. It looks like a normal smoke detector. That's why I didn't notice it right away."

"Ay-uh, Eddie knows his stuff."

Static crackled on the radio. Miller reported in with an ice-skating collision and a possible broken ankle. "Folks here are handling it, Boss. No need for a bus."

Nick pressed the mike. "Thanks, Miller." To me he said, "I'm looking into Sal's business more closely. Got two guys working on it. Sal makes decent money, but his lifestyle doesn't match. Everything about him says big money."

"So you're suspicious. What do you think he's involved in?"

"Not sure."

"Yes, you are. You just don't want to tell me." I put one hand on my hip. "Come on, Renzo. Out with it!"

"You're such a demanding woman."

"Stop stalling."

He smiled. I poked him in the ribs.

"Could be car theft. Not saying it is, mind you, but if he's into anything criminal, that's a possibility. Also money laundering. Or I could be completely off the mark. Maybe none of those things."

"Small items in a bag?" I suggested. "I bet that's the key. Floyd could have been working for Sal. Carrying or delivering stolen items. Jewelry can be small. Rings don't take up much space, watches either. Or money." I raised my brows. "Laundering money! Could Floyd have been his bagman?"

Nick's eyes narrowed. "That's a giant leap."

"Just thinking out loud. And jumping ahead to broken fingers! Could something have gone wrong? Did Floyd lose the money? Have it stolen? Maybe by Eddie? Those Mafia guys don't mess around, especially when it comes to their money."

He nodded. "I realize that. And I'm thinking about it, too. I intend to make time to view that video today, even if it's only in bits and snatches."

We were both silent for a moment.

"I have one request. Please hold off. Stay out of this from now on. It's more dangerous than I first thought."

"I know. I'll hold off."

He stared at me. "I would kiss you right now, but it might cause talk. I'm on duty."

"I understand. You need to be alert. Kissing me would make you appear . . . careless.

"Yes. And reckless."

"Imprudent."

"Irresponsible."

"Unwary."

"Lacking in judgment."

I reached up, and touched his cheek. "A sheriff lacking in judgment? Absolutely not. We can't have that."

I grabbed my handbag and shifted to get out of the SUV, then quickly, before he could say another word, before he could react, or I could change my mind, I leaned over and kissed him right on his partially open mouth.

Sometimes, it's fun to take people by surprise.

It was the first time I had ever made the first move. Quickly, I drew back and grabbed the door handle, not indulging in a backward glance as I made my escape with the speed of a fleeing prisoner.

I didn't count on his speed. The man must have had practice with escaping prisoners because seconds later I was in his arms, right there in his police vehicle, parked at Winterfest in the town of Silver Stream, Maine, in the northeastern section of the United States.

Next thing I knew he was kissing me. When we pulled apart we were both laughing.

"See you around, Sheriff Renzo," I said, this time sliding toward the door more slowly, my gaze connected with his.

"Ay-uh, see you around, Nora Lassiter."

* * *

Skirting the small groups lining the cardboard sled racecourse, I spotted the aunts near the s'mores bar and headed in their direction, although I was more interested in finding Marney. She'd vanished. Sal, too.

The camera crew was still here, now filming the sled races, and waiting, I figured, for the arrival of Big Josh, who might not even make it. Since I was not interested in movie production, I gave them a wide berth.

That's when I spotted Mary Fran talking to Sal. They stood by the huge boulders not far from the parking area. Trying to stay out of sight, I wove my way through an assortment of sleds—a spaceship, a shark, a canoe.

Finally, to watch Sal and Mary Fran more surreptitiously, I stepped closer to a group preparing to go downhill in a massive Viking ship. Even though I couldn't hear them, their body language shouted.

Mary Fran seemed calm, definitely not her emotive self, no gesticulating, no prancing around; Sal seemed restless, glancing off to the side occasionally, not focused on Mary Fran. He did not look like a man captivated by the woman in front of him. Instead, he seemed to be watching the camera crew, or perhaps the sleds. I stepped farther back.

I hoped Mary Fran would not give herself away. I figured Sal was pretty good at reading people and would pick up on changes in her demeanor. It wouldn't take much.

The kids around the Viking sled were beyond excited— laughing, talking, jumping around. "Great design," I said, pretending interest.

"Daddy did most of it," the little girl told me.

I pictured myself on the Viking sled, gliding down the hill, winning the race. Howie and I had entered one year. We never had a chance. The sled we constructed was in a different league, definitely minor league. We'd used a big carton box. Howie taped it together, and I painted wheels and windows on either side.

It never made it all the way down the hill. I had leaned

too far to one side, and we tipped. And ripped. I fell out and rolled to the finish line. No trophy for that finish.

Howie laughed, my father shrugged, my mother raised her brows and commented, "We should not be surprised. Is anyone surprised? Nora rolling down a hill she's supposed to be sledding on. Absolutely not."

The aunts finished at the s'mores booth and joined friends seated near an open pit fire. On the hill, Sal walked away from Mary Fran and headed toward the camera crew and his brother Lucca, who had changed location and set up near the trees at the edge of the lake. A good-size group of movie-star wannabes were clustered around them, so I figured I could easily blend in.

Maybe I'd see Marney. I needed to talk to her, although I was not sure what I'd say. I had a strong feeling my original impression of her didn't fit her recent actions. Something was off. The funeral, the money, the blonde curly hair? What on earth had she done to her hair! And her connection to Sal, if any, was truly mystifying.

That's when I noticed a familiar figure staring at me, unkindly, across the snow-covered field.

I stared back. Not defiantly. I'd never do that. But I did not intend to look away, either.

CHAPTER TWENTY-SIX

"She saw you. That's why," Mary Fran said, nodding toward a group of women standing near a sign indicating the afternoon guided nature walk.

"Who saw what?" I asked.

"Opff," Mary Fran puffed in disbelief. "I was talking to Sal, and I caught Arianna looking toward the parking lot with a funny expression on her face. Like she had crunched a mouthful of peppercorns and they stuck in her teeth. So I checked to see what could cause such a puss, and guess what I saw?"

Mary Fran held up her hand like an NYPD traffic cop.

"Stop. No, no. Don't bother guessing. It had to do with you and Nick Renzo—surprise, surprise—sitting in his official vehicle. K-i-s-s-i-n-g!"

"Oh," was all I said.

"And you told *me* to be careful."

"Yes. Well, I meant that. About Nick, perhaps that wasn't wise."

"Pfff. Wise? She'll dislike you now. You may have made an enemy."

"She disliked me the second she met me. I was always her enemy. She wants her son to marry Crystal, and she sees me as the roadblock."

Mary Fran agreed, then said. "I may not be the sharpest tack in the corkboard, but I'd say there's nothing you can do about that." She paused and looked around, biting her lower lip. "Now, about Sal. I played it cool. I don't think he picked up on anything. But . . . and this is big, something's definitely off with him. He's uptight. He's thinks someone is stalking him."

"Oh, gee. Wonder where he got that idea."

Mary Fran gave a huge smirk. "I told him he was safe in Silver Stream."

"Does he suspect anyone? Did he drop any hints?"

"Said it was probably a woman. He saw a flash of bright blue. From the jacket."

"So the man is color blind. Good. The jacket was aqua. The inside gray." I thought about that a moment, then said, "You don't think he'd ask around, do you? A lot of people saw me in that aqua jacket, and a few remarked on how much they liked it."

"Don't worry. Blue. He called it blue. There's only about two million of those in Silver Stream."

"If Arianna or Crystal knew, do you think they'd mention me to him?"

Mary Fran stared at me, a frown dipping her lips. "Did they see you?"

"Sort of." I explained about running into them after the incident.

"They're probably too focused on the movie and Nick to even think about it right now. I doubt they'll do anything drastic." She paused, then laughed. "Like try to poison you."

I rolled my eyes. "What about Sal?"

"I asked him if anything was wrong between us, and I didn't choke on my words. He gave me a phony smile. Nora, it's hard for me. He gives me the creeps now. I want to do physical violence to the man."

"Did he mention Marney? I saw them talking."

"Nope. But I saw her on the road by the parking lot when I was talking to Sal. She was probably on her way home."

"They were talking earlier. So they know each other.

I'm not sure if that means anything."

"He was at the funeral. They could have met then."

"She wore snowshoes today."

"Big deal, worrywart. Everybody in Silver Stream has snowshoes. 'Course, Marney's in pretty good shape."

"Really?"

"Oh, yes. She won a few events in high school. Can't recall what they were. She was athletic."

I thought about that as Mary Fran left to watch her daughter in a snow fort building event, and I headed in the opposite direction toward the aunts. Midway there, I decided to detour and talk to someone I hadn't met before. See if I could find out anything about him. He figured in the mix.

Sal's brother Lucca was busy working with the camera crew. I shouldn't interrupt. I waited. He saw me waiting and turned his back. Mister Bushy Head hid his hair and lack of it under a hood attached to his green down jacket. Despite the warm clothing, he looked cold.

I was patient.

Ten minutes is my limit. Then I become less patient. I walked over.

"Hello. Great day for filming. I rode in that magnificent sleigh over there." I said, pointing to Uncle Walter's sleigh, which was rounding the bend and in a perfect spot to film. "You should consider getting a shot of that for the movie."

He looked down at me as though I was something he'd stepped in and needed to wipe off his shoe. I was taken aback.

Unable to fathom such a reaction, I felt instant dislike for this guy I'd once pitied. I wanted to strike back, tell him to watch out or somebody would pop his other tooth. Maybe me. This was clearly a very mean thought. I tried to keep it off my face.

"I pick the scenes, lady. Move along."

Move along! Had he just told me to move along?

Over the top!

I gritted my teeth as the words *What is your problem?* took a lap through my head. Since I possessed no martial arts skills and didn't own a Wonder Woman lasso, I attacked with words.

"I saw you go into the dentist's office the other day. Hope it's nothing major. Nothing Harold can't fix."

If I hadn't been watching closely, I would have missed the tell, that flicker of anger on his face that came and went in a flash. The look he gave me qualified as a scathing rebuke. To get rid of me, he ignored me, turned his back and directed the camera guy to another shot in the opposite direction.

We were standing on a slight rise, and I had the strongest desire to shove him and send him ass over teakettle down that hill. Since that was out, I delivered a mental shove.

"I noticed your fat lip. I'm sure Harold didn't do that. If you're having a problem with someone, the sheriff can probably help. I'll send him over."

That said, I turned *my* back, and scooted down the incline.

"Don't send anyone over," he called. "I handle my own affairs."

I stopped and faced him. "I agree. Your affairs are your business, but that fat lip . . . "

I shrugged and kept walking.

Seconds later he was planted smack dab in front of me like an angry moose with hackles raised, ears flattened and nose jerking. If he were a moose I'd be shaking in my L.L. Beans. As it was, I stood my ground.

"I don't know what your angle is, lady, but stay out of my business. Out of my life. If I want to see the sheriff, I'll go see him. Understood?"

Stunned by his brashness, I didn't answer.

He repeated himself, so I answered. "I think I understand, but I'm not sure."

"Really? Then let me clear it up. You listening?

"I am." I wanted to take a step back, but since I equated that with giving in, I held my ground.

Leaning forward, the man said in a harsh whisper, "I saw you."

Unsure if he meant what I thought he meant, I said nothing.

Moving a step closer, something barely possible given the limited space between us, his eyes focused on me as if he were a sniper and I was prey in the crosshairs.

He repeated, "I. Saw. You."

His words were a two-by-four to the gut. I froze mentally. Without speaking, I turned and walked away, heart thudding like a bass drum, fear racing through me making my knees weak. I concentrated on not stumbling as I walked down the slight incline.

Incredible as it seemed, I was afraid of this man.

The people around me were laughing, playing, enjoying life. I had friends nearby who loved me and would have my back in an instant. I knew the sheriff would shoot anyone who tried to harm me.

Yet, I was afraid.

Lucca had not made a specific threat.

I saw you. The words alone were not a threat.

If I could have summoned the nerve, I would have questioned him. I should have. Maybe I was delusional, reading something that wasn't there. Or maybe my fanciful notions about Sal looking like Michael Corleone in *The Godfather* played into it.

Regardless, I wanted to share my sudden fear with someone. Nick would sideline me from the investigation, definitely. I'd never get another bit of information from him; the aunts would panic; Mary Fran might panic, too, and reveal something to Sal, which could be a disaster. That left no one. I had to keep this to myself, at least for now.

I met up with the aunts, who were seated around a shallow fire pit with glowing embers, watching Aunt Agnes heat her s'mores.

"You must try the grilled cheese, at least," Aunt Ida said when she saw me. "You need nourishment."

"I will," I answered automatically, unable to drag my thoughts from Lucca.

That's when it hit me, like a second two-by-four to the gut. Fear had tangled my thoughts, paralyzing me, not allowing me to act. I had always prided myself on my ability to think on my feet so this mental freeze was a blow to my self-image. But the thaw had set in. Like clouds parting to allow the light to shine through, my thoughts cleared, and reason returned. I knew, despite the problems that would follow, that I had to talk to Nick. Today. Soon.

Because Lucca's anger stemmed from fear.

Fear of exposure.

I walked out of hearing range, hit Nick's number on speed dial and left a voice mail. "I need to see you, or at least talk to you, before you leave today. It's vitally important."

Whatever Lucca and Sal had been discussing could have been family business, or could have had something to do with the movie. Both seemed unlikely to me.

No. This was huge. It was criminal.

The worst part was they thought I knew what it was.

"You look worried. Were you watching Arianna and her friends over there?" Hannah asked when I returned to the circle.

Glad for the excuse, I replied, "Yes, I saw them."

I turned to look in that direction again.

Suddenly, my mouth went dry. The camera crew had relocated and were now near the line for the nature walk. Sal had joined them. He and Lucca were talking again, and they stopped to glance in my direction.

Ida handed me half of her grilled cheese sandwich. "Here, eat. You look hungry."

If I took a bite of anything right now, I might choke.

I smiled at her. "Thank you, but I couldn't eat a bite."

"What happened?" Hannah said sharply.

"Nothing much," I answered. *Except that two Mafia guys are probably discussing plans to murder me.*

"Did you have a run-in with Arianna? Did she say something snotty to you?" Ida asked, the concern in her voice evident.

I had to tell them something. These women might be old, but they were sharp.

I decided to let them in on the lesser of two problems.

"I made a small mistake. I kissed Nick in his sheriff's car, and Mary Fran said that Arianna saw us and looked very angry. That woman hates me. She wants me gone from Silver Stream. Plain and simple. But I didn't actually have a run-in with her."

The *Lone Ranger* played on my cell phone.

"Nick," I told the aunts, holding up the phone. I walked away to take his call.

"Hi. I'll get right to the point. I have a strong feeling that Sal and his brother are into something criminal, definitely. Don't ask me how I know."

"How do you know?" he asked.

"I knew you'd say that. Let's talk later."

"Now! Tell me. What happened between the time you left me and the time you called?"

"Nick!"

"Nora!"

"All right. I spoke to Lucca. I got the feeling he thought I overhead something incriminating between Sal and him."

"Did you?"

"No. I told you what happened."

"So, how did you get that feeling? About the incriminating part."

"He wasn't friendly. Most people are friendly when they meet me."

"That's it?"

"Pretty much."

"No, Nora. Tell me all of it. What did he say?"

"Oh, Nick."

"Why are you resisting so much? Did he threaten you?"

I closed my eyes and took a deep feel-sorry-for-myself breath. "Okay, here it is verbatim. He said, *I saw you.*"

"You know for a fact he was referring to the station house? When he was talking with Sal?"

"It couldn't be anything else. But he didn't include Sal. He didn't say *We saw you.* Do you think there's a chance Sal doesn't know?"

"I need to check into a few things. Stay away from them. Steer clear, Nora. I mean it."

"But do you think—"

"I don't know what to think." His voice was clipped, angry. I'd never heard that tone from him before.

CHAPTER TWENTY-SEVEN

A brutal Arctic air mass swept down with a vengeance, blasting all of Maine and most of New England on kissing-scene day. How fitting. The weather reflected my feelings. Icy, icy, icy. Before I left the house, Ida informed me that the weatherman reported that way up in Frenchville, Maine, they'd recorded wind-chill temperatures at forty below zero.

My nose hairs froze with my first step outside.

Ce-ce rebelled. It took a while to get started. Good thing Winterfest was over because these temperatures might have kept even die-hard Mainers away. I could be wrong, of course. It's been known to happen, me being wrong, that is.

Deputy Miller, the guy with the eye twitch that resembled a wink, admitted me to the station house, which, according the sign on the door, had been declared off-limits to residents of Silver Stream unless the visit could be considered an urgent police matter.

Miller whispered, "Stand by the wall over there and be real quiet."

"How's Nick doing?"

The answer was on his face before he replied.

"He's been better."

"You being diplomatic?"

"Absolutely, ma'am." And there was that twitch. Wink.

I had never been on a movie set before. The main station house area was a tangle of cables, lights and cameras. Nick's office door was open, and I could see him talking to the director.

The lovely Crystal sat in a makeup chair in front of a brightly-lit tri-mirror getting her face dabbed with some concoction. Beside her, second assistant director, Lucca, gestured flamboyantly as he talked. Not far from them Arianna and Crystal's mother watched the proceedings with the attention of surgeons performing open-heart surgery.

On the platform that ran the length of the back wall, Deputy Trimble sat behind the big desk, trying to look like he knew what he was doing. Sal stood in the shadows by the hall that led to the cells. My stomach lurched when I saw him. I assumed Lucca had told his brother I was the one he had chased into the parking lot. Of course, I wasn't positive. I followed Sal's gaze and spotted the female star, an attractive blonde woman of about forty, popping peanuts in her mouth. She looked bored.

I kept glancing back at Lucca.

I saw you.

I tried to shake his words from my head. Worked to tamp down the desire to run and hide. These were dangerous men. I decided to call Howie later. Tell him what was going on.

The peanut popper missed a peanut, then reached into her cleavage to retrieve it. It was hard not to notice the masculine eyes in the room that tracked her movements. I wondered if Sal were interested in her.

She was good at peanut popping. I had a bag of peanuts in my handbag which I was saving for a snack. Later, I'd try that. Too risky to try it now.

Suddenly, the director clapped his hands. "Quiet. Let's get moving on this scene. We don't have all day. Places everyone. Josh, in here," he ordered, indicating the sheriff's office.

I thought it was already pretty quiet, but what do I know.

The peanut popper stopped popping peanuts.

Trimble picked up some papers and tried to look even

busier.

Josh Rockford stood at the door to Nick's office. So this was the guy the aunts were crazy about. The heartthrob of a gone-by era. Very gone-by, I thought as I looked at him. Tall, slight paunch, dyed black hair. The aunts were coming into town tomorrow for tryouts for the scene on the station house steps with him.

In the scene, Josh would rush up the steps and ask someone if the sheriff was in. One lucky Silver Stream resident would get to reply, "He's been here all morning." The aunts had been practicing that line ever since it was announced.

The director exited Nick's office, closed the door and called, "Action!"

Crystal got up and headed for the main desk. Was I seeing things or had she added a wiggle to her walk? She took papers from Trimble, wiggled over to the Nick's door and knocked. Nick called, "Come in."

She opened the door, and tossing her black silken mane, wiggled up to Nick and handed him the papers. Hands on hips, Josh looked on. Nick said, "Hey, Babe."

Hey, Babe? Really? That was his line?

I almost gagged.

Crystal sashayed closer, stood on tiptoes and leaned in for a kiss.

Yuck.

"Cut! Let's do that again, this time with more feeling, sheriff."

I hated the thought of watching this again, but I persevered. After the eighth time, I was disgusted. After a dozen takes, I was annoyed. And hungry. I took out my bag of peanuts. Although I was tempted to imitate the peanut popper, I decided against it, lest I drop one and shatter the *quiet on the set* command. I'd just nibble silently while the endless takes continued.

I watched Sal. So far, he hadn't glanced in my direction, which was a good thing.

"Quiet," the director yelled for the thousandth time. "Let's make this the last take. Action!"

A hush fell over the room. You could hear the proverbial pin drop.

Last take? Lots of luck with that. Who knew a scene could be done so many times in so many ways. Crystal walked to the front desk, reached for the papers from Trimble and headed for Nick's door. Just the thought of watching her kiss Nick one more time, compelled me to look away. Enough was enough, thank you very much. I should not have come.

I scanned the main room. I couldn't see Sal anymore. Maybe he'd gotten fed up and left. I hoped that were so. He made me nervous. Relaxing, I shifted position.

Suddenly, like an apparition in a scene from a horror movie, he appeared at my elbow. Startled, my hand in the peanut bag jerked wildly, sending peanuts flying, pinging their way across the wooden floor like little pebbles. Ping, bounce, ping, ping, bounce. Scatter and roll.

The director screamed.

Nick smiled at me.

Sal tore the band off the cigar he was holding and tossed it on the floor among my peanuts.

All heads swiveled in my direction with something akin to military precision. I bent to pick up the peanuts, partly to avoid scrutiny, partly for neatness reasons. I am a neat person, and I do not litter. I was amazed I hadn't noticed all this debris before, everything from candy wrappers to that cigar band from a super expensive cigar, the Churchill Stradivarius, that my dad had once won in a raffle. Nick should get after these slobs.

"Get that woman out of here. Now!" the director shrieked like a madman. "And make sure she stays out!"

After so many takes it wasn't surprising he was upset by a little noise.

I caught Crystal's haughty look, the hint of a pitying smile tipping her lovely red lips. I wanted to give her the bird, but with the entire room staring at me . . .

Head held high, I watched Deputy Miller approach to escort me to the door.

I nodded. "Miller."

"Ms. Lassiter," he said graciously, suppressing a grin.

At the door and out of earshot he said, "It's been a boring morning. You're the best part so far."

"Anytime, Miller. Glad I could break the tedium."

No way was I going to stand around outside in this cold, so I decided to visit Marney. I had the perfect excuse. I'd never returned the key she'd given me. Before leaving town, I went to the Country Store and made a duplicate key so I could keep it.

By the time I pulled up in front of her house, I'd decided to tell her about the movie, try to get her chatting about Sal. Maybe she'd invite me in for coffee. I'd never been in her house. Of course, with those ferrets, I probably wouldn't want to be. She'd mentioned nipping and biting. But I could persevere.

When I knocked on her door, something crashed inside. I waited. Knocked again. I heard animals scurrying around. The sheet on the window fluttered, but I saw a weasel. No, that must be a ferret. I did not know what a ferret looked like.

"Marney? You in there?"

Nose to the window, I peered through a tiny slit in the sheet. Mistake. In this extreme cold my nose stuck to the window. I pulled back and rubbed to get feeling back. Any longer and I'd have ripped the skin right off.

What I'd seen startled me. A huge mess. Huge. Stuff all over the place, like an indoor junkyard.

"Marney," I called again, as I knocked on the door a third time. Only the animals acknowledged me, so I carefully went down the rickety steps and walked around back. In one window the sheet was partially down so it was easy to peer in.

"Oh, my gosh!"

More mess than I'd ever seen in my life—clothes, boxes, empty bottles, milk cartons, stacks of papers, garbage bags, even dirty dishes. The most astonishing part was the contradiction to all this that occupied a corner of the room like a beacon of sanity—a small desk with a computer and books stacked next to it. And a tidy-looking notebook next to the books.

"What on earth! Marney, Marney, Marney," I mumbled to myself. "What is going on here?"

Chilled to the bone, I walked around the house, peering in every window. Consistent chaos polluted each room. I half expected to see Marney collapsed on top of one of the heaps, but no. Nothing. If she were inside, she was well hidden.

I glanced at the shed, ran back and did a quick check. Nothing. My toes were numbing, my gloved fingers were freezing, and my nose was a block of ice that might fall off any minute. I thought about frostbite and hurried back to my truck. Once inside, I started the engine and called Nick on the chance the final take was really final. It immediately went to voice mail.

"Nick, call when you've finished kissing Babe."

Next I called Mary Fran. Another voice mail. Where was everyone? Only so many people could fit into that station house.

Seconds later, Mary Fran called back.

"What's up? I missed your movie debut. Heard it was a dilly."

"You'll have to wait for the rerun. Have you seen Marney lately?"

"Not since she was in my salon before Winterfest. Big surprise. She seldom bothers with her hair. It's a real mess. I think she cuts it herself once in a while. But she wanted curls and a dye job. No cut. I didn't want to do what she asked, but she was the customer. It looks worse now. She's got long blonde frizzy hair that sticks out like someone pitched a wrinkled tent on her head. She loved it."

Hard to picture.

"Do you have her cell number?"

"Marmaduke, I mean Marney, has not moved into this century yet. She doesn't have a cell phone."

That was odd. "Really." Without mentioning what I'd seen at her house, I asked, "How about a computer?"

"Are you crazy? The woman wouldn't touch one. Once, when I was in the Country Store and she was behind me in line, some loudmouth guy was going on about his new computer, and Marney said loud and clear like she was making an announcement, 'Computers are the devil's playground. Wouldn't have one in the house.'"

"Was this before or after Floyd went to the mountain to live?"

"Probably after, but I'm not sure. I'll have to think about it. Why? What's up?"

"Do you think Floyd had a computer?"

"I have no idea. Marney never said a word about that. Come on, give. What's up, Nora?"

"Was Marney smart in school?"

"I don't know. Never heard she was dumb. Or smart."

"I have to head to the library."

"I hate it when you keep me out of the loop. I am your assistant, in case you forgot."

"Didn't I just call you?"

"Well, I—"

"I have to get moving. We'll meet later," I cut in before she could protest.

I arrived in town just in time to witness a stomach-churning scene on the broad top step of the station house. Despite the extreme cold, despite the pummeling wind, a foursome made up of Nick, Crystal, Arianna and Crystal's mom stood laughing and talking as if they were at a summer picnic. The best part was Crystal clinging to Nick's arm like a lover.

How special.

I parked a short distance from the Country Store,

which is across from the station house. I'm not sure whether Crystal saw my truck or not. Maybe it didn't matter.

No, it mattered, I thought as I noticed her looking in my direction.

Only she and Arianna faced me. As I got out of Ce-ce, Crystal reached up and touched Nick's cheek. Then she leaned in and kissed him. Although I couldn't see her face clearly, I knew she was looking at me. Just as I knew that's why she was doing what she was doing.

Crystal was on stage again, this time before a live audience of one—me. I considered her actions overly obvious and extremely immature. I *so* wasn't in the mood for this nonsense.

If she expected a display of temper, like a door slam or a huffy look, she had sorely misjudged me.

I closed the door quietly and casually walked toward them, head held high, a neutral façade that belied my true thoughts pasted on my face. Looking at me, I knew no one could tell that I wanted to jump back into my truck, drive home and hop into bed where I could pull the covers over my head.

Nick saw me as I neared the bottom step. He greeted me as if nothing unusual were going on.

"Nora."

He reached down for my hand, which I turned into a casual fist bump as I remained on the sidewalk instead of joining the quartet "on stage." I would not play Crystal's game. Crystal with the perky look on her face. I hated that perky look. So petty of me. Sometimes I'm petty.

I did smile as I said to all, "How did the scene go? I had to leave before the final take, but I managed to observe a few hundred takes. Who knew this movie business could take so long, or be so boring."

I couldn't bring myself to add a chuckle, but I did pause and look directly at each of the antagonists, and Nick. He had the grace to look uncomfortable, but not by much.

"Hello Arianna, Crystal." I nodded at Crystal's mother,

whom I'd never met.

Arianna introduced me, but the wind carried her name away, so I faked a friendly smile and lied. "Nice to meet you. Hope you all enjoyed the day."

The friendly foursome had become an awkward foursome-plus-one-interloper. I waited for one of them to pick up the conversational ball. Arianna led the pack.

"Oh, it was wonderful. Two stars in the family. Nick was a natural. Why wouldn't he be? Playing himself. And Crystal . . . well," She paused, and if faces could gush, hers gushed. "Made for the role. Perfect."

Sh-ut. Up-p. Gag me with a spoon.

I said nothing. Not even a murmur passed these frozen lips. I simply pulled my hood tighter against the cold, thought about Aunt Ida's fish chowder, and moved on to garbanzo beans. Since I didn't know what they were, I couldn't picture them. Were they green, yellow, brown, beige or white? Did they resemble baked beans? Were they round, oval. Square. I tried to imagine a square bean.

Crystal said, "Nick was better than me. For sure. He put his all into the scene, right Nick?"

"Umm," said the talkative one.

"It reminded me of old times," Crystal went on.

Nick said nothing to that bold statement, either, just looked at his watch.

Crystal rambled on. "Remember? We used to sneak into your office so we could steal a few minutes alone?"

Arianna and Crystal's mom smiled adoringly at the chosen one, shaking their heads at the antics she described.

"Beautiful moments," Crystal said, her eyes on Nick. "Good times."

Nick glanced at me and winked. This was not like the Miller twitch, it was an actual wink. The twitch was on his lips, something I considered his pre-smile.

Interesting. I couldn't help respond to him with an actual smile. I couldn't help like him a little bit more than I did. We held each other's gaze.

Seeing Crystal's lips tighten into a straight line, her mother blinked about twenty-two times, Arianna looked from her son to the interloper with disdain, and Nick looked like he'd rather be fighting a raging fire or battling a dinosaur.

"Well, let's not stand out in this cold any longer," Nick said. "I've got work to do, and I'm sure you folks are ready for lunch."

With that he turned to go, then stopped to look at me. I hadn't budged. "Nora, you have some info for me? Let's go over it inside."

Arianna frowned. Crystal strained to keep her perky look in place. Her mother stopped blinking and settled for glaring.

I nodded and stepped up. "Let's go then. We'll have to make this quick. I have things to do later."

Clearly outmaneuvered, the feminine threesome had no choice but to exchange goodbyes and be on their way.

Once inside I whispered, "You owe me, Sheriff, for my timely arrival."

"I do. Absolutely," he whispered as we stepped around cables and other paraphernalia. "You're in the catbird seat now. What would you like? Dinner? Champagne? A million dollars?"

I smiled up at him.

"Me?" he added to the list, a hopeful glint in his eye.

CHAPTER TWENTY-EIGHT

As soon as the door of his office was closed, Nick pulled me into his arms, laughed and said, "Hey, Babe," before he kissed me.

I grinned as his mouth covered mine. This was nothing like the tepid kiss I had witnessed between Crystal and him, but who knows how that ended up, what with the director calling for retakes and more retakes. This kiss held all the warmth and passion that screen kiss had lacked.

"I am not cut out to be a movie actor," he said between kisses. "I felt like I was wasting my time. How can they stand it?"

"Maybe action-adventure movies would suit you better."

"I doubt it."

We ordered lunch from the Country Store. Egg salad on seedless rye for me with pickles and chips, chicken Panini with bacon on sourdough bread for him, extra honey mustard sauce on the side.

While we waited for it to be delivered, I told him about my visit to Marney's place.

"You searched her house after Floyd was murdered, right?" I asked before I mentioned the computer.

"Of course. Found nothing incriminating. A lot of garbage. The woman's a hoarder."

"What a keen eye you have, Sheriff."

He stared at me, eyes narrowed. "Why are you asking? You didn't break in, did you?"

"Of course not. But I did look in the windows. In one

of the back rooms, I saw a computer. It was located in an oasis of clean surrounded by a sea of trash. It was an older model, an iMac, I think. Not sure."

He looked startled. "I did see it. It was tipped over, layered with debris. Didn't look like it had been touched in years." He tipped his head. "Incredible."

"This one has been touched recently."

"I'll get a warrant. I doubt she'd let me in without it."

"I wonder what she's hiding."

Someone knocked on the door. "Lunch, chief."

"Come on in," Nick called as he shoved aside the strategically arranged props on his desk, one of which was a silver-framed picture of Crystal, which he laid face down. He looked at me, brows raised as if daring me to question it.

I accept most dares, but sometimes, like now, wisdom wins out.

I unwrapped my sandwich and flattened the paper around it, making a little plate for myself.

Nick said, "Even if it is old, something on that computer could shed light on Floyd's murder."

"Could be. Did Floyd have another computer? One at the mountain?"

"There was a melted cell phone on the floor of his truck. The techs figured it was a plus-size one. They couldn't get anything from it. May have used that as a computer."

I thought about that.

"He might not have erased his tracks on that home computer." I arranged some chips neatly around half of my sandwich. "Big trouble if that happened."

"How's that?"

"Unless he changed his email address, she'd have access to his email and the sites he visited. With Apple products they all link together. What's on one can also be found on the other, unless you specifically set it up otherwise. He may not have thought of that."

"And she could pull all that up without him knowing

about it?"

"Maybe. Not sure."

I told him what Mary Fran said about Marney never using a cell phone or a computer.

"Sometimes people say things to deliberately throw you off track."

"I wish we knew more about her finances. Do you know how much Floyd took from her? What she's got left? The amount of the insurance she'll get?"

"She told me what he took from her. I'll subpoena the other financial records, including the insurance payouts."

"Will she know you're doing this?"

"Yes."

I bit my lip. "She may be totally innocent. She'll resent this very much. You could look at it two ways. Subjecting a grieving widow to more stress is heartless. But, if she's guilty she could run, maybe disappear forever."

Nick did not comment. Instead, he concentrated on opening the honey mustard container.

I knew I could find out about Marney's financial situation. He knew that, too. No need to articulate the obvious. For the first time, I thought his silence conveyed a nonverbal communication. I dropped the subject.

I placed the pickles around the lower half of my sandwich, making for a nice arrangement.

We moved on to Eddie and the hidden camera and disk. Nick said, "I assume it was money in the bag. The bigger question is where it came from. Floyd's joint bank account with Marney? Or was Floyd into something illegal? Originally, Marney told you she thought he was into something illegal, right?"

"Yes, and she wanted him to go to jail."

Nick said, "I'm going up to the mountain tomorrow. Talk to Eddie and to Beverly again."

"Good. Maybe Beverly knew about Floyd's stash. Or Eddie's."

A distraught look on his face, he said, "I should have

spent more time on this." He set his Panini aside. "I've allowed myself to be distracted by the chaos around here, as if this movie is more important than murder. I'd like to kick the lot of them out, but the mayor and the town council have the final say. The show must go on. Big bucks for the town."

"You feel guilty?"

"I'm not doing my job." He reached for my hand and clasped it tightly. "You are! You've helped a lot. Thank you, Nora. You have a good head for this. Finding that disk was a big bonus."

"Thank you."

"Any other thoughts?"

"About you or the case?"

I was happy to see him smile. "I meant the case, of course, but if you want to touch on something else I'm open to it."

"Okay. The case first. I'll leave the best for last." I paused and was pleased by the look he gave me. "I was wondering whether Eddie was ever arrested? Maybe when he was back in high school?"

"Where'd you hear that?" he asked as he dipped his Panini into the honey mustard sauce.

"The aunts. They said he broke someone's windshield."

"He was under age. That record is sealed."

"But you know about it?"

"I've lived in Silver Stream all my life."

"So he was violent back then?"

"That's pushing it. He never hurt anyone, but he did have a temper."

I lifted the rye bread and sprinkled a bit of salt on my egg salad. "So, he's got a temper. He's shifty, too. Not above planting a spy camera in a friend's room—"

"Former friend," Nick corrected.

"And is not above stealing," I continued without missing a beat. "The question is twofold. Did he find something that gave him a motive to kill Floyd? Is he capable of killing?"

"Money is a powerful motivator," Nick said.

"And Beverly?"

"Don't know. She might have known what was going on since she was well acquainted with both men."

"And the lottery ticket? Don't forget that."

"Yes. Either of them could have stolen it."

"But if they did, why would they need the money in the bag?"

Nick shook his head and took a swig of root beer. "Another mystery."

"Which brings us to Sal, the Mafia don and his soldier-brother Lucca, the guy he punched in the mouth as a warning and probably threatened with worse. Death by snake or screwdriver, or something. Or a horse's head in his bed, if he had a horse."

"Nora!"

"You saw *The Godfather*?"

"Everyone saw *The Godfather*. What's your point?"

"Sal looks like Al Pacino aka Michael Corleone."

Nick studied me as I took a bite of my egg salad sandwich. Finally he said, "That's true. Why didn't I think of that? The guy must be guilty."

We both laughed.

Nick closed his eyes. "Over the top."

"Yes, and I agree. I have to stop being . . . oh, what's the word." I paused and looked at the ceiling searching for the word. "Fanciful. Yes, that works. I guess it's because these are movie people."

I munched on the chip.

"Will you be in town tomorrow for tryouts on the front step?"

"A blizzard couldn't keep the aunts away. And there's a senior citizen meeting tomorrow about the luncheon for the cast, or the town guests as Hannah calls them. So I'll be here with them. Also have to go to see Margaret."

My cell phone sounded with a generic ring indicating it was someone other than family or close friends. I rummaged in my purse for it. Margaret's name came up.

"Hi, Margaret. What's up?"

"I just got a call from Beverly."

"I hope it was good n—"

I stopped when I heard sobbing on the line.

"She finally told me the truth. She can't find the lottery ticket. At all. It is gone!"

CHAPTER TWENTY-NINE

I drove slowly into town the next morning.

Great-Aunts Ida, Hannah and Agnes left for town earlier to attend a short senior citizen meeting to finalize the menu for the cast luncheon. After that, they'd go to the front step tryouts. I planned to meet them after my library visit. I hoped one of them got the role.

I also wanted to see Marney before Nick interviewed her. She might be more open with me. Perhaps I could find out about the computer.

As soon as I walked into the library, Margaret rushed from behind the big desk to greet me. We hugged. She cried. I misted up.

"I'm so sorry about this, Margaret. Wherever that ticket is, it has not been turned in yet. Either the thief is holding onto it and plans to cash it later, or Beverly Sue truly misplaced it." I thought that one last was unlikely. No one misplaces a winning lottery ticket.

"Is there some hope, any hope?" Margaret asked with a sob. "Is that what you're telling me?"

"Not much," I said truthfully, then reigned that in when she sobbed louder. "Well, perhaps a glimmer."

Margaret took a deep breath and went back behind the big desk, which shone with a lemon oil finish. She must have been working off frustrated feelings this morning with her cleaning cloth. She stared at me for several seconds before plopping on the stool.

I realized she needed something other than routine

library work, something that might lead to a positive outcome. "Time to go over the library records for the day or days you noticed these items missing," I said. "Perhaps I should have started there. That glimmer I mentioned might be hidden in those pages."

Nodding, she reached for a book on a shelf beneath the desk, and my hopes of finishing this project any time soon plummeted. Maybe when all was said and done, I could bring the library records into the twenty-first century. Get all her records on computer.

She opened the book to the pages in question and set bookmarks. "I'll make copies of these pages and you can keep them. No need for you to spend the day in this dismal place."

"Make duplicate copies. You need to study these pages, too. Something might strike you."

I looked around and breathed in the scent of books and old wood.

"I do have to be going, but this is not a dismal place to me. I love this library. It takes me back to happy days in my childhood." Mary Fran never came to the library so I was free from persecution here.

Margaret made copies and handed me about eight pages. "Would it help if I also listed the type of books and videos these folks usually check out?"

"Perfect. Just what we need. That'll work better than your original list."

Looking pleased she said, "This is good. I'll work on it. In some cases I may remember what time they were here. Not sure that will help."

"Good thinking. You should be a detective."

The hint of a smile brightened her face.

* * *

By the time I arrived at the police station for tryouts, a few chairs had been set up in the snow-cleared street, and an audition protocol had been established. To keep the entire town from trying out, the director had drawn ten numbers from a hat, and the lucky winners were lined up at the base of the steps ready for their chance at the role. Hannah and Arianna were among them.

Crystal stood off to the side, watching with her mother as the selected candidates were told to enter the station house and come out the door when Lucca directed and say their line. Sal stood off to the side. I noticed him glance at Crystal several times. I wondered whether he had switched his affections from Mary Fran. Or, more wonderful, she had switched her affections from Nick.

The senior citizens occupied a section right in front. Some had set up their own chairs. Bundled in down coats, scarfs, wool hats and mittens, Ida and Agnes waved me over, indicating I should take Hannah's empty seat.

"Josh is in the building. Hannah might be talking to him this very moment," Ida said.

"He's been here all morning" was heard eight times before Arianna came out. She gave a nod of her head as she delivered the line in a formal manner. Crystal smiled at such wonderfulness, then glanced at Sal. Suddenly, I wondered whether this audition was fixed, if Arianna was already locked into the part through prearrangement. I felt anger welling up. I wanted to smack Crystal. How awful of me.

Hannah came out last.

I held my breath. Ida clasped her hands at the breast. Agnes bit her bottom lip.

"He's been here all morning," Hannah said, her voice affable, her expressive eyes looking straight at the stand-in. Then with a Hannah flourish, she added a hand gesture, indicating the station house door. "Go on in," she added, going off script.

Agnes gasped. Ida's mouth dropped open, and I smiled, thinking, *Oh, Hannah, how perfect.*

After a short consultation among the powers that be, the winner was announced.

"Will Hannah Lassiter step forward please. The others are excused. We thank you all for your participation."

Ida, Agnes and I clapped wildly. Agnes added a loud "Hooray for Hannah! Hooray!" She would have continued with a few more hoorays if the director hadn't called, "Quiet on the set," looking in her direction, his words delivered with a stern frown.

Crystal aimed a killing glare at Sal. Sal glared at Lucca, who had stepped out the station house door with a microphone. A lot of glaring going on, for sure. I loved it.

Avoiding Sal's gaze, Lucca said, "We need to wrap up this scene as quickly as possible since Main Street has been blocked to traffic for the duration of the shooting. We plan to complete this within the hour. If you wish to stay and watch, you are welcome to do so, but you have to cooperate and be silent."

Before returning inside, he shot me an intense look. A threat or a warning? Hard to say. I stared back.

Due to the cold, few stayed to watch. Of course, Ida and Agnes could not be persuaded to leave so I stayed with them. Ida had been holding a wool blanket which she unfolded, and we all huddled beneath it.

As promised, the scene wrapped up quickly. Three takes and less than an hour later the aunts were in Hannah's warm Honda Pilot on the way home, and I was on my way to Hot Heads Heaven.

Once inside, I was assaulted by the usual bleach and dye smells which overpowered the pleasant aromas of shampoo and conditioner. My eyes watered. I sneezed four times.

"Hi, Mary Fran," I said, reaching for a tissue. "I need a private spot to work, undisturbed, for an hour or so. I've got my laptop. How about your back room?"

"Absolutely, boss. I'll clear off the table for you." To the woman with the foil-wrapped hair, she said, "This is super important. I'll be right back."

As she opened the door for me, she said, "Anything I

can help with?"

"Not yet. I'll let you know."

Mary Fran cleared the dye bottles from the table and placed them on the shelf.

"I need to do some research first," I explained. "Then you can help."

"I'm good at research."

No way was I going to tell anyone, even Mary Fran, that I intended to breach a few firewalls to uncover Marney's financial situation before I went to visit her today.

But maybe. . .

"One of the things I have to do is cull a list of library patrons. Look at their choice of reading and other material. When I'm finished, and I'm not sure when I'll get to it, you can take a look and tell me who might be interested in what."

Mary Fran danced around and waved her arms, then posed in her paso doble stance. "Oh, do it now! Do it. I'm feeling in detective mode. I'm in the zone."

I set my laptop down and opened it. "I'll let you know when I have the list," I said, trying to put her off.

"Do the list. Plee-ese. I'll be quiet as a mouse."

"Mary Fran," called the woman with the foil in her hair. "You coming back soon? I think I'm almost done."

"I'll keep her quiet, too."

I laughed. "Gonna hit her over the head, are you?"

"The list," she said as she walked out. "It's probably very important."

"We'll see." But I had already decided she might be right.

I turned on my computer. Instead of tackling Marney's financial records, which I planned to do first, I switched plans. Going with my gut, I looked over the pages Margaret had given me, wondering if there was a red herring in the mix.

An hour later I was finished. Stunned, I stared at four names that seemed to pulse with the energy of a Broadway neon sign. Eddie, Marney, Beverly and Floyd had made the list. Each had visited the library on the days in question, but no two on the same day. All four of them! What were the chances! Most amazing of all, some of these entries dated back several months.

I called the library.

"Margaret, I just finished the list. Do one more thing for me. Go back in your records and see the types of books or videos these people usually borrowed. Actually, focus only on Eddie, Marney, Beverly and Floyd."

Margaret said, "I can tell you immediately that Beverly took out mostly romances. She and I liked many of the same books. Eddie took out videos, ones about adventure. He's not much of a reader. Marney? Mostly books about animals. Ferrets, I think. I'll have to look her up. And about Floyd, he was not a frequent visitor. But I'll check them all and get back to you."

When we hung up I looked at the list with new eyes, wondering if I might be looking at the name of a murderer. And wondering how Sal and Lucca figured into this. All of them had some connection to Floyd.

They couldn't all be complicit.

I shelved my library thoughts, closed my computer, packed it up and put on my old jacket. I yanked a wool hat on and pulled a few locks lose. My fashion sense was not completely dead, but it was close. The downward slide began the day I asked Ida for her L.L Bean catalogue, a game changer for a woman who was strictly a designer label fanatic. An old jacket! What was next?

I walked back into the main room, amazed by the crowd. Previously empty salon chairs were now filled with older women. I figured they might be members of the senior citizens' yoga group. All four chairs in the waiting area were occupied, too. Several people were standing. Business was booming. Even the manicure table was busy, reminding me I should get my nails done.

When she saw me, Mary Fran flitted from her

customer to the reception desk.

"They all expect to be in the movie tomorrow," she whispered. "Most of them are walk-ins. Some I don't even know." She handed me the list I'd given her. "I made notes next to the names I recognized. Hope it helps." She spoke quickly, barely taking a breath. "I didn't get to finish."

"Thanks. I'll call you tonight."

As I stepped outside, I pulled up my collar against the wind and called Marney.

"Marney, I'm in town and thought I'd drop by if you have time."

She coughed several times. "No, no. Don't come. I'm in bed. Had a bout with some bug."

"I'm sorry to hear that."

I heard a crash in the background, and figured the ferrets were doing their thing.

"Besides," she continued, stopping briefly to cough, "there's no need. I told you we was finished our business. You have to stop investigating. Just stop, girl. No need to do anymore. Enough is enough."

I saw the Land Rover heading this way, driving slowly past the police station. I took an impulsive step onto Main Street knowing he had plenty of time to stop. If needed, I could hop out of the way.

"Okay, Marney. Feel better."

The Land Rover stopped, and the driver narrowed his eyes as he lowered his window. "What's up lady? You looking to get run over or something?"

"I love this SUV," I gushed as I casually pushed aside one of the blonde tresses that fluttered around my face. I stood at his door, wide-eyed, a true innocent. "I cut a picture of one of these out of a magazine once," I lied.

"Good for you. Now step aside so I can get by." He was breathing fast. Easy to see he was annoyed.

Instead of backing away, I set my hands the edge of his door and peered inside. "Ay-uh. Looks wonderful. So much room," I said, noting the retractable cargo cover that hid what he carried.

"Look lady, I'm in a hurry, if you don't mind," he said, eyeing my hands. "Unless you want to get in and search my vehicle."

I complied, slowly. "I was just admiring your SUV, Mister. I didn't mean to keep you."

Without another word he took off in a swirl of powdery snow, and I was left in the middle of the street wondering what was in the boxes he'd concealed beneath the cargo cover. I'd seen the edges, but was unable to see any lettering. One word popped into my head. Transporting.

I remembered what Margret said about the Land Rover at the scene of the accident.

I think Lucca signaled him . . . Like he was telling the guy to move on down the road. I got the feeling they were going to meet.

CHAPTER THIRTY

Before heading home, I stopped at the police station to give Nick my latest theory and show him the library list.

As soon as I walked in the door, it was like I'd set off a silent alarm. The director shot me a scathing look and yelled, "What's that woman doing here? I banished her."

Banished? Well, that was a little harsh.

"I have official police business," I said in a prim tone I hoped would annoy him further. His expression announced that it had.

The shout brought Deputy Miller out from behind the big desk. Bless him, he smiled and escorted me to Nick's door.

"Thanks, Miller. How's it going?" I asked as I knocked.

"Been dull since you and your bag of peanuts were banished."

"Come in," Nick called.

"Is it my imagination or are things a little tense on the set?" I whispered to Miller as I opened the door.

"Tense, yes. Not going well. They're setting up for the pre-yoga scene."

"Tense. Gee, that's a dog-gone shame," I said gleefully.

"Absolutely."

"Nora, I'm glad you're back," Nick said, all business. "New developments."

"Thanks again," I said to Miller.

Nick nodded to Miller, who closed the door.

"What developments?"

"I made some calls up to the mountain, talked to some of the people Eddie works with. Even called Beverly. After that, came the hard part."

I narrowed my eyes as I looked up at him, discarding several possibilities that took a rapid trek through my head. Then I stopped, smiled, said, "Waiting! Waiting was the hard part, wasn't it? You didn't call him. You waited for him to call you."

Nick's brows shot up. "That didn't take you long."

"Hey!" I countered. "I'm a private detective, you know."

He gave me a quick kiss. "Impossible not to know, Nora."

"So when—"

"He called less than an hour ago. Said he had things to tell me. Since I have other people to interview at the mountain, I said I'd be up there late tomorrow. He's nervous."

"He should be. He's far from innocent."

"Easy does it, Nora. Can't play prosecutor, judge and jury."

"I know. I'm conclusion jumping. You going to tell him what we know?"

"Can't tell him about something obtained illegally, but I have a feeling he's going to tell me. At least tell more about what Floyd was involved with."

"He thinks you know something. He wants to get out in front of it."

Nick nodded as he popped a Green Mountain k-cup into his Keurig, placed his sheriff's mug on the drip tray and closed the lid. "Something like that."

"What did you hint at with the others?"

"I kept asking questions about Eddie, his whereabouts, his work, his relationship with Floyd."

"So they got the impression you had something linking

Eddie to Floyd's murder?"

"Who knows?"

"You do. Good move. I love it."

"I'll find out tomorrow."

"Great! Can I come?"

"No," Nick said, as he opened the small refrigerator and took out the milk container. "Not a good idea. You've gotta stay clear of this."

I mulled that over. The senior yoga scene was tomorrow, so it was best I stayed. "You'll tape the interview?"

"Definitely."

I sat in front of his desk, pulled out my laptop and opened to the financial information I'd collected on Marney.

"Would you like a cup, too?" he asked.

"No thanks."

He set his mug on the desk and studied the pages in front of him.

I said, "I was shocked when I saw the insurance papers. She's getting much, much less than she implied. Maybe enough to pay for the burial, enough for her to live on for a year, tops. If she's frugal, that is. It doesn't make sense."

"Amazing. When she came to me originally about this, she told me he stole most of their, or rather *her*, savings."

"I got the feeling she was almost destitute. She's not, but she doesn't have much, including the small insurance payout."

"Right. I'm going to interview her when I come back from the mountain. She'll know she's a suspect then, and I'll get the subpoena."

"Good. Because several things are not adding up to innocence here. First, I was just on the phone with her, and she told me *again* to back off. No more investigating. I wanted to find out what Floyd did with the money he took. I thought maybe I could get some of it back for her. I don't understand why she insisted I stop. Few people turn down extra money. The only thing I could think of was she was actually madly in love with Floyd and didn't want to besmirch his memory."

I shook my head. "Do you buy that?"

"Of course not."

"Second, she has a computer set up in what seems to be the only clear area in her hoarder trash house. Third, she was talking to Sal, the gangster, at Winterfest."

Nick rolled his eyes but didn't interrupt.

"And fourth, she's on the library list."

Elbows on his desk, Nick covered his face with his hands. Without looking up, he said, "You lost me at library list. And if talking to Sal makes someone less than innocent, maybe half the town should be added, including my mother and Crystal." He looked at me. "Start with library list."

"Margaret gave me a list of people who were in the library on the days items went missing. I wasn't going to bother much with the list. I scanned it quickly. Then I saw something that that made me shiver. Definitely a telltale sign."

Nick looked up at me. I could not interpret his look. Interested? Amused? Skeptical?

"You shivered?" he asked, pretending he was seeking clarification.

Okay, now I was able to zero in. His tone said amused. Ignoring this un-sheriff-ly attitude, I plunged on. "Yes. Because Marney, Floyd, Eddie, and Beverly made the list. Doesn't that make the hairs on your neck stand on end?"

"No. But I'll admit it's interesting."

I knew I had him. I continued, "Big-time. Three prime suspects. Coincidence? I think not! I have the strongest feeling this is all related to Floyd's murder."

He took a sip of his coffee. Still silent, he stared at me, hands clasped beneath his chin.

I waited for him to say something. With each tick of the clock, tension increased and I wasn't sure what it meant, what I had missed. I wondered if I had been wrong about getting so involved, if I had overstepped some boundary I didn't know existed.

After long minutes, he put his hands flat on his desk, and his look changed. With his eyes holding me like a lover, he said softly, "Nora Lassiter, I've never met anyone like you before. Never met anyone who was so in sync with my thoughts. This financial information . . . I never had to ask. You knew."

I smiled at him. "I understood what you couldn't ask for. And why."

He nodded. "Yes," he said quietly. "You did."

I didn't know what to say.

"I never met anyone who could make my heart leap with joy just by walking into the room, who brightened my day, who made me want to smile when they used words like shiver. No one close to me has ever had this effect on me.

"I want to take you home. Hold you. Lay down beside you and never let you go."

With those words, the most awful thing happened. Fast-collecting moisture pooled in my eyes, blurring my vision. Next thing I knew the moisture spilled over. Big fat tears.

Nick had never seen this embarrassing display before. Well, once when I first met him it had been close, but it was dark and he didn't have night vision goggles so I figured I was safe. Here in his bright office there was no darkness to hide the display.

What a wuss I was! Such a coward!

I tried to be stalwart.

I brushed the tears away and cleared my throat. I'm not sure why I did the latter, but the situation seemed to call for action, and jumping across the desk and into his lap seemed inappropriate.

True kindness or compassion or love touched my heart and summoned tears that never had a chance in the face of danger or meanness or fear.

I wanted to hide.

I needed a tissue.

I grabbed my handbag from the floor beside my chair and managed to open it on my lap. Next thing I knew his hand covered mine and he pulled me into his arms, my handbag tumbled back to the floor and the open bag of peanuts made a second debut, along with assorted other items that had no business on the floor.

The tears flowed in earnest as my arms went around him, and I buried my soppy face in his neck.

"Oh, Nick. You make me cry."

"Tears of joy, I hope."

"Ay-uh. For sure," I said, realizing as soon as the words were out that I sounded like a few Mainers I knew. *Ay-uh. Really Nora!*

For an added embarrassing crescendo, unable to hold back, I hiccupped and sniffled. What a pitiful display. I had to get hold of myself.

No sooner had the thought formed, when he began an assault on the unruly tears, kissing them right off my face. Smiling, I cupped his face with both hands, turned his head and kissed him full on the mouth. We touched, lips to lips, body to body, heart to heart.

I had never wanted the way I wanted this man. Incredible for a once-engaged woman to admit. Incredible to realize. I knew and understood the pull of sexual desire, but this was different. This went beyond that place and into a new realm.

I had words and music playing in my head as I melted into him and returned his kisses. It was a song I'd downloaded and kept on my phone after hearing it for the first time in Hannah's GTO. Written and sung by John Denver, "Annie's Song" filled me with joy when I heard it. I felt that joy now as Nick filled up my senses, my spirit, my heart.

Like no one had ever done before .

CHAPTER THIRTY-ONE

"Well, that's a real humdinger," Agnes said as she smoothed her Yoga Chick shirt over her ample hips. "Two dishes. The woman made two dishes. They're in the refrigerator in the back room. I won't go near them, for sure. Jellied bouillon with organic frankfurters? Really? Prune puree with raw egg white whipped up to look like cream? That's evil, deceiving folks like that. I might have taken a big bite before I realized what she'd done. Downright dangerous. A person could die from such stuff. Salmonella and diarrhea. Killers."

"Doesn't sound good," I said as the aunts added their coats to the pile on a back table in the church basement.

"I don't know how she got to be in charge of this cast party," Ida said as she removed her hat. "Did we vote? I don't remember voting."

"I think she knows someone," Hannah said. "Got connections. Maybe because Crystal was in the movie. She seems to be friends with that guy Sal now."

Ida said, "Well, we saw her sporting a new handbag. Arianna too. One of the girls said they were super expensive, a gift from that Sal fellow."

Interesting. Sal must have given up on Mary Fran and turned his attention to Crystal.

"The place looks really nice today," Hannah said. "Smells like someone sprayed air freshener around. Sea Breeze, maybe."

"They staged it for the scene," I said, wondering what the aunts considered expensive when it came to handbags.

"The floor has never been this clean, or this shiny,"

Agnes said. "You can smell the wax."

Another group of women came down the steps to the church basement. Arianna, Crystal and Crystal's mother were among them. I noticed the designer bag Crystal carried. Louis Vuitton. Big bucks. She came over as soon as she saw me, the handbag prominently displayed in front of her.

"Are they letting you remain for this scene? The director seemed so upset with you when Nick and I did our romantic scene," Crystal said.

"Love your new bag," I said, ignoring her comment.

She held it up for my perusal. "A gift," she said, "From Sal. That wonderful man who is friends with the assistant director."

She smiled coyly, inferring she was now good friends with Sal, too. Nick had definitely dodged a bullet when he broke their engagement. He must have known.

Crystal held the bag out in an in-your-face move. I obliged by studying it as she casually turned it around to make sure it was all on display, front and back. For brief seconds I wondered what she had to do to get it, then quickly cut off that line of thought. No Mensa intellect needed for that mystery.

"Very nice," I said, staring at the kind of Louis Vuitton monogramed Tuileries bag I'd once drooled over. Of course, spending several thousand dollars on a handbag had been miles beyond my price range.

Crystal turned the bag again. I looked at the back more closely.

"Excuse me," I said.

I walked over to Aunt Ida, took her aside and whispered, "I'll be right back. I have to take care of something."

I grabbed my jacket and headed up the stairs, putting it on as I went. I knew Nick would be on his way to interview Eddie so I took out my cell phone and hit his number on speed dial as soon as I was far enough away to speak privately.

"Can I call you back?" he said as soon as he picked up. "Trimble and I are at an accident scene. Several people hurt. Had to postpone my visit to Eddie."

I came right to the point. "I think Sal is into fake designer goods. Illegal stuff."

"How do you . . . " he stopped. "Are you sure?"

"Crystal's carrying a fake Louis Vuitton. A gift from Sal. She thinks it's the real thing, or at least I think she believes that. Who knows? Either he's dealing in them, or he knows someone who is. I suppose he could have been duped, but that seems unlikely."

"This case gets more involved every day. Thanks for letting me know. I'll call you later."

I hurried back downstairs to watch the yoga scene. Only a handful of spectators were permitted, but Nick had informed the director that I would be among them. When the sheriff speaks, everyone listens, even a headstrong director who has banished one particular spectator.

I took the only vacant chair in a small arrangement that had been set up in the back of the room. Josh and another actor were standing off to the side with the director. Sal stood across the room with Lucca. I did not look at him, but noticed Crystal glance his way as she hugged her fake Louis Vuitton.

The casting director walked around studying the participants as the yoga class began with the Mountain Pose.

"Sense your feet rooting into the ground while the crown of your head reaches up to heaven. Breathe," the instructor said as she took a deep breath herself.

Agnes was intent on her Mountain Pose. She'd even remembered to use her hearing aid today so she would not miss a word. Hannah and Ida were the picture of concentration. Almost everyone in the group sported new clothes, wore makeup and had salon-fresh hairdos. Most wore ballet shoes, but Agnes wore heavy sneakers. Arianna looked completely different from the group, of course, with her long gray braid, super baggy jeans, scrubbed face and bare feet.

The instructor had chosen tranquil background music that conjured up images of a peaceful nature walk. If I closed my eyes I could be in a quiet meadow sitting by a stream, or under a leafy tree. I needed to remain alert, needed to watch Sal and Lucca, so closing my eyes was out.

The session was going well. Agnes was quiet. None of the former disharmony was evident. The peaceful nature walk music had been the perfect choice. *Music hath charms* . . . I thought. Little birds began to tweet and chirp sweetly in the background, adding a nice touch to the nature feeling.

Suddenly, Agnes looked around, frowning, her Mountain Pose morphing into a hill pose. I couldn't imagine what was bothering her. She studied the coat table in the back of the room.

"Elongate your spine. Align your head and spine," the yoga instructor said, looking at Agnes.

Agnes complied, and went back to her pose. However, she now began to study the ceiling. Unable to hold back her concern a moment longer, she called out. "Hey! Where's that bird? How'd a bird get in here?"

"Shut up, Agnes," muttered Arianna, loud enough for me to hear. "You're spoiling everything, as usual."

"Oh, like you don't spoil things with your stupid prune whip poison."

The casting director honed in on the dissention.

"I provide healthy food which is something you obviously know nothing about."

"Don't tell her to shut up," Hannah said in a harsh whisper. "So crude."

"Ladies," the yoga instructor interrupted. "Let's quiet down. Concentrate on our tadasana. It will improve our balance."

"That's a black-capped chickadee doing its chick-a-dee-dee-dee call. I know my bird sounds," Agnes said, touching her hearing aid.

"There's no bird, Agnes," Ida said, ignoring the request for quiet. "It's the music."

"Are you sure? It sounds like a bird right in this room."

The casting director raised her hand, signaling the instructor to stop the class, and walked over to the director and the two actors. Eyes on the yoga participants, they talked among themselves.

Oh gee, oh gee! I hoped they wouldn't kick Agnes out of the class. She'd worked so hard for this moment. She even wore her hearing aids today. A train wreck was coming. To avoid the sight, I forced myself to look in another direction.

I focused on Crystal's fake bag, wondering if she knew the truth about it.

Fake designer goods were big business. Sal, a savvy guy, gifted Crystal with a fake bag. Mistake? Unlikely. Running with that thought, I saw the situation as a box of puzzle pieces that had been tipped over and suddenly slipped into place. The Land Rover delivered the goods. Floyd delivered the money or maybe some of the goods, not sure about that. Eddie had seen the bag of money or small items on video and stolen them, leaving Floyd to explain the loss.

In which case Marney probably had nothing to do with it. She was innocent.

Could this be right, or was I jumping to conclusions again?

I had to talk to Nick.

The casting director approached Agnes, interrupting my thoughts. I saw Arianna's satisfied smirk. Ida and Hannah looked worried. The casting director spoke to Agnes, and the two walked over to the director and the two stars.

Agnes looked downcast.

I bit my bottom lip.

Hannah and Ida commiserated with each oher.

Suddenly, Agnes brightened. The director walked her back to the group, moved Arianna from her place at the end of one line and placed Agnes in Arianna's spot. Josh, and the actor playing the bad guy, followed.

"This will be a brief scene," the director began. "The yoga class will be in session. No rehearsal. We'll begin filming immediately. We'll take it from the beginning of the Mountain Pose. After that—What's your name, honey?"

"Agnes."

"After that, Agnes talks about the birds, exactly as she just did. The perp will come running in followed by the lead detective, Josh. The desperate perp will grab Agnes, using her as a hostage. All yoga activity will cease. The entire group, *all of you*, will back away, looking frightened. Make it look natural. You're really scared. Agnes has no lines. She will look extremely frightened. Desperate even. Can you do frightened and desperate, honey?"

Agnes made a face. She shook. "How's that for frightened?

"Perfect. Josh will talk the perp into releasing her. Everybody got it?"

There were nods all around, except from Arianna whose face seemed frozen. But I was sure she got it.

The director whispered something to the perp actor.

Then called, "Action!"

The scene began smoothly with the class in session. Then the perp charged in the room and grabbed Agnes. She made a horrendous face, her hands shook and she tried to break away. Josh came dashing in, and stopped short when he saw the gun pointed at Agnes. The director had not mentioned a gun.

The perp had immobilized Agnes, holding her arms behind her back. He pressed the gun against her temple.

Clearly, Agnes didn't like that.

"Let me go," she yelled. "You big dumb jerk."

"Shut up, fatso."

That did it. Agnes's demeanor changed in an instant,

her face morphing from frightened to irate. Tensions
mounted. I saw disaster looming. Josh stood at the bottom
of the steps, unsure of what to say. Agnes had thrown him
off. Then years of starring rolls and acting classes kicked in,
and he rescued the moment. His lines came out smoothly as
he walked toward Agnes and her captor.

"Look at her. She's twice your weight. If she steps on
your foot, she'll break your toe."

That was all Agnes needed to hear. It was like a cue.
She lifted her foot as high as she could and slammed it
down on the perp's foot. Shocked, hurt, he cried out and
released her. Josh rushed over, captured the perp and said
his remaining lines.

"Cut. That's a keeper," called the director.

Everyone clapped. The perp actor shot Agnes a dirty
look as he limped away. Agnes bowed and accepted
congratulations from the senior yoga ladies, or at least most
of them. Arianna maintained her Scowl Position.

Josh came over and gave Agnes a kiss on the cheek.
"Great scene, lady."

Agnes about swooned. She immediately forgave him
for referencing her weight. Flanked by Hannah and Ida, she
said, "My name is Agnes. These are my friends, Hannah
and Ida. We've been fans since your first movie over forty
years ago."

"Why, thank you. Can I interest the three of you in a
cup of coffee? Maybe a donut? They've set up the table in
the back room."

"Don't have to ask us twice," Ida said.

"But stay away from the prune whip," Agnes
cautioned. "It's deadly. All organic."

CHAPTER THIRTY-TWO

Although I held little hope of finding anything useful on the photos I'd taken at the murder site over a week ago, I had put it off long enough. Tonight I planned to spend the tedious hours necessary to check each of the three hundred and eighty-two pictures I'd taken.

Give certain people a camera and they go crazy snapping pictures. That would be me. Guilty, guilty, guilty.

Determined to be thorough, I located a magnifying glass, and joined Ida and her afghan squares and bag of yarn in the front room.

She chuckled when she saw me. "All you need is one of those Sherlock Holmes herringbone hats and a curved stem pipe to complete the look."

"For sure," I said, setting my laptop on the loveseat opposite her.

"What're you looking for?"

"Evidence. I don't know specifically. I may not even recognize it when I see it. That's what makes this so difficult. And disheartening."

"Wish I could help," she said, adding a finished square to the yarn tote organizer beside her chair.

"I have to do this alone. I downloaded the photos and have to check each one," I said as I plopped on the loveseat and opened the computer.

"Didn't the police take pictures?"

"They did. But since I bothered to take these, I might as well check them out."

"You are very thorough, Nora. I'm proud of you."

Ida and I spent the next hour discussing the day, especially the luncheon with the cast, with Ida doing most of the talking as I scanned pictures with an eagle eye. I heard, verbatim, every word that Josh the magnificent uttered. Even though I was not the least bit interested in this star from a bygone era, I loved Aunt Ida and was glad I was there to share her happiness at finally meeting the man she considered a "hunk."

By the time Ida and I called it a night, I had checked less than half the photos. I should have begun days ago.

I had called Nick after the yoga scene to tell him my thoughts about Sal and his fake designer item business. He agreed it was a possibility, and said if Eddie confirmed this, they might be able to wrap up the case sooner than expected.

The following morning I was up early, determined to finish this odious job. Ida stopped by my room and said she'd make a special breakfast. Her specials were beyond delicious.

Less than half an hour later, the welcome aroma of fresh coffee wafted up on the same current as the bacon.

"Pancakes are done, Nora."

"Be down in a sec," I called.

I was about to shut down, when I saw something that didn't belong. I enlarged it until it blurred, but still couldn't quite make it out. I'd look more closely after breakfast.

I wondered whether it was still back at the scene. The weather may have destroyed whatever it was. I closed the computer and headed downstairs, cell phone in hand, and called Mary Fran.

"I need to go out to the scene of the crime this morning, and—"

"I'm sick. I have a cold. I worked like a dog all week getting those women ready for their debut, and now I'm paying the price. Can you hold off going for another day or two?"

"Okay. No emergency. Take care of yourself. We'll

talk tomorrow."

I called Nick as I poured coffee.

"You're on the speaker phone," he warned immediately. "Miller's with me. We should be at the mountain soon. I already spoke to Eddie. He's meeting us later today. With what you mentioned about the designer goods yesterday, I hope we can wrap this up soon."

"Me, too. Good morning, Miller. Nick, I thought you'd still be in town."

"I know. I just took off. I've wasted enough time with that movie crew. They should be out of my station house by now. Out of town. They're incredibly slow. And annoying."

"I agree. But their presence made a lot of people happy. The aunts loved every minute. So did your mother. They brought a lot of money into the town. Can't fault them for that."

"No comment. What are you up to today?"

"Not sure. All the results of the crime scene investigation were turned in, right? I mean the photos and such?"

Seconds passed before he answered. "The report was completed days ago. Nothing of value, except the ring and a burned-out cell phone. Why are you asking?"

Suddenly I felt foolish. The Maine State Police handled homicides. I had no business second-guessing their Major Crimes Unit. Those folks had a top criminal investigation division with years of experience and training. They were thorough. I had nothing except a blurry photo of something that might be nothing more than a spot on my lens.

"I'm looking over the photos I took. I still have a ton more to check out."

"You think they missed something?" The tone of his voice implied this was unlikely.

That settled it. I couldn't tell him what I thought, not yet. I'd check the photo again, then maybe go to the site. "I doubt it."

"Keep me posted. I'll call tonight. We'll probably stay over. Depends. I may interview several folks."

I said, "Hope you get what you need from Eddie."

"Hi, Nick," Aunt Ida called from across the room. "You take it easy today. Eat a hearty breakfast."

"Tell her I said I will," Nick said.

I conveyed the message and hung up.

Ida's pancakes and bacon lived up to expectations. Wonderful. Such a treat. As I added butter and maple syrup I told her what Nick was up to today, what he hoped to accomplish. She told me she'd pass the information along to Hannah and Agnes.

After we cleaned up, I went back to my laptop. When I enlarged the photo in question, I knew I needed to go to the switchback today.

I ran off a few photos, stuffed them in my bag and headed downstairs.

Ida was in the kitchen cutting up carrots. "Starting dinner already? We just finished breakfast."

"Irish stew takes a while. I'll make it. Put it away for tonight. Where're you off to?"

"I'm going—"

When my cell phone sounded, I held up a hand to Ida. "Hi, Margaret. What's up?"

"Beverly Sue's coming to town today. She's being so sweet. She apologized and promised to explain everything in person."

"Glad to hear it!"

"She said she didn't want to talk on the phone, but she owed me some answers."

"At least you'll get closure."

"She'll be here in about fifteen minutes. I can't wait to see her. She's taking me out to eat."

Food instead of a winning lottery ticket? Wonderful. I couldn't bring myself to say anything positive. "Keep me posted. Talk to you later, Margaret."

Ida was hunting for something in the refrigerator when

I hung up, so I kissed her cheek and took off.

Because the roads were close to clear, it took less than an hour to get there. Pictures in hand, I hopped out and studied the scene. Within minutes I found what I was looking for. It was high in a tree caught on a pine needle. Because of the location close to the trunk and beneath a branch, it had been sheltered from the elements. It was as if the wind had played a game of ring-toss, and scored. The person who lost this never noticed the path it took. I would never have captured the image if I had not angled my telephoto into the trees beyond the burn site.

I stood beneath the tree, took several more shots, and enlarged them. These photos were crystal clear. And damning.

I recognized the distinctive label with the double S set back-to-back. I remembered the day my dad had shown me that same symbol.

"The Churchill Stradivarius is one of the best cigars out there. The guys bought a few as a fund-raiser and raffled them off. Smooth, mild and super expensive. I got lucky," he said. "For sure, I'd never spend so much on a cigar."

I knew who had murdered Floyd. Or was responsible for having him murdered.

I had seen the identical band on the floor of the station house the day they shot Nick's kissing scene. Sal had tossed it there.

My cell phone rang. Margaret again.

"Hi, how did it go with Beverly Sue?"

"She never showed. I tried to call her, but it went straight to voice mail."

"You think she's avoiding you?" I asked, realizing as soon as the words were out how ridiculous that was. Beverly had called Margaret.

"I doubt it. I have an awful feeling something may have happened to her. Maybe she had an accident. Should I call the police?"

"Good idea. Tell them what kind of car she's driving."

"That's easy. Same as me, a Jeep Grand Cherokee, top of the line. Only hers is silver, not red. I got mine because I loved hers."

"Let me know if you have any news."

Fighting the desire to climb the tree and grab that stupid cigar band before it succumbed to the forces of nature, I stared up in frustration. Taking it would present a problem when it came time to prosecute. A good defense lawyer would definitely challenge the chain of evidence. With reluctance, I left it and headed back to the truck to get my cell phone.

Mister Big Bucks Sal had made more than a littering mistake when he tossed his cigar band on the station house floor. I had him now.

Sal had murdered Floyd. He would pay for it.

I was about a few hundred feet from Ce-ce when a monster moose ambled out of the woods. I froze.

Oh, dear God, save me from this beast.

Shaking in my L.L Beans, I backed up, increasing the distance between us in small increments. Casually, careful not to make eye contact—I knew that was dangerous—I looked around for a tree to hide behind and maneuvered off the road one mini shuffle at a time.

From behind the tree I watched the huge animal swing his head from side to side. Then he stopped and began to lick my truck, his long tongue slurping away at the bumper. What on earth! Then I realized it must be licking the road salt. Ce-ce was covered with it.

After my last encounter with a moose in rut—I ended up sitting in a tree waiting out his antics, a scenario too scary to revisit—I'd read up on these animals. I knew that hiding behind a tree was a good move.

I heard my cell phone ring on the front seat of the truck, not a ring I recognized. It could be anyone. Interested more in his salt find, the moose didn't react.

My toes were cold. Perhaps they were turning blue. I shuttered at the thought of them being amputated. The moose might be here all day. I was trapped. I could freeze out here. No one would find me for a long time. Days. Weeks.

Snow could fall and cover me up. It would be months before anyone would find me.

Because it was the last thing I needed, I recalled a scene in some movie where someone happened upon a man frozen to death. Mini icicles hung off his nose, eyebrows, eyelashes and hair. He looked horrible.

To keep the circulation in my feet moving, I began to shuffle. It was a quiet shuffle, as shuffles go. I got a rhythm going and began to hum in my head, anything to block out thoughts of being charged by a thousand-pound animal, or of freezing to death.

The tune was interrupted by the second ring of my phone. The same person, probably Margaret, was trying to call.

Okay. Now I had to go to the bathroom. When did that happen? I shuffled a little faster, wishing the salt licker away. Just when I thought I couldn't last a second longer the behemoth took off. That was my cue to run like a crazy woman to the truck. Seconds later, I listened to the message on my phone.

"Nora, it's Margaret again. Beverly still hasn't shown up. I'm worried. Call me."

A few light snow flurries sprinkled my windshield as I returned Margaret's call.

"I guess she's still not there," I said as soon as she answered.

"No. And she hasn't called."

To me, this fit the Beverly-profile I'd arrived at. Nasty. Spiteful. Offensive. Plus a few other things I didn't want to think about. Of course, I couldn't say any of this to the second cousin once removed who was waiting and worrying in the library.

"Margaret, I'm sure you'll hear from her sooner or later. " I didn't think this was necessarily true. "Remember how long it took to hear from her after you won the lottery. She's not much for calling you."

"I suppose. But she did say she was coming."

"True. But maybe something came up."

"Maybe." I heard resignation in her voice. "I'm going to close early today and head home. Unless," she began, her voice brightening, "you want to stop by."

"Margaret, I want to support you, but I don't want to drive all the way down to town. I have a few other things to do."

"I understand."

"Talk to you later."

I did have time to run over to Marney's before I went home. I should do that. None of what I needed to talk about should be discussed on the phone. Best if I just drop by.

Ever since I saw her with Sal at Winterfest, I had a strong feeling she knew something about him that would aid the investigation. If she knew nothing, or claimed to know nothing, I owed her a warning about his unsavory character. Of course, until Nick arrested Sal, I couldn't reveal that I knew Sal murdered Floyd.

I hoped she'd offer to tell me about the computer in her back room. I suspected she'd pilfered the library materials about computer usage. Why she would take the other items was a mystery, unless she wanted to throw someone off the track. The phrase *red herrings* popped into my head. But why?

I usually went down to town and looped up and around when I went to Marney's. I seldom went the shorter way because the road was narrow. Today, I took the shorter route and approached from the opposite direction. I stopped short before I got to her driveway.

Something in back . . . something was off.

I stared at tree branches tilted oddly behind her shed. What on earth?

I backed up out of range of the house and got out of Ce-ce to take a closer look. A few snow flurries swirled around as I approached the shed. Then I saw it, the tail end of an SUV. I recognized it.

What was *she* doing here? What was going on?

I had a bad feeling about this. Nothing I came up with made sense.

Wary, I headed to the back door, keeping out of sight as much as possible, skulking from bush to bush. I was alert in a way I usually reserved for the moose population.

In the open area that led to the back door, I saw two sets of tracks.

Oh, dear God. What had happened here?

CHAPTER THIRTY-THREE

I swallowed the scream when I saw her. For one brief moment I thought I was going to be sick right there on the back step. I ducked quickly. Took a deep breath, then peered over the bottom edge of the window again.

Surrounded by garbage and vermin on a narrow path in Marney's kitchen, bound hand and foot to a ladder-back chair with electrical tape, Beverly Sue writhed back and forth, attempting to break free.

Her face red, eyes tearing, she struggled to dislodge an object that stretched her mouth wide enough to split her lips and make them bleed. A filthy rag anchored it in place.

By the kitchen sink, her back to me, Marney poured something out of a bag and into a bowl. It looked like she was speaking.

From Beverly's expression, I knew she'd heard, and it wasn't good.

Her eyes flared and more tears came. I heard a muffled screech explode behind the gag as she twisted her head back and forth more vigorously.

I remembered her words the last time I'd seen her.

"Stay away from me, Nora. Keep your distance or you'll regret it."

I might regret this, but not for the reason she originally intended.

My body trembled as much in outrage as fright. Suddenly, Beverly's jerking motion ceased. She had seen me. I shook my head furiously, hoping she'd understand that she shouldn't do anything to alert Marney to my presence.

Marney shifted. I ducked. I waited.

I needed a weapon, something to threaten Marney with, like a gun. I'd never used a gun. The thought of shooting another person was repugnant, but since I didn't have access to a gun, the thought was moot.

With desperate eyes I looked around for something to use as a weapon. The only thing that remotely qualified was the metal snow shovel next to the back door.

The shed was close. It might hold something I could use—a hammer, a pitchfork, an ax. I would have to run.

Suddenly I heard a loud crash. Reflexively, I peered in the window again. Beverly's chair had been knocked backwards. Marney stood over her.

Time had run out.

I grabbed the shovel, crashed through the back door like a an avenging goddess in a superhero movie, yelling, "Stop right there!"

Holding the shovel at baseball bat level, ready to swing, I braced for action in the narrow debris-lined path. I was gratified to see Marney stop dead in her tracks.

I had a brief advantage, a moment to act.

Instead of seizing the moment, instead of slamming her with the shovel, I chose to be reasonable. Arms shaking, I shouted, "What on earth are you doing? This is crazy. Let Beverly go! Now."

Afraid to take my eyes off Marney, I didn't spare a glance at Beverly.

Marney said calmly, "I don't think I should let her go. She has to have her mouth washed out with soap. It's what she deserves for name-calling.

I looked at the metal bowl in her hands. "Put that down."

"Ferret food," she explained, holding it up. "They haven't eaten today. They have to be fed. They're very hungry."

Off to the side, Beverly's frantic sounds increased along with her attempts to break away, making me wonder what Marney intended to do with the ferret food. Obviously, she had told Beverly.

I didn't know what to do. I didn't think I could slam a person with a shovel.

"I told you we was finished, Nora."

The shovel was getting heavy. Panting, mostly from fear, I lowered it a little, along with my voice. "I tried to help you, Marney. Tried to investigate Floyd's finances for you. I came here to tell you to stay away from Sal Baldino. I saw you talking to him at Winterfest. He's a criminal. Dangerous. He killed Floyd."

Marney took a step toward me, still holding the bowl of small pellets. "Oh, my. Did he now? Baldino killed that rotten, thieving weasel? Ohhh-myy! Is that what you think? So I did a good job. I sent you on a merry chase. Convinced you. Made you think I was innocent. I knew you talked to the sheriff."

She took another step in my direction.

"Stop!" I yelled, raising the shovel back to batting position. "What are you saying?"

Without taking my eyes off her, I inched toward Beverly, knocking over a bucket of metal cans, stepping into something that increased the stench level.

Marney paused.

"Floyd got what he deserved. I took care of it. Just like I'll take care of Beverly. She'll get what she deserves."

Had I heard that correctly?

"*You* murdered Floyd?"

"I did," she said proudly. "I had the evidence. I could send the jackass to jail. Ay-uh, I could make his greatest fear happen. He knew it, too. Dumb jerk left his computer here. Used his big cell phone as a computer. I got me some books, and I learnt it." She took another step. "I was getting all his emails, his texts. Scumbag cheater was a bagman for Baldino. I had the proof. In his own words."

Another bombshell.

If I had any doubts about her intentions toward me, her

words put them to rest. She intended to kill me.

"Take another step, and you'll get this shovel in you head. I mean business."

Nodding, she acquiesced. I relaxed a fraction.

Next thing I knew, the ferret food bowl rocketed across the space like it was shot from a canon, slammed my head hard enough to knock me off balance and cause me to drop the shovel. In one swift move, she snatched something from a pile of newspapers.

Lightning bolts of pain surged through every neuron.

I screamed.

I convulsed.

My knees buckled.

Incapacitated, I collapsed face-first into an open garbage bag.

CHAPTER THIRTY-FOUR

"You're a good detective, Nora. Better than the police, I think. You couldn't rest until you figured this all out. Could you?"

Still shuddering from the shock, arms secured to a ladder-back chair with electrical tape, I faced Beverly, who remained tipped over backwards on the kitchen garbage path, and Marney who stood behind her.

Angling my head, despite the pain where the stun gun had hit me, I wiped the side of my face on the shoulder of my black jacket.

"Why?" I asked, my voice shaking as tears puddled in my eyes. "Tell me what this is all about."

"I'm sorry, Nora girl. I liked you, but I told you we was done. You didn't listen."

"Right. I should have listened. But I found something at the murder scene. I came to warn you."

The smell in here was beyond atrocious—rotted food, animal feces, urine, mold. It was difficult to control the gag reflex.

I was surrounded by a sea of garbage—empty bottles, open cans, newspapers, magazines, clothes, hats, advertisements, dozens of hot water bottles, ornaments and oozing cans, light bulbs and plastic boxes.

Things had taken over, were piled window height, and in one case, above window height.

It was like visual noise. Maybe it took the place of having people in the house.

Shaking her head in disgust as she took the stun gun from the pocket of her gray sweatshirt and set it on a stack of newspapers, she asked, "Warn me about what?"

"About Sal," I said with a sob. "I found a cigar band from a very expensive cigar that I knew he smoked. I thought he might have murdered Floyd. But you said *you* murdered—"

"He smokes the Churchill Stradivarius."

Surprised by her revelation, I said, "Yes. How did you know?"

She maneuvered across piles of detritus to the kitchen cabinets and removed a small wooden box the length of a cigar.

"No harm telling now," she said holding up the box. "I met Sal weeks ago in a cigar shop, way before that movie bunch came into town. When I told him my name, he asked was I related to Floyd LeBeau. Imagine that. Told him I was Floyd's wife. He gave me two of his best cigars. Such a nice man."

"And you smoked one at the scene of the murder?"

"Yep. In Floyd's truck. On purpose. That man hated cigar smoke."

I heard animal squeaks and scratches behind a door off the kitchen. I dreaded what I suspected was coming. She had mentioned feeding them. I did not want to be visited by a bunch of ferrets.

"We talked, me and Floyd. Nice little chat," she said as she reached for a bag of ferret food. "Met me in the same spot we had sex the first time. We was kids. He even proposed to me on that very road."

I had to keep her talking, play for time while I waited for an opportunity to strike back. How that was possible, I had no idea.

"I'm surprised you were able to get him to meet you."

Marney scooped the pellets from the large bag into a bowl. Beverly started to go crazy. Next thing I knew, Marney was back with the bowl. She sprinkled ferret food all over Beverly, even stuffed some down her bra.

Oh, dear God, no!

I tried to stop her as she headed for the ferret door. Speaking quickly, I said, "Do you think he wanted to make it up to you? He must have realized how hurtful his actions had been."

She scoffed at that but kept maneuvering across the room. "He came to get money. His bagman money went missing. Don't know how that happened. They broke his fingers over that. Then they upped the amount he owed them. Interest. Stupid fool actually asked me for more money. In cash. It was due the very next day. He didn't have it. Desperate man."

I could see she wanted to tell me, to brag about how clever she was, so I seized that. "Why did he think you'd bring him money?"

"He offered me a deal. He told me about the lottery ticket, said he stole it, but by the time he'd be able to collect, it'd be too late. They'd break his knees. He promised to give me the ticket. Said we was gonna get back together again, leave Silver Stream and start a new life. 'Course I had to promise to destroy the evidence I had against him."

"He wanted a few thousand from you? So, a few thousand in exchange for a few million? Why not give the ticket to the guy he owed the money to?"

She stepped off the pile of garbage onto a lower spot next to the door. "You dumber than dirt? He wanted the big money. And he wanted *out* of the bagman business."

"So you agreed?"

"Sure. Good deal, right? Except I was too smart for him. I knew he intended to kill me. I beat him to the punch. Soon as he showed me the lottery ticket, I hit him with the first bullet. Was he ever surprised!"

She reached in the pocket of her dirty jeans and pulled out the winning ticket and waved it front of me. "See this. My ticket to a life of luxury."

"Why don't you take the ticket now and disappear? You don't have to murder us."

"But I do. Sorry, Nora. Else I'd spend the rest of my life looking over my shoulder. Expecting to be arrested any time. No way to live."

She shoved a clump of wild, bleached blonde hair off her face. Mary Fran had mentioned her hair, and I agreed. Awful mess that fell over her shoulders. I felt like telling her that.

"And I had Beverly's ring," Marney said, staring at Beverly. "I told Floyd to steal it from Eddie and bring it with him. Leaving it at the scene was a nice touch, I thought. Got the cops looking at Beverly and Eddie for the murder."

She reached for the doorknob.

"Wait!" I called, desperation alive and well in my tone. "Please don't let the animals come around me. Please. I'm afraid."

I began to shake, which came naturally since I was a wreck. "You're going to shoot me *and* do this to me, too?"

When I saw her hand ease off the doorknob, I continued to appeal to her sense of fair play. "I've been nothing but nice to you. Helped you all I could. I even wanted to help you today. That's why I came."

Marney considered this. I knew I'd reached her, briefly. She made her way back across the garbage. "All right. What's fair is fair. Do you want me to shoot you first?"

"No!" I cried out. "Let me live as long as possible. Please. You owe me that, at least."

Standing over me, she put her hand on my shoulder. "I did get you involved in this in the first place, by tricking you into looking for Floyd. He was already dead. I used you because I needed to look innocent."

"So you'll keep the animals away from me?"

With a decisive nod, she said, "I will."

Then she turned her attention to Beverly.

She bent over and slapped Beverly, full force, across the face, once, twice, three times. "This is your fault,

Beverly Sue. Poor Nora. Now look what has to happen. I have to kill her. She's collateral damage."

"Stop! Marney, please stop. Please."

Focused on Beverly, she said, "Nice Nora can watch what happens to bullies. Beverly the Bully! Beverly the Slut! Don't worry, Nora, this won't happen to you. I'll be quick and merciful with you. One shot to the head."

Oh, dear God. How do you reason with a crazy person?

She said, "That's one of my larger bars in her mouth. I make my own homemade lye soap. Good stuff. I use it to clean ferret poop. Use that rag for the same thing. Beverly's got a poopy mouth."

She picked up a water bottle and squirted Beverly in the face.

When she finished torturing Beverly, she said, "Nora, I'm gonna set you in the pantry before I let the ferrets loose. I'll have to take your tape off. You carry your chair. I'll follow with the stun gun. Any false moves, you know what'll happen. So be really careful."

"I will," I said, trying to sound appreciative to a woman whose postponement of my execution could be measured in minutes, not hours.

I considered trying to attack when she removed the tape, but as soon as I saw the knife and the stun gun I changed my mind.

CHAPTER THIRTY-FIVE

With Marney pressing the stun gun to my neck, I taped my left arm, wrist and most of my hand to the arm of the chair. Then she held my right arm in a death grip and secured it the same way. At least my fingers were loose, sort of.

I cried when she closed the door. Death was near. I had no chance of getting out of this. None.

I was alone in a closet-sized room with a small overhead bulb for light. The shelves around me contained enough products to fill a small supermarket, holding everything from canned soups to nail polish, toilet paper to olive oil. No weapons.

After one huge sob that left my nose running and eyes tearing like faucets, I looked around again, blinked to clear my vision. I had to get hold of myself. Had to. I bent my head to my shoulder to wipe my nose. Despite the paucity of survival chances, I could not give up. I'd go down fighting.

I focused on the shelves with the attention I usually reserved for computer investigations. Intense, complete.

That's when I saw it. Not exactly a weapon, but possibly something to give me a fighting chance. What had Aunt Ida said about vinegar? It could remove *furniture* glue.

Before a plan was fully formed, I was inching the chair next to the bottle, which was hand height, maybe my best break of the day, if I didn't count escaping the moose. If I tipped the chair slightly, I could use my index finger and middle finger to grab it around the neck.

Success.

Once in hand, I wasn't sure how to open it or pour it into the hole the dowel was set in. It looked tight. No wiggle room. Well, we'd see about that.

With great care, I set the bottle back on the shelf and concentrated on wiggling the arms of the chair, knowing this was an old chair, knowing I might be able to loosen the dowel. If I could manage to get some vinegar into even a tiny separation, it might work on the glue, help dissolve a bit of it.

I ignored the ache in my hands and wrists and arms as I assaulted the chair with a vengeance, pulling, yanking, pushing every muscle to the limit. My whole body hurt with the strain. But when you're fighting for your life, pain takes second place to survival.

Finally a tiny space appeared. Very tiny, barely visible. Elated, I pushed harder. Back and forth. Back and forth. I stopped for breath, then reached for the bottle. Once in hand, I grabbed the top in my teeth, hoping that Harold could fix whatever I destroyed, hoping I didn't crack a tooth, a front tooth in particular.

I'd look like a Halloween witch. I'd need a false tooth. I imagined smiling with a missing front tooth. I actually smiled, testing, keeping my lips over my teeth to hide my missing tooth.

Life over teeth, I thought.

It took several tries, but I finally forced the top open. Shaking the chair to and fro, I was able to empty some of the contents on the dowel where it leaked into the minute space I'd created.

Then to my horror I dropped the bottle.

Unwilling to quit, I resumed my chair attack, working the arm back and forth with all the strength I possessed until it finally came flying up in such a rush it conked me smack on the forehead. It was a double conk. First the arm, then the attached dowel hit.

Thank you, God.

Tears blurred my vision. My head hurt.

Without taking a second to appreciate my success, or bemoan the lump that must be blooming on my forehead, I wriggled and twisted my hand until I was able to work it over the end of the chair arm. Suddenly, it was loose.

Still confined to the chair by my left arm, I managed to pivot and grab the tape from the shelf. After stuffing it in my shirt, I grabbed my weapon of choice, my only choice, the detached chair arm with the dangling dowel. All set, I duck-walked to the door at a ninety-degree angle, hauling the chair on my back.

This time I would not hesitate.

Nervous but determined, I stood beside the door, held the thick dowel as high as I could, which wasn't all that high considering the angle I was standing at, and waited. I could feel the backache of the century coming on.

As soon as Marney opened the door, I swung with every bit of strength I possessed. Caught her right in the midsection. She flew back and down into a sitting position. I slammed her a second time alongside her head, and she toppled over all the way. The stun gun fell from her pocket. I was down on all fours in an instant, which wasn't too difficult seeing as how I was halfway there already.

I seized the gun and stunned her smack-dab on her rear end. She convulsed. I watched. And then stunned her again, which probably wasn't necessary, but what the heck.

She convulsed again.

Before she fully regained her senses, I grabbed the tape and secured her hands behind her back, then worked on her ankles. On a roll, so to speak, I went a little tape crazy and secured her legs all the way up to her knees, which is where I ran out of tape.

Staring at her all wrapped up, I said, "Marney, what you've done is so absurd, so inhuman, I don't know what to say. But you are dangerous. You shouldn't be loose."

Before leaving, I reached in her pocket and took the lottery ticket. I turned away slowly, my back aching like crazy. I needed a knife, fast. I had to get this chair off me.

I stepped out the door and called, "Beverly. It's over. I got her. I'm coming."

I set out across the debris field, tripping and falling beneath the horrible weight that slammed into me with every step, battering my arms, back, head, legs. Every muscle ached. It was easier on all fours, so I crawled the second half of the trip, the joy of freedom outpacing the frustration that rose with every ungainly movement.

Finally I arrived at the sink and found a knife. Minutes later, I was free of my burden and heading over to rescue Beverly from the swarming ferrets who still searched out their food all over her body. I grabbed a box labeled ferret treats, shook it to get their attention and tossed it, open, across the room. They took off after it.

I removed Beverly's gag first.

"Whereisshe?" Beverly mumbled, slurring her words together through a bruised mouth. "Didyoukillher?"

"She's taped up in the pantry. Not getting out any time soon. I tape better than I ski," I said as I cut away the bindings on her legs and arms.

Seconds later, we were both hugging and crying, survivors united by averted tragedy.

"Thankyou, NoraLassiter," she mumbled. "Iwillloveyouforever."

"Oh, Beverly, what a day."

The ferrets that hadn't gone to get more treats, pawed at my feet and legs. With a shiver, I brushed them aside. I said, "I have to go to my truck, get my phone. I'll be right back."

"No! Don'tleaveme," she implored. "Please."

Nodding, I grasped her trembling hand, and we took off out the back door, running, tripping, falling and finally making it to Ce-ce though the light snow that had begun to fall.

Once in the truck I gave Beverly a bottle of water to clear her mouth, and I called Nick.

"Hi, Nora, I've been trying—"

"I need help. I'm at Marney's. She killed Floyd and—"

"What? How do you—"

"Just listen to her," Beverly shouted, her voice much improved, but sounding like sandpaper. "And get some guys here to Marney's right away. That crazy broad tried to kill me. Kill Nora too. Send EMTs. I'm a mess."

She looked awful. Her mouth was red, bleeding. Her face scratched.

Exhausted and in pain, she sat back while I told Nick what had happened. Beverly reached for my hand several times.

When I finally hung up, she said through her tears, "How can I ever thank you? You saved my life."

"Well, I—"

"When I saw you at the window, I thought you might run. Leave me. It was your chance to get even." She sobbed. "I remembered the last words I said to you."

You are the last person I ever want to see again. Stay away from me, Nora. Keep your distance or you'll regret it.

"Just words, Beverly. Best forgotten."

"You're incredible. Some people would have held my words against me. But you confronted the monster. For me, who was so nasty to you."

"I do have a vague recollection of that."

She shook her head, smiling through her tears. "She was going to kill you, Nora."

We both cried some more, and hugged. Then I said, "There may be payback, Beverly."

Curious, she looked at me. "Okay. Tell me."

"I may need more ski lessons," I said with a straight face.

She laughed through copious tears, grabbed me and pledged, "Anytime, Nora. For you, anytime at all! Backwards, frontwards. Whatever."

* * *

While an Emergency Medical Technician cared for
Beverly in the EMS vehicle parked in Marney's driveway, I
sat across from her with a cold pack wrapped around my
head.

I called Margaret to give her the news about the lottery
ticket.

"Oh, I'm so happy. I can't believe you found it. And
saved Beverly Sue." She sounded very emotional. "I did
what you suggested, Nora. I told Harold what I'd done. He
was angry. He said he was very disappointed that I broke
our agreement. I was apologetic, but he kept his sour face.
He kept reprimanding me. That's when I said to myself:
What would Nora do?"

"And?"

"I blasted him. I told him I wasn't perfect. 'Too bad
about that, Harold,' I said. Then I did something I thought
I'd never do." She paused.

It was tooth-pulling time again.

"And?"

"I walked away."

She paused again.

"And?"

"He followed me! And he proposed!"

"Wow! Yay, Margaret! Congratulations. Here's
Beverly."

I handed Beverly the phone, removed the cold pack
and stepped out of the vehicle into the softly falling snow.
Spreading my arms, I looked heavenward, twirling around,
happy to be alive, happy to be in Silver Stream, Maine.

Less than an hour later, Nick drove up.

Despite the abundance of official personnel around, he
ran to me, and not caring what anyone thought, lifted me off
my feet and kissed me right there in plain sight.

"Are you okay? Let me look at you?" he asked, setting
me down.

Both hands cupping my upturned face, he studied the

forehead bump. "You didn't mention this. Has the EMT looked at it? You might have a concussion. Looks like you were slammed with a baseball bat."

"I hit myself with a chair dowel." I went on to explain, in detail, how I'd gotten loose, and how fast that wooden post shot from the chair.

"Putting me in the closet was her warped idea of kindness. She planned to put a bullet in my head when she finished torturing Beverly."

Nick pulled me into his arms. "What you do is too dangerous. You know that, don't you?"

"Absolutely."

He eyed me skeptically. "So you'll give up your detective career?"

"I'm thinking about it."

"Good." He gave me a quick kiss that promised more to come.

When he stepped to the side, I noticed Eddie in the back of his vehicle. "He's under arrest?" I asked as we headed over.

"Ay-uh. He's going to testify against Sal and Lucca, who've been arrested. Trafficking in counterfeit goods, money laundering and a few other things. We seized some of the goods that were being transported in that Land Rover that's been around town."

I couldn't help myself, I had to ask, "Was Crystal's handbag bag taken?"

"Yes. He gave out several. All were seized as evidence."

I showed tremendous restraint. I did not smile.

He went on, "Sal had a whole network operating. We notified police in Texas where his main supplier was located."

"How did Eddie know all this?"

"He was a busy guy with his smoke detectors, aka spy cameras. Your discovery was the biggest break in this case. You are amazing. And the fact that you recognized the fake handbag, the Louis Baton—"

"Louis Vuitton," I corrected.

"Right," he said, grinning. "Outside my purview. I'm not up on designer goods. Fortunately, you are."

"I once wanted one. Not so much any more. So, you were telling me about Eddie."

"He turned over everything he had. Video of Floyd's room, Sal's room too. Several things made him call me. First, he thought someone had been in his room, maybe Sal."

"That would have been me."

"Yes. Without a doubt. He also found out I was asking questions again. Thought I might be suspicious of him. He had wanted to remove Sal's camera, but held off because he figured since someone had been in his room they might be watching him, too."

"So he was scared."

"Terrified. But he finally risked it. He went in and changed the camera for a real smoke detector. Viewing Sal's video convinced him to call me. He saw one of Sal's men breaking Floyd's fingers. He thought Sal murdered Floyd. He wanted to get out in front of the charges. Make a deal for lesser charges."

"What did he confess to?"

"Stealing Floyd's money bag. Besides the money, there were Apple watches in there."

Standing at his SUV, Nick nodded to Deputy Miller, who opened the door and reached for Eddie.

Nick said, "Ten minutes, Eddie. She's in the EMS truck."

We watched Miller lead him over to Beverly. Less than two minutes later, Eddie walked back looking extremely unhappy. Nick and I headed over to Beverly. My cell phone rang, and I stepped off to the side to answer it.

"Nora, this is Aunt Ellie. You never got back to me about that peeping Tom I wanted you to check out. I saw him again last night. Are you coming soon?"

I hesitated, taking in the scene around me.

In front of me, Nick sat in the EMS truck listening to Beverly tell how Marney had managed to waylay her on the road, and then shocked her with the stun gun and tied her up.

Trimble and Miller were backing out of the driveway with Marney a prisoner in the back seat.

Uniformed officers were busy sealing off the area around the house with yellow tape. It had been a horrible day. Scary, so scary. And it started when a moose had licked my truck.

"Nora? You still there?" Aunt Ellie said.

"Yes. Still here." This was not a big deal, a peeping Tom, forheavensakes, certainly nothing dangerous. "I'll be over in a few days. I promise."

When Nick finished with Beverly, we walked over to Ce-ce, hand in hand.

"I'm going home now," I said as I opened my door. "I smell awful. I need to clean up."

"I have to be here a while. One of my men will drive you. With that bump it's not a good idea to drive."

I was going to protest, but decided against it. I was tired, had a headache, and various body parts ached like crazy. It would be good to have someone else drive. It would be good to get home. The thought of telling the aunts about all the new developments made me smile.

"Ida made Irish stew. I could save you some. You interested?"

"Everything about you interests me. Besides, I need to hold you close for a while, a long while. Kiss you. Over and over again."

I smiled up at him. "Me too you."

"You know how much I care about you, don't you?"

"Maybe. I'm not sure. I think . . . " I hesitated, as if I were considering his words, unsure of his meaning. Sometimes, I can't help myself. I saw he was a bit concerned. I loved that.

Finally, I said, "But you may have to be more specific. I mean I *care* about a lot of people. I care about the aunts, I care about my brother Howie, I care about Uncle Walter and—"

He pulled me in his arms, lifted me and swung my around, laughing.

"Specific? I will be very specific, my dear Nora. You will not have a doubt in your mind about my feelings for you."

"None?"

"Not a one, Sweetheart!"

The End

Made in the USA
Coppell, TX
31 October 2022